White Chapel Murders_Reaper's Edge

by

Gerald Johnson, Jr.

Chapter 1

He stood there watching as the little boy ran up the stairs. He stood there watching as the little boy screamed. He stood there as the little boy stumbled at the top of the stairs and looked back frightened before standing to run again. He stood there watching as the boy finally made it to the bedroom door and slammed the door shut unable to lock it. He could almost see the little boy pressing his body to the door hoping to keep it closed, but knowing that would do him no good. He stood there watching unable to do anything to help. He stood there watching as the woman slowly stomped her way up the stairs with the brown extension cord in her hand. He stood there watching her face, an angry mask half hidden behind disheveled hair. He stood there watching as she pushed against the door finally forcing her way into the room the little boy had ran into.

He stood there watching.

The boy was about eight… no he was nine and very scrawny. He was definitely runt of the litter material, with a freckled face that would put you in the mind of the little puppet Howdy Doody right down to the mop top of red hair. He was missing one of his front teeth, and many would think it was from him falling from his bicycle. His dark brown eyes were bruised and blood shot from tears, and across his pale face was bright red handprint.

ISBN **978-1-943159-16-1**

LCCN 2018908995

She looked nothing like him, nor did he look anything like her. Her hair was long and curly and blonde. She had wide blue eyes that seemed to see nothing any would call love for the little boy. She was a big woman dressed in something she would most likely call a night gown but it was definitely too short and the world would probably be thankful she was also wearing that tattered robe. A cigarette hung from her thin lips and she wheezed around it as she drew in the smoke and quickly released it before it actually touched her lungs. Her eyebrows seemed to hang down in a permanent scowl making her appear always angry.

He stood there listening as the little boy begged and screamed.

"Why you little shit," she screamed once she pushed the door open. "Why the fuck were you holding the door? You know it only pisses me off when you run from me, you know it only makes me want to break your little fucking neck."

"Please, Mommy," he cried out, "please. I'll go clean it up. I didn't mean to spill it."

"You stupid little motherfucker," she hissed throwing him across the bed and began to beating him with the cord, "do you know how much fucking milk cost you little ingrate?"

He stood there watching as she beat him without mercy. The sound of the cord as it whipped through the stale air of the room caused him to cringe. The sour smell of the drunken woman accosted his nose and made his stomach turn. The sound of the cord striking the boy's flesh again and again drew a tear from his eye.

"If I've told you once you stupid little bastard," the sound of her voice burned into his mind, "I've told you a thousand times to be careful when you're pouring the milk."

He stood there watching as the little boy balled his body up into a ball trying to protect himself from the flailing cord. She didn't care where she hit him all that mattered- was that he was hit. He stood there watching as she seemed to get this demonic look on her face as the cord struck the boy's little body time and time again. It was as she was enjoying it and it sickened him even more, but he could neither move away to stop her or to get away from the brutality.

"I hate you, you little fucker," she screamed over and over again as she continued to beat him. "I wish your little ass would just die."

He stood there watching as the welts rose up on the pale skin. They were long and reddening quickly. They rose up like mountain ranges all across his legs and arms where he was balled up trying to protect his face.

He stood there watching as the little boy tried to roll out of the way of the cord and fell from the bed. He watched in anguish as the woman began to kick at him even as she tried to continue to beat him with the cord. He stood there watching, planted where he stood unable to move… unable to turn away… unable to help.

She reached down and grabbed a handful of his shirt and pulled him up from the floor bringing his face up to hers. She spit into his face from the force of the words she spewed and spat out as she dropped the cord and began to shake him violently. The boy's tears did not sway her, but seemed to anger her more. One hand released the boy's shirt and she slapped him hard across his face leaving yet another hand print in his flesh. His shirt ripped and he fell from her hands only inciting her anger more.

"Please, Mommy, please," he begged as his head bounced back and forth on his neck.

"Why won't you just fucking die," she demanded before grabbing him and throwing him across the room.

He stood there watching as the little boy's body struck and bounced off of the chest of drawers that were against the wall of the room. The boy sunk down to the floor to his knees his eyes were full of tears and fear as he put his hands up to ward off the approaching woman. He stood there watching as the boy again began to cry out and plead and beg for her not to hurt him anymore… for her to forgive him, but she didn't listen.

He looked again and the boy had changed. There kneeling on the floor begging and pleading was the boy at fifteen. His hair was a lot longer and covered part of his face, but it wasn't enough to hide the bloody nose. His bottom lip was blistered and swollen and there was a fingerprints dug into his neck. He stood there watching as the boy crumpled forward to the floor and she planted her foot into his stomach. He watched as the boy struggled to breathe his hands going to his stomach to keep her from repeatedly kicking him. He watched as the boy's mom got angrier because she wasn't having her desired effect.

"I fucking hate you," she screamed, "do you hear me? I hate your little, scrawny ass."

"But I didn't do it," he boy said between gasping breaths and spitting blood out on the floor. "Please, please believe me… I didn't do it I swear."

"So the Principal and your teachers are all liars? Why would the school call and say you touched that girl if you really didn't you perverted little fuck? You sick, little animal. I know I taught you better than to go and put your dirty little hands on anyone."

He stood there watching as she kept kicking at him. He stood there knowing that for once the boy wasn't lying, that he was telling the truth about not touching the little girl like she said he had. He stood there watching as his adopted mom kept kicking him over and over calling him a liar until he was coughing up blood. He stood there watching as she finally walked out and he knew that he was wishing he could die, no, better yet wishing that bitch would die.

He stood there as the boy, now older, knelt down beside a small dog. He was out in the woods and it was getting dark. There was a bit of a smile on his face as he stroked the head of the dog and the dog yipped excitedly trying to lick his hand. The boy's breathing was excited as he looked around, but knew he was pretty safe away from prying eyes as he took the dog into his arms and hugged it. The small head bounced around trying to lick at his face and he began to laugh. He'd always wanted a puppy, but she would always tell him that he was too stupid to care for an animal.

The dog moved about excitedly, but the boy could only hear her voice taunting him. Hear her telling him why he couldn't have a pet. Her whiny voice belittling him again as he knelt there screaming into his ears even as the puppy barked. A tear slowly rolled from his eye and down his cheek as he held the puppy closer, it could barely move in his arms as he began to squeeze.

His hands moved to the dog's neck and he could feel his fingers slowly press into the soft fur and then into the muscles below. He watched as the dog began to struggle thrashing its head about gurgling as it tried to breathe. The puppy's eyes began to bulge from their sockets and it tried to bite at the boy strangling him.

"I'm so sorry," he cried as his fingers crushed the puppy's throat. "I'm so sorry."

The dog whined and wheezed through its teeth, and he could only imagine what he poor animal was feeling as its airway was completely blocked. He stood there watching as the dog finally blacked out but the boy didn't stop squeezing. Tears were streaming from his eyes as he held his head up looking towards the dark of the sky and his hands twisted and snapped the dog's neck with a sickening sound. He watched as the boy sat there on his knees looking down at the now dead dog laying on the ground before him, and a smile slowly crossed his lips.

The boy stood and kicked the dog into the underbrush and walked home. He knew she was going to be in a bad mood, she was always in a bad mood. Even before he opened the door he could smell her cigarettes, and when he opened the door the smoke came billowing out as she stood there in the kitchen at the backdoor waiting on him. She no longer towered over him, but he still cowered in front of her. her dirty, blonde hair she had pulled back into a ponytail as she held the cigarette between her lips and the belt in her hand.

"And where the hell has your ass been?"

"No where," he dropped his head and stood there shuffling his feet.

"So you think you can just come and go as you fucking please," she sucked on the cigarette and allowed the smoke to stream from between her lips. "Who the fuck do you think you are?" As she said it the belt whistled through the air striking him across the chin and down his chest.

He stood there watching as she beat him into a corner of the kitchen, and he wanted to run to the boy… to cover him with his body… to protect him. The belt made a shrill sound as it cut the stale air and a sickening smack as it struck his body. The boy was sitting on the floor balled up protecting his head and taking each strike across his back and down his legs. She was so angry and the fact that he wasn't screaming out only made her angrier as she swung the belt down harder and harder to the point she was beating her back as much as she was beating the boy.

He stood there watching as the boy slowly got his legs beneath him and he slowly pushed himself up against the wall. He was not the little boy who had killed the puppy in the woods. He towered over her and looked down at her as she continued to swing the belt at him. He grunted each time the belt struck, but he no longer covered up. He welcomed each time he was hit to the point he could feel himself getting excited and he started to grow inside of his pants. The more she struck him the harder and more excited he became until he finally had to push his way past her and run off to his room before… before she noticed.

Slowly he woke and wiped the sweat from his brow and a smile slowly creased his lips as he sat up and looked around. He ran his fingers through his red mop top of hair and took a deep breath before lying down and allowing his eyes to close.

"Yes in the end the bitch has to die."

All of them have to die.

Chapter 2

Friday

The buzzing sound of the alarm clock was so annoying that she finally reached over in her sleep and slammed her hand down on the snooze button just to shut it up. Light was softly diffusing into her room through the blinds covering the window taking away the dark that seemed to consume the room only a short time ago. The air conditioning was cold and she pulled the bed spread up tighter around her body and realized it didn't move as freely as usual.

"Shit, not again" Detective Maxine Steele murmured under breath as the events of last night slowly flooded her mind.

Slowly she rolled over and stared at the sleeping form of the man beside her and shook her head. She pushed herself up in the bed and looked over the side for anything she could throw on as clothes before she woke him to get him out. Reaching down she grabbed her panties and a t-shirt and moved to the edge of the bed tossing the shirt over her head and pulling it on before she stood up and pulled her panties up her legs. Glancing back once more she wiggled her panties quickly over her ass and pulled the thin shirt down just past her hips. She climbed back up onto the bed pressing back against the headboard as she lit a cigarette; taking a deep breath and then slowly blowing it out as she turned and again looked down at the man laying in her bed.

"Hey," she grumbled at the man laying there. "You need to wake up and go."

The man moaned and stirred a bit but did not wake and this began to piss her off. Taking a deep drag from her cigarette and holding it in her lungs she finally blew out the smoke and reached over to shake the man. Finally, he began to come around and rolled over onto his back and stared over at her.

"I really need for you to get up, get dressed and get gone."

"What's the hurry?" he smiled at her and licked his lips. "I mean we could… you know."

"No we can't. I think you got more than your share last night," she stared at him as he began to sit up and the covers fell away from his body and she began to remember why she brought him into her house in the first place. His chest was like a chiseled piece of marble that he kept bouncing to show off that he worked out, and that led down to an washboard stomach that was a defined six pack that she honestly wanted to rub her hands over again. He pulled back the covers since he knew she was watching and revealed his slowly growing dick bouncing against his thigh. She could feel the heat in the room rise and the moisture between her thighs building.

"I… umm," she swallowed and then took another drag from her cigarette before looking away, "have some things to do this morning. So, up, up, up. I need for you to go."

Without another word of protest he rose from her bed naked and searched for his clothes which were strewn about the room. She sat there staring as his body rippled and flexed and his equipment continued to come to life. She looked away with a blushing smile as she realized what he was trying to do by showing off his impressive "morning wood". She could really go for another toss, but if she were to do that it would make him think he could have his way with her again.

"Bastard," she said under her breath as she took the last drag on her cigarette and snuffed out the butt in the ashtray on the nightstand. She got up out of the bed and walked around it towards the door so she could let her nameless tryst out and she could get her day started. As he walked past her, he tried for a kiss on the lips but was met with thin air and a smile as she waited for him to walk on out and into the hallway of her apartment complex.

"Will I get to see you again, Max?"

"Damn, are we that close already?"

"You didn't seem to mind last night," he flashed her what he thought was his most award winning smile. "So, will I?"

She glanced at him and remembered quite suddenly that he was the cute guy from the apartment mailbox area. "I'm sure you will," she flashed him a stunning smile, "we live in the same complex. Thank you for a wonderful night."

She quickly closed the door without waiting for him to respond. She rushed back to her room and grabbed another cigarette and lit it and took a deep pull as she fell back on her bed exasperated. She pressed her thighs together tightly to seize the fire now burning there.

"What the fuck was I thinking?" she questioned herself aloud and then the alarm clock's buzzer went off again reminding her that she had things to do and it was forcing her to get up off her ass and get them started.

She took another long drag from the cigarette and looked at remembering that at the beginning of the year she had made another resolution to quit smoking, and she hadn't yet. She rolled over and slapped her hand down on the clock to shut up the alarm and with a groan stood up again and walked towards the kitchen. Coffee was already brewing and she smiled as she sucked in and puffed out the smoke and looked through the cabinets for the possible clean cup, and not finding one she quickly washed one and stood there waiting for the fresh caffeine to join the nicotine.

With coffee and nicotine in her system she rushed off to the shower to truly get her day started. Once she was under the water she let out a sigh as her mind went back to the events of last night. She grimaced as once again she realized it all began because she had been drinking and was well beyond the point of being called drunk. It's always a good thing that the bar she frequented was just down the street from where she lived and she never had to drive or else she would really be fucked – and not literally.

She remembered Jerry the bartender at Chapel Hill Pub telling her he wouldn't serve her anymore to drink and she had only been there a couple of hours. She remembered trying to savor every last drop of that last glass of vodka and cranberry with the shot of vodka as if it would be her very last drink ever. She remembered begging Jerry for one more drink and promising to go home afterwards and him denying her. She remembered the string of profane words she spewed out as she slid and stumbled from her bar stool and then headed out the door.

She stepped deeper into the shower of water letting it run through her hair and down over her face rubbing so she could remove any of the remaining makeup. Already in her head she could hear her apologizes to Jerry and the waitress and them telling her to forget about it and once again the alcohol would flow as if nothing had happened. She could already taste the alcohol again and already see some naked, faceless man staring up at her…

"Fuck!" she grabbed her loofa and dumped some liquid soap on it and rubbed it to a hurried lather. "What the fuck is wrong with you?"

Maxine showered and washed her hair and then hurried from the shower. She brushed her teeth and was thankful that the steam from her shower clouded the mirror so she didn't have to look at the woman staring back at her. She wrapped a towel about her body and walked into her bedroom and had set about her new mission of finding clothes when the phone rang. She walked over and looked at the caller id and answered with a look of disgust on her face.

"Good Morning, Ms. Steele, this is White Chapel Adult Living."

"Yes I could see that on my id," she fought to maintain her temper, "has something happened with my mother?"

"She's been screaming out to see you all morning and nothing we do seems to calm her. We need for you to come here as soon as you possibly can."

"What's she screaming about?"

"We can't make any sense of it, but in the end the doctors all feel that you need to come here so we can get her calm without the use of drugs. When can we expect you, Ms. Steele?"

"Well," Maxine stood there thinking, "I have an appointment that I cannot break so it will be shortly after that. If you have to give her something to at least make her relax a little until I get there then do it."

"I'll let the doctors know you'll be here soon," there was a snide sound in her response, "maybe telling her that will calm your mother enough until you make it."

"What ever she needs," Maxine answered, "and I'll be there as soon as I can."

She hung up the phone before the rude little bitch could say anything else and returned to finding clothes for the day. As she sat down at her vanity, she stared at her face completely unblemished with makeup and shook her head. *There's something so fucking wrong with you* she thought to herself as she set to putting on her "face". As she put on her makeup she would stare at her hair and toyed with putting it up in her new wild style hairdo that she had been wearing just to see how it went over with more professional types.

Stepping out of her house and onto the morning streets Maxine took in a deep breath and looked around. She pulled out a cigarette and lit it and took a deep drag before releasing the smoke into the air. She could feel the morning breeze blowing through her spiked and teased hair and she smiled to herself as she walked towards her car sitting patiently at the curb. Since she was on administrative leave from work she had opted for a pair of blue jeans and a light top over which she wore her favorite black leather jacket and a pair of black leather boots to finish the ensemble. It was mid-August and there was just a little nip in the air and she welcomed it.

She tossed away her cigarette before getting into the Dodge Charger. She turned the key and smiled again at the roar of the motor. Looking at her cell phone she saw that she had missed a call from her Captain and figured he was calling to make certain she didn't miss this newest appointment with her psycho-therapist. She tossed the phone down onto the passenger seat and shook her head.

"Oh Captain my Captain," she glanced in the rear view mirror before pulling out onto the empty street, "yes I'm on the way to see my quack, please no worries."

***

"Good morning," the receptionist tossed around her hair and smiled, "are you here for an appointment?"

"Yes, Det. Maxine Steele," Maxine answered and glanced at her watch.

"Dr. Castille is still with her current patient," the girl said still smiling, "if you'll have a seat I'm sure she'll be with you momentarily."

"Thank you."

She sat down in the lobby and glanced around at the couple of other people sitting there waiting as well. The man sitting there was a cop, not that she knew him, but it was the way he was sitting there with his eyes constantly moving around watching everything around him. He sat there with a straight back and a little stiff in the neck and he seemed to favor his left side a bit more than his right, most likely a gunshot wound close to his hip and probably the reason he was here to discuss the shooting and his injuries. She stared into his eyes and could see he was trying to figure out why she was there and she merely nodded at him to let him know she too was a fellow officer… he returned the nod and they both resumed checking out the other people sitting around them.

She turned her attentions to the lady sitting there holding her head down and looking at her shoes. The woman was definitely a housewife and from the way she was sitting there a very unhappy housewife. She didn't lack money, her husband was probably some big shot defense lawyer and she was reaping the rewards of his cases of defending some of the most ill-reputed criminals of White Chapel. He was most likely cheating on her and from the looks of the way she was shaking he was definitely beating on her and he was sending her to see a psychiatrist to help her "deal with it".

She glanced up at the young girl behind the window that asked her to sit down and noticed that the other cop was looking at the girl as well…

both of them sizing her up. To the naked eye she probably seemed quite the jovial girl, but as Maxine looked at her she could tell that the girl really hated her job, she was young but most likely had at least one young child she was trying to take care of and this was the only job that her medical office assistant title could get her. She watched her lips move and read them telling the girl who could not be seen that she was ready for the day to be over already and hated being away from little Jacen for such long periods.

Maxine shook her head.

"Detective." the girl was now looking at her. "Excuse me, Det. Steele, the Doctor is ready to see you now. Please come on back."

Maxine glanced at the cop and nodded once more before standing and walking towards the door that led to the back rooms. She took a deep breath and waited for the click of the lock before pulling on the door and walking in. As she walked through she did as she always did, she took note of the pristine clean walls and floors, she took note of the open doors and the closed doors and the ones that she could hear voices behind. Her mind worked in circles as she followed the girl ahead of her towards the room she would be sitting in for the next twenty minutes waiting for the doctor and the hour after that talking to her. She hated coming to this place, she hated it with a passion.

"The Doctor will be in with you in a moment," Maxine stepped inside the room and stared at her for but a moment. She was the girl that she couldn't see the first girl talking to, and she too had that painted on smile as she opened the door and then closed it behind her as she walked back up to her seat in the small office area.

This office was so sub clinical, it was more like another office than a doctor's client room. The walls were not a drab and painful white they were more of a soft beige color that as gentle on the eyes, and the floors were covered in a plush carpet instead of the normal linoleum tile. There was a large, comfortable looking leather sofa against one wall and the wall across from it had a large bookshelf full of books ranging from clinical books to differing story books which caused her to wonder just how many of any of these books the doctor had actually read. At the head of the room was a rather modest mahogany desk with an over-sized chair behind it and the desk was cluttered with a computer monitor and its peripherals, and the typical patient papers and folders all covering the large, desk calendar. There were a few family pictures hanging on the walls and on standing on the book shelf, but more prominently displayed were all of her degrees.

Maxine grinned and took a seat on the sofa and waited patiently. This was her fifth or sixth visit with the doctor since she'd been placed on administrative leave three months ago. This was her punishment after coming back from a deep cover investigation a little less than normal, and of course all of the suits thought Internal Affairs had it right that she was not ready to return to active duty. She pushed herself back into the cushions of the sofa and took a deep breath wishing that she could light up a cigarette or that the doctor had a bottle of anything alcoholic in this dungeon she could drink just to get numb.

She laid her head back and tried to relax but there was no comfort only more memories she was longing to forget. She had been working with Dr. Castille to help her come to terms with some of the things she'd done when she was undercover, but it seemed that the more they talked the worse she continued to feel about herself. The more they talked the more she longed to leave her couch and find a bar and drink herself into a coma. Dr. Castille's answer to everything was to stop and think and then consider an alternative.

"There are no real alternatives," she hissed out.

"I see you're dwelling on the negatives again, Detective."

"I'm not quite a detective in my current state of mind, Doctor."

Dr. Castille smiled as she stepped around her desk and sat in the chair. As always, Maxine took a moment to apprise the woman who basically could ruin her well earned career or help her to put it all back on track. The woman was rather short even in heels which she always wore. Her long blonde hair she kept in a tightly wound bun at the top of her head and of course she wore the half glasses that she surely thought made her look more educated. Her blue eyes were bright and her face was rather pretty and definitely didn't show her to be the age Maxine knew… what great work plastic surgeons could do.

"So beyond the negative," she smiled as she began to read through the notes in Maxine's folders, "how are you feeling today, Maxine?"

"Not too good, Doc. I woke up this morning to a hangover, another naked man and of course the home called about my mother needing to see me. If that's not enough, my Captain called and I missed his call but I'm sure he was calling to make certain I'd be coming here and I'm going to get an earful when I do call him back. All in all it's been a great start to another great day."

"Sounds like a full morning. Did you take the time to work on any of the exercises I asked of you or did you do as you've been doing and dranked away more of your precious brain cells?"

Maxine sat there a moment and considered lying to the woman just to get a rise out of her, but she was truly trying to make her way back to work. She closed her eyes and pictured herself smoking a cigarette and then slowly opened them exhaling the air before looking back at the other woman.

"Actually," she tried to smile, "I worked on the exercises and for the most part they did seem to help some, but the truth is there's a lot of shit I know I need to work through. That operation totally fucked me up, I know it did, but I honestly think that getting shot is still messing with my head. I can't seem to get past any of it."

"Maxine," her stern voice kicked in, "those exercises were not given to you to help you to forget but to accept. I understand completely that you went through a lot when you were undercover, and I understand completely that being under so deep that you were expected to do a lot of things that you were not trained to do or expected to do. I don't completely understand it, but I'm sure there are more than just physical scars that you have to deal with concerning the shooting.

"The way I see it, you're ready to go back to work, but it is you who is holding you back."

"You mean you could sign the papers for me to get back into the department?"

"Yes I could do so today and you could be working again as soon as Monday."

"Dr. Castille, I need to get back to work. I mean I really need it because I feel like I'm going stir crazy sitting at home. If I'm out of work much longer I swear I feel I'll get lost in some Facebook nonsense, or I'll wind up finishing what someone else started."

"I'm sure you'll find a way to keep yourself out of such dire dramatic situations, but seriously, how much do you want to go to work?"

"I really need this, Doc," Maxine was sitting up on the edge of her seat. "I can honestly say I'll do almost anything to get my real life back."

"Then I need for you to give me one thing," the Doctor smiled at the raised eyebrow she got and the quizzical look. "One story, it has to be about the most regrettable thing you had to do and what you feel must be done to get over it."

The most regrettable thing? It had to be that incident with the young girl.

Rico Garvey is considered the most dangerous man in White Chapel with connections to both the Italians and the Columbians and no one had ever been able to get in close to him to bring him down. That's where she came in, released from the force because she used excessive force and then an eight month stint in Corrections when she was released she was a bonafide shoe in with Garvey' crew. After a few small "jobs" she had to perform to prove she was no longer a member of the White Chapel Police Department including some petty robberies and transporting some minor weight in drugs she slowly moved her way up to meet with the man himself. But, to prove her worth finally she had to "lay down the law".

The girl was a baser, so strung out that she couldn't even tell you her name. She looked to be in her late teens or early twenties but she had it bad. The girl couldn't sit still, even handcuffed and shackled to a chair she was trying to scratch at her arms and legs digging into the sores she had tracked across her limbs. She was such a pitiful looking creature, her dark hair hacked off just short of her shoulders was all over her head like she'd been pulled from a bed. Her strangely bright blue eyes were stretched open in either need or fright. Her skin was unusually pale and sunken in around her cheeks and eyes. She was a complete mess, and from the way she was fidgeting around she was jonesing for a hit.

The story Maxine had been given was that the girl was being tested. At one point she was a trusted delivery girl, but it became apparent that her habit was getting the better of her. She had been caught stealing and using up the product she had been given to deliver to one of the corner boys, and for theft there was zero tolerance.

"If I let just one person steal from me and get away with it," Garvey explained as he walked around the seated and blubbering girl, "well then everyone will think that they can steal from me, and everything that I've worked for will be for nothing. That is something that I cannot have."

Standing at a little over six feet tall, Garvey made an impressive image. He was of dark skin like a cross between an Italian and Spaniard. He was well muscled and enjoyed walking around in a wife beater just to show off how well defined his muscles are. He was a very handsome man and knew it, and he always had a partially smoked Cuban cigar between his lips. Clean shaven because he didn't want anything cover up his unmarred skin and his hair was oiled down and slicked back away from his forehead.

"The law of the land states," he said aloud from memory, "the life of he who steals from the family is forfeit and should therefore be rendered property tender and canceled forthwith."

Maxine took a deep breath as she again looked down at the blubbering little girl. She sat there begging and crying, those big blue eyes staring deep into hers and pleading for her life. Her skin was mottled and almost ashen from her lack of sunlight and use of drugs. She looked completely sickly.

"Her contract ends and you're the one to make certain it's paid in full," he pulled the Dessert Eagle semi-automatic from his shoulder holder and held it out to Maxine. "You must take care of this now."

Without hesitating Maxine took the offered pistol and held it to the girl's head. She swallowed hard as she pulled back the hammer and looked up the man waiting for him to give his final edict. A light sheen of sweat slowly dripped from her forehead and down the side of her face as she stood there staring once more at the back of the girl's head. *Damn, what in the fuck have I...*

Garvey nodded and her finger moved just slightly and felt her hand jerk back as the gun fired. Her subconscious watched in horror as the girl's head exploded and the blood sprayed back at her and then again out of the front of her head as the bullet passed through. Her stomach lurched and she felt the air squeezed from her lungs as the dead body slumped forward to lie dead at the man's feet, but she managed to keep her face serene showing no signs of care or concern. Her stomach churned as her entire body suddenly realized that she had never killed another person before, but she forced her knees to keep from buckling. She wanted to cry, she wanted to scream, but she did neither instead she looked up at Garvey and handed him pistol back and walked off.

"Now that was impressive," he said with a sick smile. "I honestly didn't think you'd do it. I was sure that you were some little undercover bitch the police thought they could plant in my little organization. I mean I've looked over your little resume and I was completely impressed with what I read."

Maxine sat there remembering his face, that smug smirk as if he knew she was his and that there was no way she could ever go back. He stood there with that confident look of sitting on her back or holding her over a rushing river and knowing that he held her life in his hands. She remembered swallowing hard but only smiling at him not letting him know that he scared the absolute hell out of her. Her palms were sweating, but she held her hands at her sides and never let her eyes leave his.

"This is what I live with," she whispered. "That's something that has never gone into any report, and the only other person who even knows about it was my handler at the time.

"I've cried many nights over that, Doc. I can see that girl's face every time I glance at a mirror… every fucking time I close my eyes. I can hear her begging me every time I close my eyes. And, if that's not enough I see him just standing there watching as if it was just something natural. I was so sick and I couldn't do anything but stand there. When I finally got a chance to throw up I think I passed out."

Castille took a deep breath and stared down at her notes. She was prepared for something, but she was not so prepared for her patient to come clean with this. How could she allow this woman back on the Force, and yet she'd got a call from Capt. Salter stating that he needed her back to full duty as soon as possible due to her being needed on a very primary case. She looked over the rim of her glasses and stared at the woman sitting there on the sofa. *This woman is a walking time bomb and she's going to explode very soon… what am I to do and maintain my integrity?*

"So, what would I do to get pass this, Doctor?" she grimaced and choked back the urge to vomit as the sight of the hole in the girl's head was now clearly visible before her eyes. "I'd turn that gun on Garvey and shoot him and take that poor girl to some treatment center for the help she needed. Or, maybe I'd just turn the gun on myself and not have to continue to live with her face floating around in my head."

"I really didn't know," Dr. Castille finally said, "but now I understand why you feel as if you have to hold on to all of this. But, Maxine, you have to let it all go or it will continue to eat you up from the inside. Look at it this way, Garvey is now behind bars for all of the atrocities he's committed and it was because of your undercover work."

"And for a lot of the shit I did," Maxine dropped her head, "I should probably be in a cell right next to his."

Dr. Castille took a deep breath and stared at Maxine as if trying to look into her, but she could see nothing more than what the woman cared to show and that was baffling. She sat back in her chair and exhaled slowly as she thought to take another route. "How are you handling the shooting?"

Maxine's hand went to the spot just above her right breast and pressed against the indentation it made in her flesh. She began to grind her teeth as she felt a sudden burning and she closed her eyes against the phantom pain. She could almost feel the wind blowing that night as she made her way from her favorite bar towards her apartment complex. It had been raining and the smell of it was still thick in the air but it was so fresh and so soothing that it didn't matter that she was almost too drunk to walk straight. It had been two weeks since the end of the undercover case and she was on leave pending an investigation of everything that had happened in the last two years.

She was whistling in her drunken state. She was almost skipping to the point that she almost tripped when the heel of her boot hit a crack in the sidewalk. As she fell forward, that's when she felt it. It was a severe burning that was cooking in to her shoulder and the force of whatever hit her tossed her backwards until she bounced off the wall of the building. She could feel herself screaming out just before her head hit the wall and she blacked out. From there things went black, but the pain and the burning continued.

"Ms. Steele, can you hear me?" the sound of his voice was like an echo in the dark and just bounced around in her head painfully. "My name is Dr. Soroyan, you've been shot."

"Where am I?" the words were nothing more than a whisper.

"You're in White Chapel Medical Center," he stood over her, "we had to remove a bullet from your right shoulder. It was a little touchy because the bullet was pretty close to your lung and we didn't want to risk you bleeding out. You're in recovery right now but we'll be moving you to a room here pretty soon. Is there anyone you want us to call?"

She looked up at the man and shook her head. The pain in her shoulder was unbearable and the burning seemed to be consuming her entire body. She could feel her eyes watering up as she fought to keep from crying, but the only thought that kept running through her head was… someone had tried to kill her.

"Maxine," Dr. Castille broke through her mind, "how are you handling that you were shot?"

"What can I say," she smiled as she stared at the doctor, "I'm taking it one day at a time. I mean how else can I deal with it?"

Dr. Castille pulled her glasses off and placed them on her desk. She steepled her fingers together and placed her chin on the tips. "Are you sure you're ready for this, Maxine? I mean I can sign these orders and this will put you back on the street, but are you sure that you're ready to do this?"

"I need this, Doctor Castille," she stood and walked up to the edge of the desk and stared deeply into the other woman's eyes. "I have to get back out into this shit or I will definitely consider a bullet."

She stood there watching as Dr. Castille pulled out a pen and scribbled her name across the release forms that would be passed on to the Internal Affairs department and to her Captain. Again she wanted to smile, but the most she could do was pull up one corner of her mouth into what most would consider a smirk and she nodded her head in accomplishment.

"Thank you, Doctor Castille, thank you."

"I do this under one condition," the Doctor glanced up as she read through the paperwork and made a few quick notes. "If for any reason you need to talk that you will not hesitate to call, and even though you will hesitate I need for you to make me that promise."

"You have my word," she put up her right hand with three fingers up. "I promise I'll call at the first sign of trouble."

"Excellent, I accept."

***

"Ok I'm here," Maxine announced as she walked up to the front desk in the administrative office of the White Chapel Adult Living Facility. "Can someone please tell me what's going on with my mother?"

The young lady behind the desk looked at her completely confused and picked up the phone unsure as to who she needed to call. There were no others in the office with her for her to ask.

"I'm sorry, Ma'am," she started putting down the phone, "but how can I help you?"

"My name is Maxine Steele and I'm here about my mother, Janice Rollins," Maxine was peeved because she figured the girl should know without her going through all of this. "I guess you need to call Dr. Thine or somebody in the back who will know what the hell is going on."

"Yes, Ma'am," the rattled girl answered and picked the phone back up punching a number on the keypad. She spoke quietly for a moment and then sat there waiting on the person on the other side of the phone. Her eyes never left Maxine's and she never seemed to calm down.

Maxine stood there watching the girl with a stare that obviously frightened her, and that was her intentions. Her life kept her busy enough and she had more pressing things to contend with than to have to deal with a mother she didn't truly get along with. She turned her back on the girl and walked away, her main duties where her mom were concerned were taking care of the bills; namely paying off what ever her insurance didn't pay to keep here her at this place and out of her hair. Years of pent up anger welled to the surface and threatened to boil out and she needed to get away from the girl before she bore her wrath.

"Det. Steele," an older woman's voice called out behind her, "Detective, thank you for getting here so soon."

Maxine looked at her watch and grunted. It had been over three hours since they'd called her this morning, but then maybe they had given her mother something to calm her down and the need for her to bet here wasn't as pressing. She walked up to the woman waiting for an explanation that never came and watched in aggravation as the lady turned and walked off expecting her to follow.

"Is it possible for someone to tell me what's going on with my mother?"

"I'm sorry, Det. Steele," she woman was walking fast and glanced over her shoulder to make certain she was keeping up, "I'm not privy to what's going on but Dr. Thine has been with her since the start of her episode."

"So you have no clue?"

"None," the woman answered.

They walked on in silence and she cringed at the very ominous sounds and smells that surrounded her. Now it was her time to be nervous because this place always had a way of making her feel out of place and the main reason she tried to avoid coming here unless absolutely necessary. Unlike where she'd come from this place was the epitome of clinical. Even as an adult living facility there were on-call nurses and doctors as well as nurses aides to keep a watchful eye on some of the more needy residents. At one point her mother was more self-sufficient but within the last year her mother's mental instabilities have falter calling for her to be moved from her private apartment to one of the patient rooms located here in the main building.

She stepped up her pace and was quickly walking beside the woman who had been leading her to her mother's room. Up in the distance she could hear the sounds of one of the patients screaming at the top of her lungs begging and pleading.

"I need her now! You must get her to come see me today! She has to know he was here… she has to know he was here."

As they got closer, she recognized that the voice was that of her mother's and she sounded completely erratic. Maxine jogged away from the woman and right into her mother's room to see what the hell was going on. As she got to the room, she watched as a couple of large, burly men tried to hold down a frail, little 90lb woman to her bed as she thrashed about like she was possessed. Her mother looked like a wild woman with her long hair completely disheveled and her eyes wide and she was sweating as if she had been running.

"What the fuck are you doing to her?"

A rather tall, lanky black man walked up to her and she immediately recognized him as Dr. Thane. He was holding his ever present clipboard as he stood before her in a very authoritative manner. He pushed his wide rim glasses up on his nose and ran his hand across his bald head. For all his need to feel in control of every situation, as he stood before her, he seemed very unsure of himself at this very moment.

"Det. Steele, thank you for finally making it here," his normally deep voice cracked just a bit. "Your mother seems to need to talk to you most urgently."

She jerked her eyebrow up as she stared at him. "Who is this person she's going on about that she's seen?"

"We have no clue," the Doctor answered, "no one has been on schedule to see your mother since you were last here two months ago."

Maxine shook her head as her mother got louder and louder screaming out that she needed to see her and that she had to tell her that "he" had been there. She looked at the Doctor and was tempted to ask him if they'd given her anything to calm her, but just from the way her mother was tossing about the two Orderlies she knew that they hadn't. Her mother had been suffering all this time, and even though there was no love lost between the two of them it angered her that her mother had been suffering.

"We'll discuss your treatment of my mother once I've talked to her," she hissed through clenched teeth. "This bullshit here is unacceptable. Now tell your bulls to get off of her and everyone get the fuck out now."

The Doctor turned and called out to the two men for them to let go and leave the room. He turned back to say something to the Detective and she had moved passed him into the room to try and comfort her mother. He watched as one of the two men bumped her in passing and made no effort to apologize and this brought a smirk to his face.

"We'll talk when you're done then," he pushed his glasses up on his nose and straightened his shoulders as if he'd had the last word and he was proud. He moved out of the room and closed the door watching as the elderly woman slowly calm down.

"Mother," she called out trying to get her attention away from the men as they walked by. "Mother, it's me, Maxine."

"Maxine, oh my god," she began to cry and reach out asking for her daughter to come forward so she could hold her. "Maxine, they wouldn't tell me when you would come. They wouldn't tell me if they had called you. God thank you for sending my baby to me."

Maxine stepped forward and allowed her mother to pull her into her arms and they held each other. She could hear her sniffling and shaking as she petted her back trying to soothe her.

"Mom," she pulled back looking into her eyes. "What's this all about, Mom? What's going on?"

"I'm so sorry. So sorry for everything but I needed to see you, Baby. He was here. I saw him… I saw him as clear as day. He was here."

"Who was here?"

"I saw him and I know he saw me. He stood there … right there in the door and he smiled at me."

"Mom, Mom you're not making any sense. Who are you talking about?"

Maxine stood there staring at her mother. Age had finally caught up with her and it showed in her face. Wrinkles and crow's feet decorated the corners of her lips and eyes. Her skin was pale and pasty from a lack of sunlight and her hair needed to be combed but it was a snow white with streaks of the dark hair it used to be. She was so thin like she didn't eat and hadn't eaten in ages, and this was so different from the full figured woman she had grown up with. Thin, long nailed fingers gripped her hands and held them tightly as she stared at the door.

"Mom, I'm going to get the Doctor to come in and give you something like a sedative to help you calm and rest ok."

"You have to believe me. Please say you believe me, Maxine, please. He was really here standing there like a ghost sent here to haunt me."

"I believe you, Mom," she answered as she pulled her crying mother back into her arms. This was disheartening seeing this woman breaking down like this after all that she went through growing up. To stand here holding her as she completely unraveled caused Maxine to weep herself as she finally called out to the doctor she knew was waiting just outside the closed door.

"I want her to have a sedative, Dr. Thine," she said when the man opened the door. "I want her to relax and to sleep this off and I don't want any bullshit from you or you'll have a serious problem with me. Do you understand me?"

"Yes, Detective, completely."

Maxine watched as her mother slowly sunk into the bed her eyes fluttering closed after the doctor administered the shot. She took a deep breath and stood over her protectively hoping that she would just sleep while she tried to figure all of this out. Her thoughts were scattered as she looked about the room trying to decipher what her mother was rambling about.

Damn I could really use a cigarette right now, and a really strong drink.

"Ok, Doctor," she moved around the bed towards the man at the door. "You now have my full attention and your best bet is to make the most of it because right now I'm really not in the mood to be dicked around."

Chapter 3

a week before

He stood there watching as she made her way up the stairs and into the boy's room; she wasn't a big woman but with all of the smoking she could barely breathe at times. She was dressed as she always seemed to be dressed, in her night gown and a short robe that she never kept closed and it was good that she didn't have large breasts or they would be flopping all over her chest. She had a cigarette hanging from her lips and a belt in her hand as she pushed the door open and stared down at the sleeping boy.

"Wake up you dirty little shit," her voice always scared him. It always seemed to pierce his dreams and wake him. "It's time for your bath."

For him a bath was never just a bath. For him a bath was her trying to scrub his skin off of his body with a pot scouring pad until parts of his body would bleed. It was as if she loved to see and hear him screaming out in pain. Sometimes he could see her standing over him with a sick smile on her face as she rubbed and rubbed while she prayed or called him names. The baths were never quick, and he moaned and rolled over hoping that she was truly not there.

"I said," she swung the belt down across his body hidden beneath a thin sheet, "get your little nasty ass up."

He stood there watching as she brought the belt down again and again watching as the boy wailed and writhed on the bed. Even in the dark of the room he could almost see the welts the belt was causing and he longed to grab the woman and just shake her until she passed out, but he could do nothing more than stand there and watch.

"Please, Mommy," he begged as he tried to run from the belt and was backed into the wall the bed rested against. "Please not a bath."

"Why not you nasty little beast," she screamed out as she grabbed the sheet and pulled it back, "you need one because you pissed in the bed again." She struck him with the belt again and again as he covered his head and rolled up into a ball to protect himself.

He stood there staring at the large wet spot on the bed and felt sorry and ashamed for the little boy. Why didn't she just understand? Why did she beat him like that and scare him more?

"I've got the water ready now get your ass to the bathroom and get out of those nasty, dirty clothes."

The boy got up and ran to the bathroom and tried to close the door but wasn't successful as she kicked it open and stood there watching as he removed his clothes. She could see him physically shaking as he stood there trying to hide his little private area. She pointed to the tub and watched as he stepped over the edge and into the hot water moaning out as he forced himself to get in and sit down. She stepped up to the bathroom sink and grabbed the scouring pad and knelt beside the tub.

"You nasty little freak," she growled as she grabbed the soap and began to rub the bar against the pad. "It's the same shit every single night. Do you think I enjoy getting up and washing your fucking sheets every day? Do you think I enjoy airing out that stinking room every day just to make it tolerable for you to sleep in?"

He stood there watching as she began to rub the scouring side against the boy's skin harshly, and he began to scream out. She began at his arms and went around his back and shortly after beginning he started to bleed. She went down his back and had him stand and then around his stomach, and she was praying as the rough surface ate into the boy's sensitive skin. She went down his legs and then back up swatting his hands out of her way as she made it to his penis.

"Dirty little bastard," she grumbled as the boy wailed out. "Dirty little bastard with your dirty, filthy no-nothings. Pissing in that bed and now I have to wash you up like you're a fucking baby.

"Dear God," she began praying again, "forgive the sins of this body. Let my cleansing carry him through the day and the rest of his life. Forgive him for the thoughts going through his young, sick mind and let not my hands stray from cleaning every inch of him in this blessed water."

He stood there watching as she pushed the boy down into the hot water, and the boy screamed out as the water hit his fresh wounds. Tears streamed down from both of their eyes as he too felt the boy's pain. He touched the different spots on his body as if the water was washing over his flesh. He wanted to strike out. The little boy wanted to run. He swallowed hard as he felt the heat of the water burning into his flesh especially his raw penis, and his hands automatically cupped the overly sensitive area and he grimaced in more pain.

"Now," she whined, "now we need to absolve you of your sins. We need to baptize you and wash away all of those things God thinks are dirty of you."

He stood there watching, transfixed as she grabbed him by the hair and dragged him to lie out in the tub. Her eyes were glazed with an anger that he never understood and to this day he completely feared. She held him with the back of his head just barely above the level of the water and she began to pray over him.

"Father God, we stand here as witnesses to this child's profession of faith in your Son, Jesus Christ. The scriptures declare that the old nature dies and a new one is born at the moment of that profession. Grant that this child grows in the power and nature of a believer in Christ, receiving the Holy Spirit as a counselor and teacher. Give him the strength and wisdom to live before you in righteousness, as a faithful member of your family. Amen."

And with that… she dunked his head under water and held him down. She didn't hold his nose. She didn't care that as he screamed in terror his body was filling with water. She didn't care that his eyes were stretched, begging and pleading with her. She knelt there watching as he choked and sputtered under the surface of the water until he seemed to take his last breath before she finally pulled him up. The little boy coughed out the water from his abused lungs almost vomiting and she never took her hate filled eyes off of him.

"Amen," the boy finally coughed out. "Thank you, Mommy."

He slowly sat up in the dark room and looked around. She wasn't there. He wiped the sweat from his brow and took a deep breath as the dreams still filled his head. How could anyone be so goddamn cruel and have no regrets. He could still taste the soapy water in his mouth and this forced him to cough as he tried to clear his filled lungs. She wasn't there… the tub wasn't there… there was no baptism and he was lying in his bed. He finally pulled the covers from his body and looked down at the large wet spot underneath his body. He could feel himself shaking as he fought to keep from crying. He jumped up out of the bed and rushed around to find clean bedding.

"I'm sorry, Mommy," he whispered as he pulled the soiled bedding away and quickly changed to the clean. "I won't do it again. I'll go bathe and clean myself."

His cries echoed through his home as he finally made his way to the bathroom to bathe. He stared at the sink counter and couldn't force himself to blink. He looked up into the mirror and wiped away the tears in his eyes with the back of his hand as he stared at the scouring pad and the soap laying there waiting for him.

"I'm sorry, Mommy," he whimpered, "I'll bathe and I'll never do it again. I promise."

***

He sat in his van watching her just as he had been her for the last week. He knew her complete schedule from the time she got up in the mornings to the time her husband left for his job and she finally left for hers. He knew the times her two college age kids went to their schools on Mondays and got back home Friday evenings. He knew when the housekeeper showed up, left for her lunch and then left to go home. He had been inside of the house and knew the complete layout like the back of his hand and could move around in there as easily and freely in the dark as if each room was brightly lit.

She was a beautiful woman. Her long curly hair was blond and highlighted with bits of a copper-ish auburn color. She had deep blue eyes and if one was to look really close, as he had on a number of occasions, there were flecks of grey in her irises. She was statuesque in build, the kind of woman who dressed as she dressed because she always got that second look from the men she passed by on the streets or in her office building and she seemed to enjoy the attention.

He licked his lips as he sat across the street from her home watching her and her family through the open windows of their home. They didn't seem to care about privacy, and he was sure it was because they didn't feel threatened in any way from anyone. They held themselves above everyone and there was no worry about looking down their nose at those below their station. He pulled a cigarette from the pack that had been sitting on the dashboard and he lit it. As he drew in the smoke, he looked around to make certain that he was not gathering attention before turning back to her family.

It was early still, almost too early, but he needed to get into place because it was going to be a long weekend. He ran his fingers through his short, straggled hair and then pulled the cigarette from his lips and exhaled. He had it all planned out and this was going to set the stage for everything else to come. He pressed his head back against the headrest and finished the cigarette and smiled… soon, everything was going to work out soon.

"You'll be the one who will get her on the case. You'll be the one to intrigue her to investigate. They'll be sure to call you in this time and I'll let God show you the way because you've lost your way."

***

"What time does your plane leave?" he heard her ask her husband from his hiding place in the basement. Everything said was clear through the vents it was as if he were in the room with them.

"It leaves at 7 in the morning," he answered from the bathroom where he was probably brushing his teeth as a part of his nightly ritual. "I've already called a taxi to come pick me up so you don't have to take me."

"I could have driven you there, Jonathan," he could almost see her smiling, "it wouldn't have been a problem and it would have put me downtown for my meeting."

"Yes, but way too early. The cab will be fine, Margaret."

"Yes, Dear," she giggled in that way that caused his "no-nothings" to jump and he wiped his hand across his forehead.

"Why you nasty little shit," he could hear his mother hissing in his ear, "always thinking with that damned little head. That's why you'll amount to nothing."

He pulled out a picture of Margaret Fitzwilliams and stared at it shaking the sound of her voice from his head. For all her beauty there was something very familiar about her and that's what drew him to her. He stared at her face studying it as he had for the last few weeks getting to know her better and better. He slid a finger along the contours of her jaw and around her chin as if he was caressing it and again he felt jump in his crotch that caused him to breathe in deep. She was so very successful and her husband was equally successful and anyone else would probably be jealous, but he was not.

"Do you need me to pack anything for you?" she asked her husband.

"No, I think I got it all put together this time. I'll only be gone for a few days but I should be back by Wednesday night, these guys want to check out a few properties and I've researched about five that I know should work out just fine."

"Damn, so long? And whatever shall I do with myself until you get back here?"

He sat there listening wishing he could be closer, but knowing that he could never get closer to their room this early without being seen. The basement was the best he could do since all of the vents undoubtedly led there and he could listen in to almost every part of the house, but it was ok because he had learned to be a very patient man. Thanks to his mommy he had learned to do a lot of things really well and to appreciate them all.

He sat there in the basement listening as the couple made love that night and it caused him to sweat. The sounds she made had him sitting there wiggling upon the cold concrete floor wishing he could actually watch them. In his mind he could see it all and he licked his lips. He could imagine her naked body glistening with her head thrown back as her husband leaned over her humping and grunting and sweating all over her as he wiggled and moved between her spread thighs. She invited him into her by keeping her legs up and wrapped around his body grinding and swearing beneath him until he finally released himself as deep inside her body as he could push. Then in the end she would lay there stroking his face as he cuddled her naked body close to his.

"God I'm going to miss that while you're gone."

"I'm going to miss you, Baby," her husband answered completely out of breath like he'd run a marathon.

He sat there listening through the night as the husband snored like a buzz saw gone wild in a forest of trees. He could barely hear her, and he wondered how she slept next to a man so damn loud. One of the kids quietly snuck into the house very late and slowly made their way upstairs to their room and closed the door. He allowed himself to doze off lightly for a moment as he sat there in the house like a shadow.

Before the sun rose the cell phone in his pocket silently vibrated waking him for his light sleep, he stood and stretched and pulled on his gloves and face mask before moving towards the stairs leading up into the house. Slowly he made his way from the basement up into the main part of the house, and walked about the house as he has on a number of occasions. He moved through the living room and sat in her favorite chair and moved his face about the upper pillows to get her smell. As he pressed into the seat he could feel her arms wrapping about his body holding him, comforting him, keeping him like a nurturing mother would. He softly moaned before forcing himself to get up out of the chair.

He then moved into the kitchen and looked through the cabinet and found her favorite coffee cup and he brought it to his lips as if he was drinking from it; the feel of it pressing to his lips was just like kissing her. He moaned softly before putting the cup back into the cabinet. He stood at the cabinet holding on to it as his body slowly yet fiercely reacted to being so intimate with her, he shook and his knees felt weak, and he bit his lip to keep from moaning out louder. His eyes closed and rolled back into his head and his fingers gripped the edge of the counter top as he took deep breaths to try and calm the storm raging inside of him. He grunted as he released himself in his pants, and behind the mask a tear slowly ran from his eye. Afterwards, he adjusted his "no-nothings" in his pants trying to avoid the mess he'd made and then he slowly made his way up the stairs towards the bedrooms missing the one that creaked just as the one child had earlier when they were sneaking in and moved to the room doors.

First he checked in on the two kids. The oldest was the girl who looked a lot like her mother except she had dyed her hair a dark auburn color to contrast with her pale colored skin. She was a little shorter than her mother but more athletic so she was a lot thinner than her mother. He felt a shiver run up and down his spine as he stared at the girl and wondered if it was she who had come in so late and was now sleeping so peacefully. Next he slipped into the boy's room and stared down at him sleeping on top of his covers in nothing more than a pair of boxers. The boy was tall, much taller than his short and stocky father. He was most likely another athlete, easily a basketball player, and most likely very good with the girls in his school. It was probably him who had come in so late after having a night out with his friends drinking and being stupid at some college bar. He took a deep breath and left the room and moved down the hallway.

Finally, he opened the door to the Master's bedroom and moved inside closing the door so he was alone with the parents. He walked up to the end of the bed and stood there in the shadows of the room looking down at them as they tossed around on the bed. They were sleeping so peacefully to the point the husband wasn't even snoring as forcefully as he had been earlier. He wished he could ignore the fact that the man was there but each time he turned his attention to her the man would move as if he knew someone was there ogling his wife.

She was the highlight of the bedroom, laying there in her thin night gown. There was just a sliver of moonlight coming into the room and as it shone down on her it cast an eerie glow making her look like an angel. He licked his lips as he gazed upon her body. She was lying out on top of the covers with her long legs bent and her feet tucked under her husband's legs. She was so pale that she looked almost translucent, and her body still had that damp just fucked look. He stood there sweating wanting to grab her right at this point, but it's been this way for a couple of weeks. She was absolutely appetizing and soon she would be his.

The alarm clock went off and he stood there watching as she reached a delicate arm out and tapped the top. She stretched and rolled over hugging up close to her husband and kissing him at the back of his neck. The man moved a bit at her touch but didn't seem to awaken.

"Dear," she said softly in his ear. "Jon, its time to wake up, the cab will be here in about 30 minutes to pick you up."

He slowly faded back deeper into the shadows of the room and then walked towards the bedroom door. Quietly he opened it and slipped outside into the hallway as her husband began to stir and awaken. He looked back once more and could barely make out her leg as she slowly pulled up the covers over her feet and was lying there now watching her husband and he pushed his body up and finally out of bed. His mind was a whirl as to the time he would now have to wait for the kids to leave and finally they would be all alone. She would be his … all his.

He made his way back to his hiding place in the basement with a smile hidden away by the face mask. Yes, everything was working out just as he had planned, and soon she would also be involved because there was no way they could leave her out from this point on. There was absolutely no way.

***

"Right this way, Detective," the portly officer held the front door to the home open and allowed the well-dressed man to step inside. "The body is upstairs in the Master's bedroom."

"How's it look, Grady?"

"It's bad, Sir," the man dropped his head as he closed the door. "Really bad."

Detective David Raymonds pushed his blazer back away from his pants pocket and stuffed his hand inside as he moved towards the staircase leading up to the rooms in the house. He stopped and looked around trying to see if there was anything out of order or anything missed that his well experienced eyes would see more so than those wannabe detectives from the crime scene lab. He could hear someone talking most likely asking questions of the husband who he would talk to a little later, but in his mind the guy was the most likely of suspects; that was just the way most of these cases worked out.

As he walked up the stairs, he noticed that the stair about four down from the top made a creaking sound as he stepped down on it. He quickly made a mental note of that and he will write down in his notebook and in his finally report back at the station. At the top of the stairs he quickly pulled on a pair of latex gloves as he took note of the placement of the rooms. He walked into each of them just so he could get a better layout of how the home was set up, this would give him a better idea of what his subject was thinking as he moved about before he moved in to kill the victim. Just incase it wasn't the husband he would know how someone who didn't live there made it through without disturbing or possibly waking anyone. He was being very meticulous in his investigation of this home because his Captain was not in a good mood about this entire situation.

Raymonds stepped into the Master's bedroom and noticed that there was a small vestibule before you got right into the main part of the room. The over-sized bed was against the wall to the left once you got past the corner and from the door you could just barely see a small portion of it. There was the traditional chest of drawers and a dresser of drawers close to where the large walk-in closet doors were, and right at the door going into the Master's bathroom there was a lady's vanity. He glanced into the walk-in closet and stared at the over abundance of clothes and shoes in there; he quickly took not of the lack of room in there for anyone to hide and then turned back to the room.

Raymonds cursed under his breath about how people with money just always seemed to go overboard, and then he turned his attentions to the bed. Everything just from his initial glance seemed way to clean to be a murder scene, but there was indeed a body lying there in the bed. Kneeling on the edge of the bed just to the left of the victim was the White Chapel Chief Medical Examiner Melanie DeLong with her long hair pulled back into a pony tail and her medical bag opened as she studied closely at the victim.

She was laying there as if she were sleeping. Her hair was perfectly combed and seemed to just lie around her head and shoulders. Her nightgown was a pristine white and flared down near her feet. He walked up on her and gazed down at her face and noticed that she looked as if she had applied make-up, there was a light face powder with an eye shadow and even a light lipstick.

"Damn," he said to himself, "someone took a lot of time to make her look even prettier than she already is."

There was a guy from the crime lab walking around snapping pictures and another moving around with a dusting brush lifting prints. He took out his pad and began making notes that he would need for his final report.

"Make certain you get pictures of her face and feet and hands for me," he told the cameraman and then he turned towards the guy dusting for prints. "Have you dusted here near the bed?"

"No, Sir, I just got up here after printing the husband and the children so that their prints would be on file for comparison later."

"Ok, good," he reached down and moved her head about looking for any marks around her neck that would show signs of strangulation.

"Dr. DeLong," he finally addressed her, "can you tell me the cause of death please?"

"To be honest," she looked up and pushed her glasses up on her nose with the back of her wrist, "I was baffled at first, but then a closer look and well it completely shocked me because she's so clean."

Slowly she moved closer to the foot of the bed and grabbed the hem of the woman's nightgown and pulled it up until she finally got it pulled over her waist. Raymonds stepped back for a moment and then quickly pulled himself together as he stood there and stared down at the woman's abdomen and pelvic areas.

"Judging from the number of stab wounds here, I'd definitely say that this poor lady bled out. I won't have exacts until I get her back to my lab but just from my preliminary exam I'd say there's over 30 stab wounds."

"Goddamn... 30?"

"Yes, he definitely went overboard on this lady."

Raymonds could feel his stomach lurching and was very thankful that the killer had the "decency" to clean her up, but this also meant that he washed away very important evidence. He stared down again at her pelvic area and took note of how the stab wounds were very concentrated around her vagina.

"With him washing her up," DeLong broke into his thought process, "I cannot tell if the victim was raped prior to him stabbing her to death."

"Can you tell how long she's been dead?"

"I'd have to say approximately 36 hours, but again I'll be able to give you an exact on that once I get her back to my lab."

"Well that gives me a little something to work with so thank you, Doctor."

He couldn't pull his eyes away from the stab wounds until Dr. DeLong finally pulled down her gown and told her assistants that they could finally place her in the body bag and load her up on the gurney to take her downstairs. He moved in close to the bed hoping to find anything under her that may lead to finding out who could have done something like this, but the bed was as clean as she was.

"Anything else you can tell me, Doctor?"

"Yes," DeLong pulled off her gloves and stood up from the bed, "she was bathed in her own body bath. You didn't get close but you could smell the vanilla on her skin, and I had one of my techs check the bathroom and there was a vanilla based wash in there. I have a feeling he may have even bathed her in her own tub."

"With the number of stab wounds there would have been a lot of blood, have you found any here at all?"

"The room has been luminoled and there's absolutely no blood in this room at all. This poor lady was not killed here; they will be checking the house just in case, but…"

"She wasn't killed here," he said again. "She was most likely taken from here, killed and then brought back so she would be found. That's a lot of work wouldn't you say? Thank you for your time and help."

He walked away leaving her to finish getting the body ready to be carted away to her lab for an autopsy and more examinations. He swallowed hard as he again thought of the number of times this woman's pubic area had been stabbed and literally sliced open by a knife. He removed his gloves and dropped them into the prepared waste bag as he walked out of the door and into the fresh air of the hall. Immediately he noticed that he had indeed smelled the vanilla, but was unaware of it because it just seemed a natural smell. He moved towards the staircase and almost touched it and then quickly pulled his hand back and called for one of the crime scene techs.

"I want this entire thing printed from top to bottom."

"Right away, Detective," the young man said and ran off to get it taken care of.

Raymonds walked downstairs and made his way towards the living room. His mind was filled with everything he'd seen thus far and he was sure there would be more to come. The house in itself was a very beautiful living space and he was sure the decorations were all done by the woman upstairs and had very little to do with the man he could see sitting on the sofa with his head down in his hands. He would try to make this quick, but there was still so many things he needed to know from the man he had at first been sure was the culprit. After what he'd just seen it was almost impossible it was the husband, who ever had committed this crime was a very angry and remorseless animal.

The man sitting before him was rather short and from the spot on the top of his head he was balding. He was a bit pudgy around the middle and looked like he spent a lot of time in fast food restaurants. He looked like a man who may not have a lot of problems walking but definitely made a lot of noise sleeping, and possibly the grunt or two leaning over to tie his shoes. He looked up as Raymonds drew closer to where he was sitting and his deep blue eyes were bloodshot from crying and the crow's feet at the sides of them were very pronounced. His face was clean shaven with deep dark colored eyebrows over wide set eyes.

Raymonds took all of this in as he approached the man and put out his hand.

"Mr. Fitzwilliams," he watched as he stood and accepted the gesture, "I'm Detective David Raymonds, homicide; I'll be in charge of your wife's investigation. I want to start by saying I'm sorry for your loss, but I do have a few more questions before I leave. Are you up to it, Sir?"

"Yes, please let's get this over with," he looked over to his daughter who was sitting next to him and then his son who was in the arm chair just to the right of the sofa. "My family and I need some time together away from all of this noise and all of these people. I still need to call her parents and explain all of this to them."

"I understand, Mr. Fitzwilliams, I'll try to be quick and brief," Raymonds pulled out his pen and notepad. "How long had you been out of town and when did you get back?"

"I was picked up Friday morning by Blue Line Cab and I didn't get back until this morning around ten. I walked in this morning not even expecting to see her home, she should have been at work, but when I got upstairs and found her… I…" the man broke down putting his head back down into his hands.

"What were you out of town for?"

"I'm a co-owner of a commercial property investment company and we own land parcels across the US and I was out of town showing a few properties to some potential buyers. I was only gone for a few days… just a few fucking days. How did this happen? Why was she killed?"

"I'm not sure, Mr. Fitzwilliams, but we're going to do everything we can to find out what happened here. I hate to ask but I have to… were there any problems in your marriage? Your wife wasn't," he paused to look at the kids, "involved?"

"No!" he looked at his kids and shook his head. "No! That's completely absurd. My wife and I had a good marriage and she would never go outside of our marriage."

"I'm sorry, but I had to ask. We have to eliminate all possibilities to get to the bottom of all of this. I know right now all of this is hard to understand but its all necessary. What kind of work did your wife do? Do you know if she had any enemies?"

"She was an attorney. Um, she was an Assistant District Attorney, and I couldn't honestly tell you if she had any enemies. She never brought her work home with her so we never discussed any of her cases. She used to always tell me that what she did had no place in our home so when ever she got to our front door she left it all right there and picked it back up the next morning. You would have to go there and ask them about any of the cases she was working on.

"Do you think it could have been someone from one of her cases? Could one of those bastards got out of prison and hunted her down?"

"Again, I'm not sure but it's definitely something worth looking into. I want to thank you for your time, Sir, and again I'm sorry about your wife. If I have anymore questions I'll be sure to give you a call."

Before the man could say anything else Raymonds turned on his heels and walked away from the grieving family. He stuffed his notepad back into the pocket of his blazer. He stopped at the foot of the stairs and looked up and again his mind was full of the sight of a beautiful woman who's lower abdomen was completely eviscerated from a animal who undoubted did not like this woman. His stomach lurched again as he finally walked out of the front door and took a deep breath.

"What a great way to start a morning."

Chapter 4

Two days later

"Raymonds, my office."

Raymonds looked up at his name and stared over at his Captain. The man looked the part of a seasoned hard-ass standing there in the door of his office. The suit he wore looked like it was something out of the late 80s and quite tight. It was faded from being over washed and a little high around the ankles. Underneath the jacket was the making of a potbelly from years of being behind a desk and not being out on the streets and a lack of still making it to the gym. He knew for a fact the man kept a bottle of gin in his bottom desk drawer and would slip some into his coffee when he was sure no one was looking. He was balding but wore a very moderately made toupee and he kept a neatly lined mustache over his thin, pale lips.

Captain Jeffery Salter had been on the force for close to 25 years and was looking forward to retiring soon. He had seen too much and done even more than he cared to think about over the course of his long work hours, and often looked forward to leaving the job and going home to an empty apartment. He took a deep breath as he looked out over his squad room at all of the bland faces in there. Most were like him, just looking forward to leaving for the day, but there was the occasional face that had that gleam of excitement because they had fallen upon something new in their case. He almost envied them as he longed for the days when this job made any kind of sense.

He walked back into his office and around his desk to sit down. He picked up the coffee cup that had more gin than the normal office coffee would have and took a big drink of it. He let out a satisfying "ahh" as the harsh liquid slid past his throat and into his stomach and he wiped his mouth with a napkin he kept on his desk. He glanced up at the wall clock and shook his head; dammit it was only ten in the morning and a full day to go. He took another drink and watched as his detective finally stepped into his office and closed the door.

"You needed something, Captain?" Raymonds took a seat before being offered to sit down.

"We have a problem that needs to be addressed on the Fitzwilliams case."

Raymonds sat down into the chair across the desk from his boss and crossed his legs not sure he wanted to hear what the older man was about to say. He'd only been on the case for two days and was still running down leads just as he stated daily in his reports that he placed on the Captain's desk at the end of every night. There was absolutely no way he could be pissed at him already when he hadn't had time to even get the final report from the medical examiner.

"Look, Captain, I'm just getting into this case," he stared across the desk, "I need a little time to run down a few things before you begin to chew off what little ass I have after the last two cases that I've had to add to the cold files."

"This ain't about you, Raymonds," Captain Salter raised his hand to slow him down, "I just got something back from the M. E. and you need to see it right away."

Slowly he slid a plastic evidence bag across his desk with a piece of paper inside. The paper had been folded up a number of times based on the number of creases in its normally flat surface, and of course on the front of it there was writing. Raymonds picked up the plastic by the corner and glanced at the paper and then held it more firmly to read it. His eyes widen and then he looked up at his Captain.

"Was this mailed in to the department?"

"No," Salter teepeed his fingers and stared from man to paper and back. "It was found by the M. E. on the body."

"Where? On the body? How's that possible? I was there and she didn't mention it then."

"It was wedged into the vic's mouth almost down into her throat. It was almost missed and had to be pried out by a pair of forceps it was forced in so deep. The doctor's sure it was done postmortem because there was no bile or vomit on the paper, but our primary problem is who it's addressed to."

Raymonds read it again and his face clouded. He had more or less read over that part because the content of the letter itself quickly drew his attentions. Even as he re-read the letter he couldn't make his mind comprehend that it was actually written to a specific person because the killer was basically letting everyone know the Fitzwilliams woman meant nothing to him… he was merely calling her out.

Dear Det. Steele,

*The time has come for you have
indeed lost your way. I am thine path and
through me you shall find the truth, sayeth
God. For the sins of the Mother are the
burdens of the child to carry forth. Let me
rid thee shoulders of thy sins, be then the
Reaper of what thee shall sow from this day
forward. In me cast thou faith for in you I've
found mine.*

Raymonds took a deep breath and sat up laying the plastic covered paper back on the desk. He looked over at his Captain and knew he had to ask.

"Have you called her?"

"No, I was waiting to talk to you to see if you were ready to have her as your partner. The last thing I need is you and Steele butting heads because right now her state of mind is not completely stable."

"Well, we all know that she's been on med-leave, but you think it's that bad?"

"I've been on the phone with her doctor and she seems to feel that Steele is ready. As a matter of fact, she has an appointment today and I need to make certain she shows up for it, if all goes well she may be back in here on Monday."

"Damn." Raymonds sat back again before standing to leave. "Shit, well I guess it is what it is, Captain. This maniac is calling her out, maybe she can add to the case. I do have one question."

Raymonds bent his lips into a crooked smile as he watched the man fidget a bit in his chair. It was like he knew what was coming and was hesitant to get it over with.

"What is it, Raymonds?"

"Am I working with her … or is she working with me?"

"I really don't give a fuck. You can be lead on this as long as we get this killer off my streets. Is that understood?"

"Loud and clear, Captain, loud and clear."

Salter stood and stepped from around his desk as Raymonds left his office. He glanced out again around the room and shook his head. *Damn I need a fucking vacation* he thought almost saying it out loud. He closed his door and went back to his desk and picked up the letter reading it once more before sitting down and picking up his phone. He took a deep breath and wished that she wouldn't pick up just so he wouldn't have to talk to her until possibly Monday morning when she would undoubtedly show up for her first day of work.

He dialed her number and waited. It rang once and then twice and then a final time before it finally picked up.

"Thank you for calling, unfortunately I am unable to answer my phone at this moment so please leave a brief message and a number I can reach you at and I'll make certain I call you at my earliest convenience. Thank you again for calling."

He took a deep breath. Since she hadn't answered most likely she wouldn't call back, and if she wanted her job back then she would most definitely make it to her scheduled appointment. He looked at the orders he'd gotten from the Chief telling him to get Steele back up and running before any of this hit the press. He shook his head, this was either going to work out really well, or this was going to be a real cluster fuck.

***

He sat there in front of his television watching the news. He was sure they had found the body, he was sure of it. He played their conversation over and over in his head and he was positive that the husband had said he would return on Wednesday. He should have gone back and just watched the house to make certain someone found her because he didn't want her to lie out too long… but he was sure of what he had heard; he was sure of it. He looked up at the clock and it was just past five and the news had come on and still no breaking news about the murder of an Assistant District Attorney.

"Why!" he growled out and threw the glass he was drinking from across the room to shatter against the wall. "She should be all over the news. Why are they not saying anything?"

He sat there through the entire broadcast and it was nothing more than a bunch of useless drivel about a rise in taxes and oil prices and some other nonsense about a shooting in some wasteland of a neighborhood but no one had been shot. He sat there breathing hard as he picked up his pack of cigarettes and pulled one out stuffing the filtered end into his mouth and lighting it up. He sat there with his eyes glued to his television as he started flipping from news station to news station looking for his story. He sat there wondering if she'd been found, questions running through his head about his victim's husband and what if he hadn't made it home.

Finally, he gave up his search and he just sat there as the pictures of some random show flickered across the screen. He felt worn out. He felt completely exhausted, and completely used. He felt like there was someone out there holding back everything that he needed. He felt… empty.

"Once they get you on the case they will have to break the story to the news," he spoke aloud. "Have you got my letter yet? I wish I'd sent one with the other, but what's done is done."

He turned off the television because he never watched it. There was never anything worthwhile on it and what he'd done was worthwhile to be watched. He moved from the living room towards his bedroom and closed the door; he never left it open for her to just walk in on him. He slowly looked around before he stripped off all of his clothes and found a corner and slowly crouched down into it with his knees up and his head resting on it hoping to find some sleep. He knew that if he slept it would be light because of the dreams and because he always expected her to come into the room… she always came into the room carrying her belt and smoking her cigarette.

He closed his eyes and he waited. It would be either sleep or her, either would be welcomed after his day. Either.

Chapter 5

Monday

Slowly she rolled over and hit the top of her alarm clock and she just laid there hoping that for once her bed was empty except for her. There was no movement and no other sounds in her bedroom other than the dripping sound from her shower. She slowly rolled to her back and looked over and smiled as she saw an empty pillow and no one hiding his naked body partially under her bed covers. She slaps her hand down on the empty space and laughed out.

Maxine rolled out of bed and sat up on the edge. She shook her head and was amazed that she didn't feel dizzy and then remembered that she hadn't had a drink since before Friday when she talked to her doctor. Her body really wanted a drink but she had promised herself that if she could get back on the force she would put down the bottle for a while. She took a deep breath and pulled out a cigarette and lit it … this vice here would be next, but for now she took a deep, long drag inhaling the smoke into her lungs holding it before finally letting go.

"Up and at 'em girl," she said as she pulled the cigarette from her lips, "you're back on the job."

Her morning went by quickly as she walked off to the kitchen to get a cup of the coffee that was fresh brewed. Then she rushed off to the bathroom and took a shower washing away the weekend blahs to prepare for her first day back to work. She stepped out of the bathroom with her towel wrapped around her body and ran her fingers through her still wet hair. She sat down at her vanity and quickly worked out her make up and once again decided on her new wild style hair-do before getting up and finding something to wear.

As she walked through the room, she pulled out everything she needed to put on and tossed them on the bed. First from her dresser the underwear she would wear. Then from her closet she chose a pair of black slacks and a white blouse to put on. Also from her closet she pulled out her shoulder harness and tossed it on the bed thinking she would wipe if off incase it had got dusty. She then reached in a pulled out a pair of low heeled flats because she wasn't sure what kind of day she would be having, but hoping that she would not be riding her desk. She glanced at her bed and was pleased with her choices and set to the task of getting dressed.

Standing in the mirror and studying how she looked, she was pleased. It's amazing how the feel of that empty holster made her feel as if she mattered again. Gone were the thoughts of what had happened last two years that she was undercover. Gone where the all of the thoughts of lying up in the hospital healing from the gunshot wound. Gone were all of the thoughts of sitting there on that couch while feeling as if she were a bug under a microscope. She smiled and noticed how her grey eyes seemed to shine and she lit a new cigarette and puffed on it before leaving her room to go and get another cup of coffee. As she stood at the counter sipping at the strong black coffee she listened to the voicemail once more from her Captain last Friday when all of that madness with her mom had taken place.

"Steele, its Capt. Salter. This is a reminder to make it to your appointment with your doctor; it's pertinent and important if you're looking to get back on the force full time. Also, I need you to give me a call or report to my office first thing Monday. I need to talk to you before I allow you back out on the streets. I'll talk to you soon and I will be calling the Doctor to make certain you made it there today."

Damn, a meeting with him first thing could not be good, and she could just imagine the line of bullshit he would feed her. Ranting and raving mostly about nothing. Telling her he would be keeping a close eye on her and everything she does from this point on. Most likely he will want to keep her at her desk and threaten to send her back on medical leave if she gives him an ounce of a problem. She would walk back to her desk mimicking him and gagging just at the taste of the words, but she would play by the rules just so she could get out of the house.

Maxine grabbed her purse and phone and rushed out of the door making certain to lock her door. She raced down the stairs and out the door of her complex to her car waiting there at the curb in her usual parking space. She unlocked the door and jumped into the driver's seat starting up the car and taking off. Today was bound to be a good day… at least it was starting out as one and she was even looking forward to hearing what the Captain had to say. She turned on the radio and turned up the volume as she made it to the highway and sped off towards the downtown cityscape.

He sat there watching from his van as she drove off. She seemed to be in the best of moods as she pulled away from the curb in her car. He pushed his hair back from his face and looked about the empty street making certain there was no one around before he stepped from his vehicle. His black boots hit the pavement and he pushed himself up from the seat. Instinctively he turned and looked at the seat and breathed out heavily that it was still dry. He'd been sitting there all night and hadn't moved to relieve his bladder at all. He walked across the street and up to the building she had just exited and pulled at the door, and it was locked.

Cursing he picked a number and pushed the button on the panel and waited to see if there would be anyone in there to buzz him into the building. After a moment of waiting he tried another button and waited looking around to make certain no one walked up to see him standing there. He pushed a third and then a fourth button all meeting silence and he was starting to get antsy. Finally, with the fifth button he got a response.

"This better be the fucking pizza I've been waiting on for over an hour," and the lock on the door clicked with a buzz and he pulled the door walking into the building.

Everything was quiet as he pulled the hood of the sweater he was wear up over his head and down low over his eyes and he started up the stairs. He'd been to her building before but never inside of her apartment because she was almost always home and when she left he could never be sure when she would return, but today would be different. Today he would have all the time he would need.

He started in the kitchen picking up the cup of coffee she had left on the counter. He sniffed at the contents and gently placed the ceramic cup to his lips and he tasted the contents. It had gotten cold from sitting there on the counter but it was still good and strong – something in common. He smiled as he took another swallow and placed the cup back down. He slowly went through her cabinets and then her refrigerator taking note of what she seemed to like. He went through the cabinet where she kept her plates and then the one where she kept her pots and pans and decided that at some point he would go through and organize everything.

"For a Detective," he grumbled, "you're not very orderly. How do you keep up with your cases?"

He moved from around the counter in the kitchen and out into the living room. He sat down on the sofa and slowly moved her magazines about on the coffee table taking note again of what she seemed to like and was a bit surprised by the recent issue of *Home & Garden Magazine,* but not so much for the issue of *Guns & Ammo* that was hidden underneath it. He stacked the magazines back up neatly and placed them back on the table and noticed the fine sheen of dust that had accumulated on the glass of the table. He shook his head again, he would need to hire a damn cleaning crew to come in and take care of this place just to get it all in cleaned up and in order.

"I guess you need someone to come in and take care of you."

He sat back on the sofa and then stretched out across it turning to rub his face into the pillow. He took in a deep breath and drew in the smell of her and licked his lips. She smelled delicious. He could almost taste her just from the scent of her in the pillow. He stood and removed his clothes and fell back down against the sofa's cushions sinking down into it. He rolled over onto his back and slowly he began to stroke his penis. The smell of her filled his head as his hand moved up and down his length, he felt dizzy laying there wishing she could see him, wishing she was there. He tried to keep his voice down as his hand's movements quicken, it wouldn't be much longer and he needed this release, he needed to let go.

With a grunt he felt his release. She was there in his head, naked and wet from the shower with her towel in her hand and her hair still wet. She had one leg kind of bent as she stood in the door way watching him and licking her lips. He moaned and groaned as it sped up his shaft and then out and over his hand and down onto his legs and the sofa beneath. His eyes held her as she walked closer and the heated smell of her body wash caused him to shake. She sat on the edge of the sofa and ran her hand down his bare chest and his body spasmed.

"Why you nasty little bastard," he stared at her as his Mommy's voice spilled from her beautiful lips. "You sick, nasty little fucker. Look at you! Look at you!"

He quickly sat up and looked down at his hand holding his now flaccid penis. He shook with fear as his mother stood there looking down at him with her belt in hand. She was dressed as she was always dressed and the smell of her cigarette burned his eyes and nose. He quickly let go of his privates and struggled to cover himself up without using the pillows and soiling them. He stood with his head down trying not to look at her with his fears shaking him to his bones.

"That nasty shit cannot be cleaned out of linen. I'm so sick of cleaning up after you, you nasty motherfucker. I just want you to die."

"Mommy, please," he closed his eyes and took a deep breath, "please, I'll clean it up. Please don't hit..." he reached down and picked up his underwear and wiped his body clean as tears formed in his eyes.

He opened his eyes and he was again alone inside of the apartment. He sat up on the sofa and moved to the edge of the cushion. He stood and looked around realizing he was sweating. He wiped his forehead and took a deep breath.

"One of these days, you bitch," he growled. "One of these days I'll finally be rid of you."

He looked at the time and slowly dressed. He finished his tour of the apartment taking note of anything else of interest he saw. He spent most of the day in there and after he had gotten comfortable he finally decided it was time to leave. She would be home soon and he wanted to make certain she got in safely. He slowly opened the door and glanced out into the hall, he stepped out after making certain all was clear and he made certain to lock the door. Everything was back in its place and he left just as quietly as he had entered. He made his way downstairs and the finally across the street to his van and he sat there waiting for her to return home.

It had been a good day for him… a very good day.

***

Maxine walked into the office area and watched as everyone stopped what they were doing. She suddenly felt like a circus freak on display in center stage and just wanted to slink away into a corner of the room. She walked in nodding to those she knew and raised an eyebrow as she looked up and saw the Captain standing there with his hands on his hips with a scowl on his face. She took a deep exasperating breath and moved towards her desk to pull off her coat and drape it over her seat. Her hand hit the empty holster and she smiled as she turned and walked towards his office.

"Good morning, Captain," she said patting the holster, "I think you have something for me."

Salter moved away from the door allowing her to walk inside and then he closed his door and drew the shades on the windows facing the squad room. He watched as she moved to one of the chairs in front of his desk and she stood there as if waiting for him to offer her a seat. Now would be a good time for a drink, but he hadn't got around to adding anything to his coffee cup this morning so he walked around the desk, sat and just took a big swig from of the strong black coffee.

"Smells strong enough to get up out of that cup and walk off," Maxine smirked.

"Have a seat, Steele," Salter grunted out over the lip of the cup. "I have enough to deal with besides your smart ass mouth this morning." He reached into his desk drawer and pulled out her sidearm and her credentials and slid them across the table. "Do Not make me regret this."

"Thank you, Captain," she holstered her gun and held onto her badge and identification. "Now, why do I have a feeling there's more going on than you having to return my property to me?"

"Do you know Margaret Fitzwilliams?"

"Yea, she's the Assistant D A, she rarely works anything less than the high profile cases such as murders, rapes, and some kidnappings. But, her main focus is organized crime. Why do you ask?"

"Her body was found by her husband last Wednesday. She'd been left in their home and staged in their bed for him to find when he returned from a business trip."

"I never saw anything about it on the news."

"So far," Salter ran his fingers through his thinning hair, "so far we've been keeping this hushed and out of the news, but I don't know how much longer we can."

"And, seeing that you said she was staged this wasn't something random," she pulled up to the edge of her seat, "what do you know about the killer?"

"Nothing yet, but," he reached into a folder and pulled out the plastic evidence bag, "he left this… for you."

Maxine's eyebrow rose as she reached across the desk and took the offered bag. She held it up so that she could read the note inside and shock slowly eased across her face. She sat there motionless and read the note again and then looked up at her Captain speechless. Never has anyone ever just called out to her and she wasn't sure just how to handle this and it quickly unnerved her. She laid the note back down on the desk and sat back in the chair.

"So what do you make of it?"

"Besides the fact that it's addressed to me," she stared at the bagged note, "this is not the unsub's first time killing and he's pretty much letting me know this. Have you checked for anyone recently missing or assumed missing?"

"No. Our first line of investigation has been working on leads. I've had Raymonds running lead on this since her body was found, but I've been waiting for your release from medical leave because of this letter."

"Where do you want me to start?" she picked up the letter and read it once more trying to get a feel of what the killer was saying to her and the part, *For the sins of the Mother are they burdens of the child to carry forth,* stuck a cord after the events with her mother just this past week.

"I think you need to start with this letter since it's directed to you. He undoubtedly wants your full attention and therefore there's got to be some kind of connection between you, him and the victim. We have to get ahead of him quickly because when the news gets a hold of this, and they will, it's going to blow up in all of our faces."

"Well I don't know about any connections, but I'm definitely betting this clown has priors. I need to see all of the pictures of the crime scene and do you think that the family will allow me in to see the house I need to get a feel for how this was done."

She held the letter without really looking at it, "What little I can tell you is that your killer is most likely an intelligent individual and undoubtedly manipulative based on the fact that he wanted me to find this. It makes me wonder if he knew I was on administrative leave and figured this was his way of getting me back on the force, so you're right there is definitely some kind of connection between he and I. The puzzle of it is… what?"

"From this point on, Detective," Salter stood and more or less stared down his nose, "that's your puzzle to work out. You'll be working with Raymonds and please no stepping out of line. I need this one worked by the numbers because like I said, once the press catches on its going to be a feeding frenzy.

"Now get out of here and get to work," he watched as she stood completely wrapped up into her own head. "Oh and Steele, welcome back."

It was dryly said but she smiled and nodded. She held on to the letter as she left his office and walked to her desk. It was going to be a long day, so yeah, welcome back to her.

"Good to have you back, Steele," the man's voice almost startled her as she dropped the letter on her desk and turned around.

David Raymonds stood there with his hands in the pockets of his dress slacks. He wasn't a bad looking man, definitely had something Hispanic in his chemical make up, but the European in him was dominant. His hair was a dark black and close cut and combed back away from his face. His eyebrows were just as dark and thick but well-groomed and seemed to match well with his expertly clean shaven face. Without appearing to look too closely she could see pock marks in his face from what she could only assume were from a childhood case of chickenpox. He was tall and of course she had to look up at him but he wore the height and the musculature well. He was very well dressed even on a cop's salary wearing a tailored suit and a pair of high end wing tipped dress shoes.

"Still looking like you belong in the FBI, Raymonds," she smiled as she thought of the time he called himself hitting on her. "Haven't got that call yet?"

"Not yet, but I'm sure it will be soon."

"Yea I'm sure. I need access to the pictures and we need to see if we can get back into the Fitzwilliams home so I can look around."

"I'll have Sheryl call and set up a time and I'll get the file that I've put together so far on your desk in a few, I just want to finish up my notes one it. Ok with you?"

"That will be great, David, thank you." She looked at him and noticed he was just staring at her with a very cocky smile.

"Did he tell you?"

"What?"

"The Captain, did he tell you?"

He was standing there needing his ego stroked and she could see it. For a moment she wanted to crush him under the heel of her shoe, but figured it would go against the "by the numbers" remark Salter made. She shrugged her shoulders and acquiesced to his needs.

"You've got lead on this one, David," she flashed him a warm smile and fluttered her eyes, "I'm not here to step on your toes."

"Looks like we're on the same page," he seemed to fluff his feathers like a proud peacock.

"One other thing," she picked up the letter again and studied it, "I was telling the Captain that this doesn't feel like his first kill so we need to find out if there are any recently missing persons. Someone out there is dead, most likely a female, approximately the same age as the ADA, and if he holds to this present M.O. she will be prominent in the community."

"I'll get someone right on that for you," his tone was completely condescending but Maxine ignored it as she turned and sat down at her desk.

As he walked off, she pulled out a notebook and sat there staring at the note in the plastic bag. There had to be something that would give way to his train of thought but for the moment the only thing that caused her concern was the line about "mother." She picked up her desk phone and dialed the number to the adult living facility.

"Thank you for calling White Chapel Adult Living Facility, this Ashley how may I help you."

"Ashley, this is Detective Maxine Steele and I'm calling about my mother. How has she been for the last couple of days?"

The girl on the other end of the phone was quiet for a moment, "Det. Steele, what I'll have to do is transfer you to the back to speak to Dr. Thine about Ms. Rollins, but as far as I can tell there have been no incidents."

"Thank you, I appreciate that."

"Give me just a moment please."

The line clicked and then there was a beep and another ring tone. Finally the familiar voice of Dr. Thane came over the phone.

"Good afternoon, Detective, how may I help you?"

"I'm calling to see if there have been any other incidents with my mother?"

"Since the day you came Ms. Rollins has been in a very good mood. She's not exhibited any signs that she even remembers the other day and we've not had to medicate her anymore."

"Good, good. No more mention of the man that she said stood at her door."

"None what so ever. Why the questions, Detective?" Thine asked quizzically.

"I'm just following up with what happened last week. She really seemed scared or something and I just don't know why." Maxine stared at the word "mother" once more on the letter unable to shake that it had a more direct meaning. "Will you please contact me if she says anything more about it or has another episode like the last one?"

"Post haste, Detective," he answered before hanging up the phone.

"Where are you going with this, Buddy?" she whispered to the letter before laying it on top of her notepad. She needed a drink and a smoke but decided on coffee no matter how strong.

As she made her way back to her desk with a steaming cup of stronger than ever coffee, she saw Raymonds standing by her desk. He was in his normal pose with his hand buried deep in the pockets and his eyes riveted to her desk. He didn't see her approaching so she cleared her throat to let him know she was behind him.

"Oh, there you are," he turned to face her, "I brought you the file with all of the pictures and notes so far. You'll also find notes in there from the interviews I did at the DA's office about the cases she had currently been on."

"Thank you, I'll get right into it and see what I can see. Any word on when we can get into the house?"

"I'll have to check back with you on that, and I have a couple of rookies going through missing persons to see if anyone has been reported within the last two months that fit that small profile you gave me."

Maxine nodded as he walked off and dropped down into her seat. She spent the remainder of the day going through the file with a fine tooth comb. She studied the pictures but knew that she still needed to get into the house to look around; something was definitely missing. She pulled out the picture of the full body layout of the victim and sat there studying it. This is where she needed to start.

"So much about you reminds me of my mother when I was growing up," she whispered as she stared at the woman's face. She placed the picture on top of the file folder and shuffled through pictures that had been given to them by the husband of her alive. It was amazing that who ever made her up upon her death bed made her more beautiful than she had been alive. Flipping from picture to picture she took a deep breath and started going through some questions forming in her head.

She picked up her phone and dialed the number to the Sheryl and sat there waiting for the young analyst to answer. She picked up the note once more and read it and then stared at the death photo when the girl finally picked up her phone.

"Hey, Sheryl, this is Maxine Steele, I need you to do something for me. I know you're looking for missing persons for the last two months, but I need you to do a deeper search for me. I'm looking for cold cases of similar M.O.s and try looking back... well to start go back a year and let me know what you find.

"Thank you," she answered after waiting for a moment for the girl to make notes or whatever it was she had to do. "You should have my number, just call me direct and let me know what you find, and if you can find the work cases on those please have them sent up to my desk."

She dropped the note back on top of everything. There was definitely something missing from all of this. Him calling her out like this had to mean something more than he's just killed before... damn, where should she really start?

***

The day had passed quickly and as she pulled up to her apartment she took a deep breath. There was still so much to do, but it was good to be back to work. She glanced around her neighborhood as she always did and noticed a van that seemed out of place but for now she let it pass and walked inside to get out of her clothes and relax. Tomorrow would be a new day and she would need all the rest she could get.

"Rest well, my Maxine," he whispered as she walked into her building. He settled into his seat preparing for a long night. He lit a cigarette and sucked on it deeply blowing the smoke from the window then laid his head back on the headrest.

"Rest well."

Chapter 6

He sat in front of that stupid television again trying not to throw something at it. It had been over a week and still no reports on them finding her body. There were still no reports of how she died so brutally at the hands of an unknown assailant. He was beginning to wonder if maybe they were trying not to draw any attention to the fact that one of their star Assistant D.A.s was killed. This brought a small smile to his face, but it took the wind out of his sails because he wanted to see her face plastered on all of the news stations. He took a deep breath and shut that foolish contraption off once again and moved towards the kitchen.

Once in the kitchen he pulled out a cigarette and lit it drawing in the smoke into his lungs as he looked around. Everything was spotless but he could feel the need to clean welling up even as her voice filled his head calling him a dirty pig. Her face was right there in his face with her putrid breath yelling and threatening to beat him as she pulled the belt from its usual perch on her shoulder. He flinched. His shoulders tightened as he forced himself to realize that she was not standing there, and that he had nothing to fear.

Shaking off his moment of dread he moved on to the door that led down into his basement. He pulled the key from a pocket in his wallet and unlocked the door and walked down the steep stairs into the cold and dank space. At the bottom of the stairs he reached up by habit and pulled the string that turned on the little light bulb and he suddenly felt relieved. As he looked around, he stopped at the wall that was covered with pictures of Maxine and he walked up to it. He noticed immediately how pictures he'd taken weeks ago she looked so depressed and now his newer photos she actually looked like she was happy.

"Hmm," he grinned, "someone has a new sense of purpose." He slid his fingers down a picture as if he were touching her face. "Just wait, there's so much more to come."

He turned away and on the side wall he had pictures of A.D.A. Margaret Fitzwilliams there were quite a few of her alive as he had followed her about the city and of course there in the comfort of her home. He was amazed at the pictures he had of her and her husband as they were lying in their bed asleep; she always looked so peaceful without any of the day's make up covering her naturally beautiful face. His eyes moved from picture to picture as he had taken more of her taking care of her daily routines. Then there were more of her after she was laid out on the bed looking just as peaceful as if she had been sleeping. Again he slid his finger down a picture like he was touching the woman's face and he licked his lips. He was so pleased.

"You were a star… you were my star, and they snuffed you out and buried you like you didn't even exist. I shall make them acknowledge you, I will make them shout out your name very soon because you need to be out there on that pedestal."

He moved to the left of the Fitzwilliams pictures and stared at the beautiful faces there. Long blonde hair framed their faces and her shocking eyes seemed to stare at him in differing colors, but one caught his attention and held it.

She had been sitting on the park bench when this picture was taken, sitting there having lunch as she always did and watching the birds as they would swoop in and feed on the pieces of bread she threw out. She had what he thought was a cute button nose and there were these freckles in a near constellation patter on her neck that he thought was the sexiest thing he'd ever lain eyes on. She wasn't much about up to date fashions but she dressed smartly making her look casual at almost all times. On this day in the picture she had worn a simple skirt and blouse with stockings and heels that all just complemented her belying beauty. He stood there staring at her.

"Hello, my beauty," his voice was low and his eyes downcast as he stroked her pictured face, "you were my first this time, and now its time for them to meet you."

He turned and looked across the room just where the light missed shining brightly at the chest standing there against the wall. He strolled up to it and tapped on the surface placing his head to it as if listening. He smiled and knocked again before pulling the hinged cover open and staring at the body within. He stroked her hair just as he had her picture only moments ago and then he closed the cover once more leaving her to rest behind once again. He ran his hand down the front of the chest and walked away turning off the light as he ran up the stairs two at a time.

***

"Hey, Steele," Raymonds called her from across the squad room as he came running in. He had the look of someone who had almost ran a mile and not too pleased about it. "We got the results of that missing persons search and we have 10 possibles in your pool."

"Damn, I wasn't expecting that many."

She sat back in her chair trying to figure out how to lower the number but nothing came to mind. She took the paper with the list of names and the time of disappearance and began to scroll through them all making mental notes of each. She glanced down at the picture of Margaret Fitzwilliams and saw something she could add as a filter.

"Do one more thing for me please," she looked up from the picture, "see if the filters will allow you to remove all of the women who are not blondes. Hopefully this will drop the numbers significantly for us."

Raymonds didn't like her giving him orders even though she made it sound like a request or even a suggestion, but it was a damn good idea. He pulled out his cell and punched in a number and stood there waiting for a moment before the phone was picked up.

"Sheryl, I need for you to add something to the search to see if we can get this number down a little more. Filter in blondes for me…yes I'll wait." He stood there watching as she stared from picture to list and back again wondering what she was thinking. "Yes I'm still here… that dropped the number to three? That's excellent, which names… Grace Muldoony, Amber-Lyn Addison, and Michelle Wiggins. Thank you, Sheryl. I'll be in touch.

"Did you get those names?"

"Yes, and that's perfect. We have addresses on all three, you ready to roll, Partner?"

Raymonds looked stunned at the use of the word "partner" and merely nodded as he walked towards his desk to grab his coat and then followed her towards the door. He reached into his pocket pulling out his car keys automatically assuming he would be the driver as they headed out the door of the police station and down the concrete stairs towards the curb where the detectives were allowed to park. He hit the button on his auto unlock and watched as she finally looked up to see where they were going and smiled as she made no qualms about him driving.

"Where to first?" he asked as he slide behind the steering wheel and she slid into the passenger seat.

"Third and Windover to see Mr. Muldoony, seems as good a place as any to start."

"What's the story on her?" Raymonds pulled out into traffic heading west towards the part of the city known as Elegies Village.

"Grace Muldoony sat on the city council as one of its chief chairpersons. She was reported missing approximately a month ago. She 45, married and mother of three all of whom are in college. Her body was never found but they did find her purse with seemingly nothing missing in Westwich Park by one of the groundskeepers around 8 in the morning.

"Hmm," she flipped over the paper she was reading and then flipped it back again. "What's missing is how long they did the investigation and who all was interviewed. At this point we really have next to nothing to go on."

Raymonds pulled out his cell and hit the call button and waited for just a second before it was promptly answered. "Hey, Sheryl, David again… I need for you to pull the files on those three names and have them sent up to Homicide for me. I'll need them by the time I get back into the office. Thanks again. I'll be back in touch if I need anything else."

Maxine was impressed but said nothing as she continued to go through the notes she had on the three ladies. They were entering Elegies Village and she whistled as they drove through the gate and past the first house. These were definitely prominent million dollar homes and that meant that Muldoony's family was very well off. The houses were large and the yards were all well manicured, the cars were all expensive looking and even though she was dressed nicely she felt completely out of place.

She looked over at Raymonds and smirked. "Damn, you should fit right in out here."

Raymonds huffed as he drove around the central fountain and drove down looking for the address she read off to him. He remained quiet to keep from cursing her for her little snide remark. He glanced down at what he was wearing and decided that it wasn't a bad thing that he wanted to and was able to afford to dress well, and he would make no excuses for it. He found the house and pulled into the drive way that drove up to the front door area and they both got out.

"Would like for me to question him?"

"Sure," Maxine answered, "I'll follow your lead if you don't mind."

They both pulled out their badges and credentials as Raymonds made it up to the door first and rung the bell. It was a nice cool afternoon and it was quite possible that no one was home. Maxine moved towards the large French style window and tried to look in through the light curtains but she could see no movement. Raymonds glanced and her and she shrugged as he rung the bell once more and the waited a little longer. The locks on the other side of the door clicked and clacked as they were undone and the door slowly opened.

"Yes, may I help you?" the elderly black man asked as he stared at the two people holding up badges.

"Yes, I'm Detective Raymonds and this is Detective Steele, Homicide White Chapel Police. Is Mr. Muldoony in?"

"Yes, Sir, please come in and I'll get Mr. Muldoony and let him know that you're seeking an audience."

They both stepped into the large foyer and looked around. The flooring was ceramic tile of a light sandstone color and the walls were just a little darker giving the room a large and long feel. There was an actual suit of armor standing just to the left of the door and a cross from it a shield with crossed swords. Along the same wall and on the other side of a bank of mirrors was an old looking tapestry with a coat of arms embroider on it. Overall, it was a rather gaudy scene but definitely told that this man had money and was not afraid to flaunt it.

"Mr. Muldoony will see you out on the deck. If you will follow me please."

The butler led them through the house that was equally gaudy with hunting trophies of stuffed animals and fish. As they passed by the kitchen are Maxine took note that there was a rather portly woman in there cooking and another younger girl helping with the vegetable peeling. As they got closer to the back of the house, she could hear a lawnmower going so she was sure it was a paid service taking care of the work. They stepped through the large wooden French doors and out onto the stained wood deck and were greeted by Derek Muldoony.

"Good afternoon, Detectives," he held out a hand to shake both of theirs. "How can I help you today?"

"Mr. Muldoony, we were hoping we could talk to you about your wife if you're up to it?"

"Of course, Det. Raymonds, what would you like to know?"

"How long had she been missing before you file a missing person's report?" Raymonds began.

"Well," Muldoony sat there rubbing his chin, "I remember calling on the that Saturday and the officer I talked to told me that she would have to be missing at least 48 hours before I could file a missing person's report. So, it would have had to have been on Friday that she went missing. I remember waiting through Sunday and calling again first thing Monday morning because she still hadn't come home."

"Can you remember where you were that Friday before you realized your wife was missing?"

"Yes, I had a meeting out of town earlier that week, so I was just getting back to town that morning, but the thing is," he looked down at the table and then looked back up with tears in his eyes, "I hadn't talked to her for almost three days because we had had an argument just before I left. I figured she was still steaming and didn't want to be home when I got in so I waited. Around 8 that night is when I made that first call."

"Mr. Muldoony," Maxine stepped forward from behind Raymonds, "if you don't mind, what kind of work do you do?"

"I'm an international banker," he answered, "and as such it keeps me in the air both here and abroad. We were arguing because I was always gone and I'm never around and she was preparing to run for an open Senate seat."

"One more really personal question if you don't mind? Whose money was it?"

"Grace comes from a very affluent family, but we've built our own wealth out of almost nothing because her father left the bulk of his estate to charity. We did all of this over the course of almost 20 years together."

"Thank you, Sir," Raymonds interjected. "We're just trying to tie up a bunch of loose ends. Did you know if your wife had any enemies?"

"Gracey was ruthless about her politics but not towards people. She was always saying that she was looking for a way to make a difference. She was always complaining that our government was broken and she was looking for a way to fix it. But, real enemies… no, or at least none that I can think of."

"One last question, Sir," Maxine was scratching notes out on her pad. "Did you ever find anything missing from your home, maybe something very personal of your wife's?"

"There was one thing." Muldoony stood and walked off into the house and then came back with a picture in his hand. He placed the picture down so that the two detectives could see it. "I still cannot find this Heirloom necklace. It was something that her mother gave her and she only wore it on special occasions. She generally kept it lying out on her dresser so she could see it in the mornings, and I noticed that it was missing when I got home that Friday morning. I thought maybe she had it, but I'm really not sure anymore."

Maxine was satisfied. She looked at the woman in the picture. She had long blonde hair with striking blue eyes. She had a cupie nose set softly over thin lips making her a very beautiful woman. There was something strikingly familiar about her but right at this moment she couldn't put a finger on it. She could see that the man was definitely hurting and most likely regrettable for how things were between him and his wife before he got back home.

"Sir," she glanced at Raymonds as if expecting him to stop her, "is there any way possible for us to have this picture or one like it with the necklace?"

"Sure," the man grabbed the frame and flipped it over to remove the picture. "Please, if you find my wife… just let me know something."

"Well thank you for seeing us, Mr. Muldoony," Raymonds reached out his hand and the man quickly took it. "We appreciate your time and we'll be in touch if we find out anything else."

"Thank you, Detectives," he extended his hand to shake Maxine's hand, "I hope to hear something soon so we can get this all closed and my wife can finally rest in peace."

Once they got outside and made it to the car Raymonds finally spoke up. "So what are you thinking, Steele?"

"Well we need to talk to the other two," she stared at the picture as they walked down the stairs, "but just from what I've seen and the fact that that there was a possible trophy taken I believe Mrs. Muldoony was our first victim and I really wouldn't be surprised that when we find her body it will staged much like Mrs. Fitzwilliams."

"When?" Raymonds stared over the roof of his car. "What do you mean, "when we find her body? What the fuck are you thinking, Maxine?"

She stood there glaring at him for using her name. "This is just the beginning. I'm almost sure he's going to place her body and soon because he didn't get nothing for killing the A.D.A. He's called me out and now he's ready to put this game in motion."

Raymonds considered what she said for a moment and then opened the door. He stepped in and started the motor as she stood there staring back at the house. There were whispers around the squad room that she was a tough nut to crack; that she was a damn good detective with a profilers tendencies, but she just didn't play well with others. He knew for a fact that she'd had just two other partners, one of which got killed when they were both undercover, and that she was completely rattled after that assignment was over. He sat there wondering if he was going to have to worry about her getting this job done.

"You ready to go? We still have those other two to go see about."

Maxine couldn't take her eyes off of the house. There was something wrong. There was something that she was missing and she couldn't put her finger on it. She could feel it in her gut that this lady had been one of his first victims and he was going to put her on display very soon, but why? Why was he killing them in the first place, and why did he address that letter to her? What was her part in his sickness? She looked the house up and down and trying to play out in her mind how she would go about killing this woman, but then Raymonds was calling out at her.

She took a deep breath and almost asked him to give her a moment for cigarette just so she could think on it a little more, but she didn't have the patience for his impatience. She opened the door and stepped into the car, sitting down she closed her eyes and allowed her mind to build everything around her and she studied it quickly. As the car pulled off she looked up and across the street and could almost see something as large as a van sitting there with a faceless man watching the house.

"Damn," she whispered. "He literally sat here and watched them. He knew their full routine and he stalked her. Stalked her until he was ready to take her."

"What?" Raymonds glanced at her as he drove out of the housing development. "How the hell do you know that?"

"Because that's exactly what I would do."

They drove off in silence and as they passed the park she could see him stopping his vehicle and getting out to purposely leave her purse to be found. He was setting the stage and had most likely decided how she was to be killed and who his next victim was. He was meticulous. He was ruthless and very meticulous. She could see him standing there just before dawn making certain it was laid out just perfectly before calmly walking back to his vehicle and driving off into the morning's fog.

"He's just getting started, Raymonds… this shit is just getting started."

The rest of the day was routine. They went to talk to the families of the other two women but neither case seemed as positive as the Muldoony case. The first woman had been found raped and murdered two months after she'd been reported missing so she shouldn't have made it onto the list, and the second woman wasn't very prominent in the community even though she did own her own business. Grace Muldoony was the most likely subject. There was also the fact that Muldoony's necklace was missing, that's something she needed to know of Fitzwilliams.

After they made it back to the squad room Raymonds rushed off to his desk and returned to her with the three case folders. Maxine looked through them but gave him back the two she was sure didn't matter and kept the Muldoony file. She pulled out the pictures of both the women and looked at them and made note of how similar they both looked and then took out her notepad and jotted down a few more things.

Raymonds' cell phone beeped and he pulled it from his protector and stared at the screen for a moment. "We can go to the Fitzwilliams home tomorrow to talk to him, but from a personal note you need to tread really careful with this."

"What do you mean?" Maxine looked up from her desk.

"This man has already gone through a lot and he found his wife dead in their home in their marital bed. The last thing he's going to need is you asking a lot of questions he's already answered."

"All I'm looking to do is get some answers to help find his wife's killer and hopefully prevent another woman from getting killed."

"How do you know another woman's going to be killed? You've only been on this case for right at two days."

Maxine sat back in her chair letting it recline back and she placed her hands behind her head. Her grey eyes seemed to burn with a fire he couldn't quite explain and he was sure she was about to erupt and go off on a tangent, but she merely smiled. He glanced over at the windows at the front of the Captain's office and noticed that he had stood and was walking towards the door standing there to see what was going on.

"Look, Raymonds," she sat forward in her chair placing her elbows on the top of her desk, "I'm not trying to harangue these people, and I'm not trying to step on your toes. I'm just looking for answers and right now the questions are leading me into this direction that there's going to another killing and this kidnapped lady is going to show up dead very soon.

"I'm working with you on this," she took a deep breath and looked him squarely in the eyes. "I've answered every question you've asked and when you interview Muldoony I never once interrupted. I'm not sure what you're expecting or suspecting of me, but I'm just here to do my job."

Raymonds looked over at Salter who shrugged his shoulders and went back into his office. He was stuck for anything more to say and just walked off towards his desk leaving her alone with her thoughts and half-baked theories. He was going to allow her to continue on the path she was on and sooner or later she would trip up and fall flat on her face. He just wanted to be there to see it.

Maxine spent the remainder of her day going through everything in both file folders. She spent time studying both of the women's faces and how closely they resembled. So many pieces of this puzzle were missing, and she was sure he was masterminding how each piece was going to fall into place. Again she read the letter and again the word "mother" caught her attention and she wondered if it had anything to with her mother; she was definitely sure it had something to do with his mother but just what she hadn't determined yet.

She had written the word down on her notepad and had circled it.

"There's more to this letter," she mumbled to herself, "than meets the eye."

She rubbed her head from the headache she was getting. Her stomach grumbled from a lack of food. And, her lungs ached from a need of a smoke. Just too many things keeping her from thinking clearly, and a drink would definitely take the edge off.

No fucking drink, Maxine she thought to herself as she rubbed her eyes and went back to going through the files. She only had a couple of questions for Fitzwilliams, but her main concern was the *how*? Just from looking at all of the crime scene photos not only did he kill her but he had to have killed her away from the scene so there was a primary murder scene not yet determined. Then he'd brought her back to her home, bathed her, dressed her and made her up, and then posed her in bed to look as if she were just peacefully sleeping. That meant he had time, a lot of time.

She closed her eyes and again she could see the Muldoony home and it again played out with him sitting there watching the home, or maybe… She allowed her mind to walk through the house again looking around as she did trying to place where she would feel the most concealed as she lay hidden amongst her prey and her family. With members of the family moving about it wouldn't be easy. There would be so many chances of being seen or if she were to move of her being heard. The hiding spot would have to be some where the family didn't frequent and most likely dark most of the time.

"Maybe a closet," she said as she wrote it down, "or the basement."

Chapter 7

Janice Rollins sat up in her bed and looked around. For some reason it seemed unreasonably quiet. She didn't hear the normal sounds of the medical ward she'd become accustomed to since they'd moved her from her apartment. There were no sounds of people constantly moving around just beyond her door. There were no sounds of monitoring machine constantly running or beeping. There were no announcements for medical staff to report anywhere within the building. It was just… quiet.

She brushed her unruly hair from her face and looked around. For the first time in a long time she felt… Normal. Her mind felt clear. Her thoughts were not all jumbled and bouncing all over the place. For the first time in a long time she didn't feel as if she couldn't concentrate. It was like being her old self again and she loved it. She pinched herself and whispered out a small ouch and smiled.

Slowly she turned on the bed and hung her feet over the edge and slowly moved forward until she felt the cold of the floor. She giggled as she slid her feet into the soft warmth of her house shoes waiting there on the floor, and she slowly stood up on legs she hadn't used in what felt like years. She pressed back against the bed until she was sure she was balanced enough to move away, and then she laughed as she took that first step. Stopping, she noticed at that point that she didn't have a catheter in nor was she connected to the IV pump that was normally pushing fluids through her veins. Shaking her head she smiled again as she slowly stepped away from the bed and off towards the door.

"Oh my God!" she exclaimed as she walked under her own power without the need of some orderly holding her under her arms. Tears stream down her eyes as years of being unable to do for herself seems to have come to a joyful end.

The door that had always seemed so far away as she had lain in her bed now seemed to be just a couple of steps away. She was amazed that her muscles didn't shake or quiver and that her body felt comfortable; it was like she'd never been sick or hospitalized all this time. She moved with a surprising pep in her step that she hadn't had in so many long ago years. She almost felt the urge to run towards the door but she moved very tentatively until her fingers finally closed around the cold metal handle. Turning she pulled open the door and looked out into a very empty hallway.

She was dressed in her hospital gown and reached behind her to hold the back closed, and she stepped out into the hall looking around for anyone. It was so quiet, and there was no one walking around or even standing at the nurses' station just down the hall from where she was standing.

"Hello," she called out. "Hello, is there anyone there?" It had been so long since she'd heard her own voice and it not sound like she was speaking incoherently.

If she'd been outside she would almost expect to hear crickets chirping in the silence. A shiver went down her spine as she stepped out and walked down the hall towards the nurses' station. As she passed the couple of rooms between hers and the desk, she noticed that they were all empty and again the silence became quite obvious. The silence became completely eerie.

"Hello," she called out again.

"What are you doing out of your room?" a very deep voice spoke up from behind her and she spun almost falling to see who's there.

He was just standing there staring at her, but she cannot see his eyes. As she looked closer, she realized that she could not see his face at all. It was as if he were standing in a thick shadow that kept him covered, but she could see that he was wearing an orderly's white uniform. He's a big man, not fat, but big especially in the chest and thighs. She couldn't tell what his hair looked like or if he even has hair, but she can tell that he's tall and muscular looking. Just from the way he's standing there he's very scary. She shook and could feel sweat forming on her forehead.

"Why are you out here, Janice? Why are you out of your room? Why are you out of your bed?"

His voice was deep and thick like something out of an old horror movie. He stood there like a menacing threat with no weapon.

"Did you think I would never find you?" he suddenly asked from behind her whispering in her ear. "Did you think I would never find her… never find Maxine?"

"What do you mean? Who are you? What are you talking about?"

"How could you get rid of me and think I'd never come looking for you? What are you going to tell me, you were too young, that you didn't have the means to take care of me, or that your parents made you do it? Why not tell the truth, you didn't love me."

"I don't know what you mean," Janice stood there with tears in her eyes as he placed his hands on her shoulders and slowly moved them towards her neck.

She more heard the sound of the knife being locked in place before she felt the blade pressed against her neck. His breath was hot against her ear as he leaned in breathing heavy. She reached up and her frail hands squeezed at his thick forearms as it pressed against her chest holding her in place against him. The cold edge bit into her neck and she could feel him pulling it gently against her flesh as she held her breath.

"I know where she is," he whispered into her ear, "and what I'm going to do to you is nothing compared to what I'm going to do to her."

"Why are you doing this? Who in the name of God are you?"

"I think it's so good you've forgotten, and even though it's taken a lot of time for me to get past what you've done to me. Death is all I know now. Death is all I can give."

She shivered as she felt his lips pressed into the back of her head. A tear slowly slid down her cheek and she tried to choke back her cries as the knife pressed harder against her neck. She took a deep breath and tried to look over her shoulder at the man behind her, but he held her firmly in place.

"I can almost taste the sweet of your blood, and hers… well hers, I'm going to fucking bathe in. I'm going to drain her dry and bathe in her sweet blood while staring into those beautiful, dead grey eyes."

He pulled the blade away from her neck and then placed it back against her flesh just under her right ear. Slowly he pressed in and drug it across her neck from right to left not stopping until he reached just under her left ear. Over his hand he could feel her blood rush out and spray across the room. He could smell that sickly, sweet aroma and his face split into an eerie smile. He looked down and saw Janice standing there shocked as the blood rushed from her throat. Her mouth moved as if to scream but nothing came out but a sick gurgling as the more blood spilled from her mouth.

He stood there laughing as he body shook and trembled. Quickly the life rushed from her body and her eyes rolled up into the back of her head. She could hear the thumping of her heart slowing down, and feel the blood slowly stop moving through her body. As her knees lost strength, he let her go and she dropped to the floor into the pooling mass of blood.

For the sins of the Mother are the burdens of the child to carry forth.

Janice suddenly sat up in her bed screaming. Her hands went to her head and she grabbed her hair pulling it as her mouth fell open in a scream that just seemed to go on forever. Her eyes were stretched wide as she looked about the almost dark room and now things seemed normal as she pulled at the hose running from her arm to the machine beeping just to her right. She screamed again and again as she began to thrash about the bed. She screamed until they finally came rushing into the room and began the near impossible task of calming her down.

"I need Maxine. She has to be warned. SHE HAS TO BE WARNED." She looked wild eyed. "He's going to… kill her."

***

Maxine stood leaning against her car waiting for Raymonds to show up. She was in the prominent living community of Whispering Cove. It was another housing development of high range homes with man-made lakes, an 18 course golf range, and a private country club where the elite of the community would meet to "hobnob". As she looked around the houses looked even larger than the homes in Elegies Village with their steeped roofs and dramatic layouts all set off on what were most likely an acre or two of land so that they were not crowded upon one another. Another group of fantastic homes with their beautifully manicured yards set off in a community set away from the rest of the city. She whistled and smiled as she looked around.

"All of this beauty set away behind its guarded gates and he was still able to get in here and take away so much. They are not as protected and guarded as they believe."

She closed her eyes and allowed her mind to reconstruct the entire area and she stood there looking over the lay of the land in her head. She could see the large vehicle just as she had seen it at the Muldoony residence. He was sitting there in the front seat watching the home as the family inside moved about their lives. He watched as Mr. Fitzwilliams ran out the front door to jump into the cab that was waiting for him to rush him off to the airport. Then the boy and the girl each left to go to their respective colleges to begin their weeks, and this left Mrs. Fitzwilliams alone in the house as she prepared for her day. He sat there watching… watching and waiting until the time was just right and then he…

No, something about all of this was wrong.

Raymonds drove up and parked his car. He stepped out and stared at the woman he was partnered with as she stood there with her eyes closed. He wondered just how she made it back to the force just from what he'd read in her files. He pulled down on his vest and straightened out his slacks as he stepped from around the driver's side of the car and walked up to her and stood there as she seemed to be off in dream land.

"I guess I should have bought some coffee, but I didn't realize I'd be standing out here waiting for you to come back down to earth."

"Good morning to you as well, Raymonds," she opened her eyes and smiled. "If I told you that he sat out here waiting for her, what would you say to me?"

"That you're wrong, but then it would be hard to say when he grabbed her because her car was still in the driveway and there didn't seem to be any signs of any kind of struggle outside of the house."

"See this is the problem I'm facing as well," she looked around. "He had to have been watching her and waiting for her to be alone so he could take her. But how? Where? If he had grabbed her outside of the house someone would have seen something, and there were no reports of any strange vehicles in the neighborhood at the time of the abduction. So how did he keep such a clear watch on the family?"

"That's a damn good question. What are you thinking?"

Maxine looked at him and smiled. "You're not going to want to hear this and you're not going to believe me when I tell you."

Raymonds stood there with his hands on his hips as if he were waiting for her to say something completely ridiculous like an alien abduction. He looked around hoping that something would pop out to give him a clue as to what she had in mind, but as far as he could see there was nothing. From the front door to the garage nothing gave a clue as to anything being out of place.

"I don't see anything out here, Steele," he kept looking wondering if he'd missed something. "What the hell are you talking about?"

"I'm almost sure he was in the house."

"Bullshit."

"Look at where we're at," she nodded towards the area around them. "How would he be able to just sit out here and not be noticed? He had to have figured out a way past the guarded gates and then into the home where he could hold up until things were just right for him."

"But how would he get back out and then back in with the body?"

"I'm still working it all out, but if you think about it him holding up inside of the home makes sense."

"It would keep him from being seen out here sitting around suspiciously."

"Yes," she reached into her jacket and pulled out a cigarette and placed it in her mouth, "but then the next question would be… did he kill her here or did he manage to get her away from here and then back here after he was done torturing and killing her. He had to have a way of cleaning up the body."

"All of the tubs and sinks were tested for blood," Raymonds scratched his head, "and nothing was found."

"Then he was either very thorough with his cleaning, or he left and came back. That would mean he had to have a way in without looking out of place."

Raymond pulled his notebook from his inside jacket pocket and flipped through the pages. He read them a couple of times flipping between a couple of pages and then he looked up at Maxine with a confused look on his face.

"We have a problem," he began, "either the perp has another way in and out of this community, or one of the gate guards is lying. We interviewed them all and no one seen anyone they would have considered suspicious coming or going all that week or the weekend before."

"Yea that is a dilemma," she lit her cigarette and took a deep drag. "I'm missing something and I know it's staring me right in the face."

"We need to get in here," Raymonds pointed towards the house, "I'm sure Mr. Fitzwilliams has other things to do besides waiting for us to come and disturb him and his family."

As they stood in the grand room, Maxine looked around and quickly tried to take in everything she saw. Dark hardwood floors covered everything from the main room all the way back through the vestibule out into the main hall before the two large oak doors. A plush, leather sofa large enough for maybe six people was surrounded by two large easy chairs and a coffee table and an assortment of decorative flowers. Light filled the large room from the French doors that led out into a very large and decorative back yard complete with an extended deck with a complete outdoor kitchen and furniture.

Just off from the living room was a very beautiful kitchen that Maxine was sure from the cabinets and counters Mr. Fitzwilliams had more say in than the Mrs., but the remainder of the house was definitely a decoration project of hers. She was looking forward to getting upstairs just to see how the rooms were including those of the two kids just to see if they had any their own personality in their respective rooms.

"Again we're sorry for bothering you, Mr. Fitzwilliams," Raymonds was standing there looking uncomfortable, "but one of lead investigators wasn't available when we were initially here and requested to have a look around at your discretion."

"It's no problem at all, Detective, we're just trying to cope with things as they are. I've made my kids go back to school so that they could concentrate on something other than all of this and I've been trying to work from home, but it's been very hard, but I do want to thank you for keeping this out of the news. I don't know how I would have deal with dealing with all of that nonsense."

"I understand, Sir, your privacy was our primary concern. This is Detective Maxine Steele."

Maxine shook the offered hand and noticed that he didn't hold back in how he took her hand. He looked relaxed but from the bags under his eyes she could see he was not sleeping much. His hair was a bit unkempt so he hadn't been to his barber in a while, and he could definitely use a shave. There were no staff personnel in the house so she doubted that he'd been eating properly. She smiled as she stepped back and continued to look around.

"If you don't mind, Mr. Fitzwilliams," Raymonds turned back towards the doorway leading from the room, "we'd like to start in the bedrooms."

"That will be fine, but I must say I've cleaned up since you were here last."

"Excuse me," Maxine broke in with a smile, "Mr. Fitzwilliams, do you have a basement?"

"Yes I do. Why do you ask?"

"Was it checked by the Crime Scene guys when they were here last?"

"No, well not that I know of," he glanced from her to Raymonds and then back. "Is there a problem?"

"No problem, but I was wondering if I could start there first?"

Fitzwilliams stood from the sofa and led them through the house to a hall just off the foyer and then out into the garage. They moved around the front of the Range Rover SUV that was parked there and towards a door that looked to lead outside. That door opened into another small foyer with a door leading outside and then a set of stairs leading down. He hit a light switch turning on a small bulb over the stairs and walked down with the two detectives following. At the bottom of the stairs he flipped another switch that turned on a series of lights that lit up the entire basement that ran the full length and width of the house. He stepped out of the way and allowed the two to stand beside him.

"As you can see," he looked around, "it's a fully finished space. We had intentions of making it an entertainment space for the family, but as you can see, we just never got around to completing that part of it."

"Is there another way out besides the door at the top of the stairs?" Maxine asked as she slowly walked around looking.

"No, the only door is the one at the top of the stairs and we keep it locked by dead bolt and chain at all times."

Maxine nodded and moved around the room now not paying much attention to the two men. She sniffed the air and could smell something that was completely out of place in this very well cleaned house. She moved towards the back of the stairs and noticed what looked like a stamp in the carpeting as if someone or something had sat there. Again the smell was there and it was stronger. She looked around and noticed that she was pretty close to the furnace.

As she stood there, she could almost see him sitting on the floor listening to everything above him through the vents. He would be a patient man knowing that the husband would be still be there until morning. The question would be how did he get in and when would he have done it. She moved from under the stairs and glanced up at the lights taking note of how they were spaced, and then she stared back towards the stairs and noticed that it was dark enough to conceal someone if no one was really paying attention. She walked up towards a small window that was on the overhang above the floor and wondered if a man could squeeze through it.

"Do these windows open?"

"I believe that they do," Fitzwilliams scratched at his chin, "but to be honest I've never opened them or know if they are locked."

"Would you mind if we sent someone back over to have that window dusted on the inside and out?"

"I'll make certain that someone is here to let them in, but that won't be a problem at all."

Maxine nodded her head and moved towards the stairs. They made their way up the stairs and she found herself counting the number of steps. At the top she took another look at the door and noticed that the chain was indeed in place but she didn't check the deadbolt as they walked past and into the main hall. The smell she had noticed downstairs in the basement hadn't followed her upstairs to the main floor, but she was sure it was because of the number of people that's most likely been in and out of the house since the body had been found. She followed Fitzwilliams as he led them upstairs to the bedrooms.

For the remainder of the time in the house she said almost nothing, but she did have out her notepad flipping through the pages and then adding in smaller notes where she could find space. She looked into the kids rooms but did not stay for long before moving on towards the Master's bedroom and her looking became more intense. She sniffed the air and noted again the smell she had detected in the basement.

"You haven't slept in here, have you?" she looked back towards the door where Fitzwilliams was standing. She took note that he wouldn't enter the room.

"No, no I haven't. I don't think I can." He dropped his head and stared down at his feet. "I had to have a cleaning crew to come in here and clean out the room, but I can't even get rid of the bed or the bedding she always used."

Tears welled in his eyes as he stepped back out into the hallway.

"How did you know he hadn't slept in here?" Raymonds asked her quizzically.

"I cannot smell his cologne in the room and it should be rather strong."

She watched amused as Raymonds sniffed the air and then shook his head; he would never understand what she understood. She only wished she could tell what the other smell was, but it definitely wasn't something from anyone that lived or worked in this house. In her mind she could almost see him standing there at the foot of the couple's bed watching them as they slept, and then again watching her after everyone had left the house the morning he abducted her. She most likely didn't know anyone was there with her until his hand clamped down on her mouth and she opened her eyes from a dream in fear.

Where the hell did you take her? She asked herself as she continued to look about the room. Nothing would have been left out of place, she was almost sure of it, and she planned to look through the notes again once she was back at the office. He would have cleaned up behind himself to make certain everything was pretty much better than how it was before he had stepped into the room. She stepped into the bathroom and again she was assailed by that scent now mixed with the bath soap of the victim. She moved to the tub and envisioned him kneeling there almost lovingly bathing what would be a dead Mrs. Fitzwilliams, and he would be talking to her as if she were alive. She backed out of the bathroom and stared at the two men as they watched her move about.

"Thank you for letting us look around again, Mr. Fitzwilliams," Raymonds called out as they walked the steps towards their cars.

"I'll meet you at the office," Maxine called out as she stepped into her car without allowing her partner to say anything.

As he drove off, she sat there going through her notes and looking around. Her mind played through the images she kept of the basement, the smells, and of course the bedroom where the body had been placed. Thoughts of where he would have to park to get in and out, of how he would get past the guards at the community gates, where would he take her and why bring her back? All of this rushed through her head as she looked around.

"So many pieces," she pulled out a cigarette and lit it. "So many goddamn pieces and not a one of them are fitting together. What the fuck?"

Chapter 8

Maxine slumped down on the sofa staring over the back of it to the rain gently beating at the window. It had been a long day and ended well with the rain which kept her mind off of the bar down the street. She was nice and comfortable in a pair of her sheer boyshorts and the dress shirts of one of her former lovers with just one button right between her breasts fastened. She felt refreshed after getting a shower and washing away the smells of the precinct from her skin and now laying there she stretched out on the sofa pointing her toes towards the ceiling. Her head was filled with the sounds of the rain and everything that's happened since her return to work. She took a deep breath as she reached over to the coffee table and grabbed her cigarettes.

The rain was extremely soothing as she turned back towards the window allowing herself to daydream just a bit. The smoke from the cigarette filled her lungs and she held it deeply before slowly releasing it slowly into the air of her apartment. The cloud of it is heavy and seems to linger about her head before slowly dissipating leaving nothing but the lingering smell of ash and menthol. As she closed her eyes, she took a deep breath allowing the nicotine did its job, attempting to relieve her of the stress she was continuously under. She pressed her body down into the sofa's cushions as she took another drag and again slowly released it.

So much was missing in this case. Where was the other body she knew he would put out there for them to find? Who was this guy and why would he address a letter directly to her? What was their connection to one another? She had only just got back on the job and already she felt as if her entire world was up in the air.

She glanced once more over the back of the sofa to the window and watched as the raindrops bounced on the glass and then slowly rolled down the surface. No other sound filled the room as she sat there contemplating this is exactly what she needed just to figure out what it was that was missing from this entire case. She turned on the sofa and snubbed out the cigarette before standing and moving to the window. Her feet sunk into the soft plush of the rug surrounding the sofa before she stepped onto the cold of the wood flooring.

As she is standing there, thoughts of the two houses once again build and stretch out inside of her head giving her room to just walk about carefully looking at everything. Both are in guarded communities so that means he had to be able to bypass manned guard booths without much effort. Both were out in the open so that means he had to be inconspicuous and not stick out. He himself had to be someone that everyone in these neighborhoods would trust, someone that seemed to be a natural fit in these neighborhoods and that could be anything from a resident to a maintenance worker.

"Could you be a resident?" she said it aloud just to see how it would sound and she tried to picture him dressed in his business attire carrying a briefcase and talking on his Iphone handling business as he walked towards his Mercedes Benz. He would be clean shaven with an always fresh hair cut, and the press of his pants would be sharp and crisp with a tie over a fresh pressed Brooks Brothers shirt. Was it even possible for him to be a resident? That would easily explain how he could move the body about without being seen, but that would also mean he'd have to have two or more homes all over the city. She smirked at the thought and then shook her head.

"Definitely not a resident, it would get you in and out of at least one community but I doubt you'd put your money out so freely as to own more homes. So how the hell would you move about the other communities? No, some kind of maintenance man makes better sense still."

She looked down at the street below through her raindrop streaked window. The night had settled in with the storm and the street lights were on shining down on the wet black of the street. Off in the distance streaks of lightning glazed the horizon and the slow rumble of the thunder lightly played a tune on the window's glass. The pitter patter of the rain dancing on the glass was like a soft song that would rise and lower in tempo with the wind. The street below was empty of people including in front of her favorite little pub; just looking down at it caused her to lick her lips, but she was determined to stay away and stay clean. She glanced at her car and then her eyes went across the street and she found herself staring at the van parked there.

It was so familiar and yet it seemed to stick out like a sore thumb. At one point it had been painted black, but now the paint job was mottled and it was sitting on very dull uncapped wheels, the windows were all darkly tinted, and the small port window facing the street was cracked. She could almost imagine the inside; there would be no other seats besides the driver's seat and the passenger's seat; the back of the van would be gutted and most likely carpeted with something he could pull out and dispose of. Along the walls he would have it covered so that he could pull all of that down and dispose of it in the event that he got blood or anything else on it. He would have a toolbox back there with everything he would need to keep his victim tied down and muffled so that he would not have to worry about her moving about as he drove.

Yes, he would definitely need something just like that to move the bodies around. Something that he could feel as safe in as he would his own home, and yet have no problems sliding the bodies in and out of once he got to where he would kill them and to haul them back to be staged. He would have to be a man who was pretty strong, maybe not a bodybuilder type, but he definitely would be someone who kept in shape. He would be a simple looking man and able to fit into any surroundings without a problem. She stood there in the window staring down at the van; it was so nondescript just sitting there at the curb that most people would just drive right by it without so much as a blink. That's exactly what he would be counting on, fitting in as if he were a part of the scenery.

The rain had picked up obscuring the outside world from her but she stood there staring down at the street. From here she couldn't tell if there was anyone in the van but her mind allowed her to imagine that he was sitting there just as he would have been at each of the victims' homes. He would be so very patient sitting with the tinted windows rolled up so no one could see inside but he could see very clearly out of them. For hours on end he wouldn't move from that spot until he was extremely sure no one would see him make his way from the vehicle across the street to the point of entry he'd already prepared. He's very meticulous. He's studied his victim and her family to point he knew every members schedules and set his own time table by their schedules. He'd want as much time as he could have in order to enjoy the moment before and after he'd killed her.

She could see him dressed in dark colors with the hood of a sweater over his head so that he could completely blend into the dark of his surroundings as he moved to the house. Again he would wait, wait pressed against the side of the home as he moved around it making certain no one inside was up or in a place where he could be heard slipping into the house. There he would wait again… wait in the silence of the home… wait until he was positive they were all asleep… wait until he could move about as he wanted to. She could see him just sitting there listening to the quiet as it enveloped him.

Then he would move out of his hiding place and he would slowly walk around the house. He would be getting a feel for it. He would be memorizing every inch of it so that he could move around without any hindrances. Slowly and methodically he would walk about the house like he owned it, like there was no one else there besides himself, and he would get to know his way around. He would feel powerful as he walked into the bedrooms and he would stand there looking over the family. It would be as if he lived there and he was making certain everything was in place.

She could see him standing there at the foot of the couple's bed, breathing in deeply their mingled scents as he longed to just grab her, but he wouldn't at this moment. He wouldn't chance the man waking up and then having to deal with him on top of keeping her from squirming away. He wouldn't chance the man making enough noise to wake the rest of the house and have anyone contact the police. No, he would just stand there looking over them and making certain that everything else in his plans were well in place. Then he would leave them with visions of her swimming around in his head and he would go back to his hiding place and once more he would just sit there and he would wait. He would move about the house slowly as if he had all of the time in the world.

"That kind of patience is not something you come into on your own," she wiped away the light sheen of moisture on the window. "Abusive family life, or military trained, which are you?"

She stares out of the window as she leans against the frame. The rain's coming down harder and it's giving the outside world a watery kaleidoscope appearance. She can still see the van but it's so distorted now and she finally walks away from the window to get another cigarette. There are so many thoughts running through her head, and again she thinks back to the Muldoony home. Would they happen to have a basement like the Fitzwilliams' home? If not then how did he gain entrance into their home? If he's keeping to his pattern he would have watched her before he abducted her.

She paced through the living room smoking and thinking. Still so many missing pieces, and then her thoughts once again went back to the note addressed to her. The mentioning of mother, and then the problems with her mother just seemed too much of a coincidence to her. She could see the fear and terror in her mother's stretched eyes, and the fact that the staff seemed to be just forcing her to remain in her bed with nothing to calm her or soothe her… bullshit, that was such bullshit. What was that about seeing him? Could it even be possible that the killer was in her ward, but how? How and why?

"He did address that note to me," she keeps pacing the room, "but I wasn't even working at that time. Could he have known that?"

Maxine takes the last drag on the cigarette and then presses out the butt of it in the ashtray on the table. As she blows out the smoke, she stares at the kitchen wondering if there's a bottle of something to drink in there, but then remembers that she dumped it all right after getting home from seeing the doctor. Her head's hurting from all of the thoughts running through it, and she suddenly feels tired. Her stomach's reminding her that she hasn't eaten anything since she's been home, but she resists the urges to go to the kitchen and heads towards her room turning off the lights as she leaves the living room. Tomorrow she would start this all over again, and hopefully there will be more to work with.

Hopefully…

***

He steps out into the rain and tosses away the cigarette he was smoking. Her light had finally gone off and he was prepared to go visit her… again. His visits had quickly moved beyond just watching her window a long time ago, but now he was truly getting comfortable. He'd found a way to actually sit in there with her that he'd not found until recently. Now he could basically come and go as he felt just as he would with any of his other houses. He glanced up once more to make certain she hadn't come back to the window and then he quickly made his way across the street.

Using her code, which he'd finally figured out, he stepped into the apartment complex and slowly made his way up the stairs to her floor. He opened the door and stared out into the hallway to make certain it was empty before he walked out and towards her door. *Just like sheep,* he thought as he placed his ear to her door and listened, *forever sleeping away life as if it all stopped when you got home and closed the fucking door.* He glanced down the hall once more before pulling the key he'd made from his pocket, and he quietly let himself into her apartment closing and locking the door.

She was in the bathroom humming and brushing her teeth as he moved towards the window she had been standing at moments ago. He looked out and down at his van sitting there across the street making certain she could see nothing of him as he'd been sitting there watching her. Even if the window hadn't been smeared with condensation she wouldn't have been able to see into his van windows because they were too dark. He took a deep breath and sat on the floor behind the sofa to wait for her to go to bed and get comfortable.

He allowed his eyes to close and he relaxed against the back of the sofa. Under any other condition he would have never relaxed so much being out in the open, but she had gone into her room and he was positive that she was sleeping. For over and hour there had been no sounds coming from her room or any other part of the house. She slept quite soundly once she would fall off to sleep giving him opportunities to get very close to her on a number of occasions, but tonight his mind was so full that all he could do was sit there and just imagine her laying there waiting for him.

Slowly his mind began to relax and he found himself standing in a small field that he didn't recognize at first. It was such a beautiful day with the sun shining so brightly in the blue sky above him. Clouds were slowly floating by on a gently Spring breeze, and this had him wanting to just lie out and bask in the beauty of the day. There were wildflowers growing everywhere in every color he could ever think of and there were bees and butterflies dancing around the flower buds all over the field. He was so comfortable here, and he couldn't begin to explain why.

Everything about this place was so amazing, and the normal pains he felt he suffered all seemed to just disappear. For the first time in a long time he was happy, very happy, from the top of his head to the bottom of his… feet. He looked down and his feet were bare and pressed into the soft of the grass, and he grinned as he curled his toes and watched them dig into the soft ground. He wanted to just take off running. The breeze was so gently like it was touching his bare skin and he just wanted to enjoy it before… before she came and ruined it all. His shirt was opened baring his chest and he was wearing shorts that allowed his very pale legs to show, but he was happy.

All around him everything was unlike anything he'd ever witnessed. There were singing birds flying around whistling. There was a pond and he could see the fish and turtles splashing about and playing in the water. The breeze that was blowing was perfumed with the fragrances of the wildflowers. He felt like he was in heaven. If only this dream would never end and he could just live here forever.

"Wake up you dumb little shit," it was her words in his ear and then her hand across his face that abruptly pulled him from his dream of peace. "Get your pussy ass up from that floor before you touch yourself again."

He jumped up from the floor looking around unsure of where he was. The room was dark and it was quiet, but it was not his home. He could smell the stale scent of menthol cigarettes in the air along with the light faint scent of a woman's perfume. He stared out the window and shook his head at his own darkened reflection staring back at him as the rain water beat against the window, and then he saw her standing there beside him. Not the owner of the apartment he was in, no he knew how she looked and her visage was more welcoming… more beautiful.

"What are you doing here?" he asked her in the window as she glared at him. She stood there staring at him with her cigarette hanging from her lips, her night gown and robe hanging from her shoulders showing more flesh than he cared to see, and that belt hanging over her shoulder.

"You cannot be here, if she wakes and sees you…" he turned and looked and he was alone in the room, but when he turned back to the window she was standing there looking a mess. Her hair was a mess and her eyes were dark and sunk into her head.

"You filthy little animal," her voice was inside of his head, "what dirty thoughts was going through that small brain of yours? Laying there with your hands in your pants."

He turned away from the window again and moved around to sit on the sofa. He loved sitting on the sofa because it smelled of Maxine. He turned and pressed his face into the throw pillow so he could smell where her head laid and filled his nose with the scent of her shampoo. He ran his hands along the sitting pillows as if he could feel her laying there and smiled at how soft her skin was. He turned and pressed his face into the back pillows so he could smell her body wash and her perfume. His head was swooning from it all and he could once again feel himself getting excited. He stood and removed his clothes and folded them up neatly and placed them on the coffee table and then stretched out on the sofa.

He looked around before taking his penis into his hand and slowly stroking it. It felt so good to do this when he knew she was right there in her bedroom, but he was always so fearful that his mother would show up. He was so excited as he turned his head and again pressed his nose into the throw pillow sniffing in deeply. His hand moved quickly up and down his length as he pictured her laying there in her bedroom with nothing on as she always slept. He held his breath as he stroked himself closer and closer to an end, but then he stopped; he could feel "her" watching him, and in his head he prayed that she wasn't but he knew she was.

He stood and looked around the room. He was sweating from his exertions and sweating from his fears as he quietly walked around the living room looking for any signs of his mother, but she was not there. He stroked his still hardened erection and then moved off towards Maxine's room. He had to see her laying there. He needed to be in the room with her watching her as she breathed, watching as she tossed and turned.

Gently he turned the knob and slowly pushed the door open. Quietly he moved into the room standing near the foot of her bed comfortably cloaked into the dark of the room. The curtain on the window was opened just a bit and the little illumination from the night filtered into the room just barely highlighting her there on the bed. She was laying on top of her bed covers and just as he knew she would be, she was naked and he had a full view of her beautiful body. She was on her side and her hands were above her head and he could see her breasts gently moving against her chest as she breathed.

Standing there in the dark of the room he began to stroke his hardened length once more staring at her naked body. He breathing hissed through his nose as his hand moved faster and faster and his knees suddenly felt weakened. His excitement was to the point he could hear the slapping of his hand meeting the base of his penis as he testicles swung freely between his thighs. His heart was pounding in his ears and he suddenly felt cool from the sheen of perspiration covering his body. He was so close as he stood there staring at her laying there just waiting for him.

She moaned and suddenly sat up staring right at him as if she could see him. Her hair was so wild on top of her head as if they'd just had a crazy night all over her bed. She was breathing so slowly and the sight of her breast only excited him more as they moved up and down on her chest. As she crossed her legs, he held his breath and continued to stroke his penis as she tried to see into the darkness of her room. Slowly she turned and stretched out on her stomach and sunk back to sleep lightly snoring. He pressed against the wall to support himself as he finally felt his orgasm surge up from his testicles to drench the floor in front of him. The rug she had around her bed covered the sound of the splatter and he slowly sunk to the floor breathing heavily.

"Why you nasty… dirty… filthy little son-of-a-bitch!" he jumped from the floor and almost hit the dresser he was sitting next to. He quickly turned and looked at Maxine to make certain she hadn't awakened. "Look at you sitting here playing with your little nasty man. You sick fucking dog."

He moved towards the door hoping that his mother would leave before him, but she remained behind him berating him. He took a last look at Maxine before quietly opening the door and moving out into the hall. He closed the door as the tears slowly began to crawl down cheeks to drip from his chin. His embarrassment at being caught by her filled his head as he looked around for her to be there and he was alone in the hall. He quickly walked off to the living room and dressed, and then he froze as he remembered what he'd left staining the rug in her room. He suddenly wanted to scream, but couldn't chance going back in there to clean up.

Slowly he backed up to the front door and unlocked it. Peaking out into the corridor he slipped out and made his way quickly to the stairs. Sweat was beading his forehead as he opened the door at the bottom of the stairwell and looked out into the lobby to see if it was clear. He could see the rain softly beating against the door as he pushed open the door and made his escape from the building.

Maybe… just maybe everything will be dry by the time she wakes up.

***

Maxine stirred in bed once more. Her dreams had her restless as she tossed and turned on the bed. In her dreams he was there in the room with her just standing there watching. He was completely hidden away in the shadows of the room so she couldn't see his face or anything about him that she could use to figure out who he was. But, she could just make out his eyes; so cold and almost an ice blue as he stood there just staring at her. She wanted to just wrestle him down and put him in the hot seat and just grill him, but he wasn't real.

"Soon, Maxine," his voice filled her dreams like thunder rolling across the skies, "very soon you'll get all you think you want and more."

As his hand suddenly reached out of the darkness to grab her, she screamed and woke up lying on her bed. She quickly turned over and sat up and began looking about her room, but she could see nothing. Grabbing her blanket and pulling it about her naked body she stood from the bed and began to walk around the room. She stepped down into something wet and sticky and she quickly wiped her foot off onto a dry part of the rug as she stood trying to think of anything she may have dropped earlier.

"Fuck," she said to herself as she moved towards the door and then out into the living room of her apartment. She turned on lights looking to see if anything was out of place and the area looked cleaner than she remembered as if things were just in a more organized position than she'd left it going to bed. A shiver slowly went up her spine as she walked to the front door to make certain it was locked.

An eerie prickle crawled up the back of her neck as she found the knob locked but the deadbolt was unlocked. Again she turned and looked around to make certain there was no one about to pounce out at her. She quietly made her way to her room and grabbed her gun and this time made a thorough search of her entire apartment until she again felt safe enough to finally sit down.

Her nerves were on high alert as she sat there trying to remember everything she'd done before going to bed. She recalled shutting off the lights but she could not remember walking to the door. Her mind was in overdrive because she's always been a stickler to locking up her house, but tonight was a complete blur. Her only recourse was to assume that she'd locked the knob when she came in from work, but had not gone back to lock the bolt. She stood shaking her head and went back to her room with a sly, nervous smile on her face.

"You're slipping, Max, ol' girl… you're slipping."

Chapter 9

"Good morning and thank you for joining us," the newscaster's voice filled her apartment as she stood in the mirror in the bathroom brushing her teeth, "this is White Chapel News 9 I'm Aaron McMannis and in our top story… an update on a story that we brought you about a month ago on the missing Chief City Council Grace Muldoony. This morning her body was found by groundskeepers in the city park of Elegies Village, Westwich Park. She was discovered approximately in the same place that her purse was found. We now send you out to Westwich Park where Daniel Forthsythe has the story.

"Daniel, good morning, what can you tell us?"

"Good morning, Aaron," Daniel said as he stood with the park in his background filled with the bustling of Police and Emergency Response units moving around, "as you can see its pretty busy here as the police and the EMS are on the scene trying to preserve the sight, but what I can tell you at this point is that they are pretty sure that the body found is Chief Councilwoman Muldoony and from the initial reports she has been dead for quite a while."

Maxine rushed from the bathroom and stood in front of the television. A part of her felt she should have been surprised that the body of Mrs. Muldoony had been found, but after the night she'd had she was almost expecting her body to be placed out. She stood there studying what she could see of what was going on behind the reporter, but it was impossible with all that was going on within the scope of her small screen. She cursed under her breath as she ran back into the restroom to finish what she'd started so she could dress and get out the door before she was…

Her cell phone began to ring and she walked from the bathroom into her bedroom and picked it up. "Good morning, Chief."

"I don't know if you've been paying attention to the news but I need for you to get your ass to Westwich Park right now."

"I'm dressing now," she answered over him talking, "and I'll be out the door in a few moments."

"This is a complete clusterfuck, Steele, Raymonds will meet you there. So get your ass there A.S.A.P. and don't fucking talk to anyone. There will be some kind of official response given to the press later today."

"I understand completely, Chief… I'm on my way."

Pulling up at the crime scene and it was like driving into a circus catastrophe. There were people everywhere and it seemed as if the throng was getting larger by the second. Maxine parked and stepped out of her car and immediately began to look about the crowd of people standing there trying to see anything they could. There were more cell phones out trying to record the area than there were news reporting crews there trying to legitimately record the scene.

She stood there a moment studying each face trying to discern and decipher their reason for being there. Most stood there in horror staring at their first crime scene. Other stood staring in wonder at the fact that they were staring at an actual murder in such a very affluent neighborhood. There were those few who were actually fascinated and she made a point of remembering their faces to have them questioned later, but the one look she was searching for was not present. Undoubtedly, he was not there, he didn't care that the body was found. Most likely he was sitting at home watching everything fold out over the news.

"Bastard," she hissed under her breath and turned to walk towards the actual crime scene.

"Detective Steele," a voice off to her right yelled out her name and she turned to see Daniel Forthsythe rushing towards her mic in hand and his cameraman in tow. "Detective, its good to see you're back on duty. Can I ask you a few questions please?"

"I've just got here and I really don't know anything yet," she turned to walk away.

"But, Detective, we've been told that this is not the first body. What do you know about the murder of A.D.A Margaret Fitzwilliams?"

Maxine slowly turned careful to keep her face as neutral as possible. "There will be an official statement made downtown. That's all I can tell you right now."

"Are you sure that's all you have, Detective?" Forthsythe called out to her back as she turned away from him. "I'd swear there was more to this story than anyone is telling anyone. What are the police not telling the public, Detective?"

"Have a good day, Daniel."

She scowled as she walked off. How could he have known about Fitzwilliams? They were supposedly keeping that story under wraps, and then for him to ask that on camera. Damn… the family would surely see this on the 6'oclock news. She shook her head as she stepped up to the yellow police tape cording off the area and flashed her badge at the young cop watching the line to keep everyone not involved with the case away from the area. As he held it up, she looked back at Daniel Forthsythe once more taking not that he was standing there staring at her with the weirdest of looks in his eyes and a smile. She quickly shook it off and kept walking.

"Over here, Steele," she looked up and saw Raymonds waving her to him.

"What do we have here?" she stepped up to the people surrounding the tree and looked down at the body propped up against it.

"How did you know, Maxine?" Raymonds asked as he stuffed his hands into his pants pockets. "You more or less called it, so how did you know?"

Maxine didn't answer as she knelt down to study the body. It was as if she'd been placed in some kind of human sized humidor and preserved well. Her skin was dried but not flaky and hadn't lost a lot of her muscle tone. Her eyes were sunk in some, but not as much as they would have been if she'd been left out to the elements to slowly denigrate. He had taken good care of her, and just like Fitzwilliams she'd been bathed or rather cleaned up and dressed before she was placed out to be found. Her clothes were neatly ironed and her Mary Jane style shoes had been polished. She looked like a baby doll laying there against the tree.

Maxine stood and walked around the tree staring at the ground, but was not surprised when she didn't even find a footprint. There was just too much going on around the entire area that she wanted to just scream for everyone to get away while she looked around, but that wouldn't have happened. Being outside took away certain things like dusting for fingerprints because most likely nothing could be removed from the tree bark or even her clothing. She did notice that one of the CSI officers was dusting her shoes, but she was certain that he'd worn gloves to prepare her.

"These aren't his first murders," she said more to herself.

"What do you mean?" Raymonds squatted down beside her.

"Look at the way the two bodies have been laid out for display. He's not nervous at all in his actions because he's had practice. He's been doing this for a while. Even the stab wounds are not erratic they are very well placed."

Raymonds glanced away from the body and looked at her as if to ask if she'd pulled up the woman's clothes to check her privates here in the open.

"No," Maxine answered raising her eyebrow, "I haven't looked but just from what we know of Fitzwilliams I'm almost sure he stabbed her as well. But look at her, she's so well preserved. He'd have to know how to do this to keep her from decomposing."

Raymonds reached out and lightly touched her face and was amazed at how soft and not brittle her skin felt even through his gloves. As he stared at her face, he thought quickly of the other victim and looked around for a free CSI.

"Hey, I need you to open her mouth and look inside for me."

The young lady moved to the other side of the body and slowly opened the mouth and flashed her light inside. "There's something in her throat," she responded before looking in her case to pull out some forceps. She reached in slowly and tugged at what she'd seen before slowly pulling it out.

"It's another note," Raymonds said before reaching out to take the folded paper from the forceps. He looked at it not knowing if he should just open it or hand it to Maxine automatically assuming it would be written to her.

"Want me to read it?" Maxine asked reaching out for it. "Or should we just wait 'til we're back at the office?"

"I need an evidence bag," Raymonds yelled out waiting for someone to hold out a plastic bag for him. "What else do you see?"

"Not much. He's very careful to the point he even made certain there were no footprints for us. Again I'm almost positive he's done this before and he's very thorough and precise. We're definitely looking for a serial here."

The word had been said out loud and everyone stopped doing what they were doing to look at her. Maxine didn't flinch as she continued to look around. There was everything there and yet she couldn't put her finger on what was missing. It was as if he wanted them to think that these were his first two victims, but just from the way things were set up even a rookie could see that he was too well advanced in his art for this to be his first try.

Raymonds stood and called in for the coroner to move in with his gurney. He and Maxine stood back and watched as the coroner and his assistant carefully lifted the body and placed it in the black bag that was lying atop the metal bed and then slowly zipped it up. After she was rolled away it gave room for the CSI technicians to move in like a bunch of ants quickly gathering anymore evidence they found. Raymonds slowly turned and began to walk away before looking back.

"What are you thinking?" he asked as Maxine stood there staring at the area around the tree.

"I didn't see the necklace," she turned and looked at him staring at her perplexed. "The necklace her husband said was missing. The one she only wore on special occasions. I was kind of expecting to see it."

"What if he's keeping it as a trophy?" Raymonds answered. "Maybe it's his reminder."

"I guess." Maxine stuffed her hands into her pockets and looked about aggravated. "I think he's fucking with us. I believe he's just getting started with this new round of killings."

"You keep saying that," Raymonds lowered his voice and looked around, "and now you're saying he's a serial killer. We only have two bodies, Steele, a 'serial' usually requires more."

"This I know," she stared at him feeling a little argumentative, but then she relaxed. "I just have a feeling that there have been others before these two, and I have a feeling there will be more to come."

She turned without allowing him to say anymore and began walking down the hill towards the throng of people. She could almost see him standing there with his hands shoved into his pockets watching her walk away and his mind was trying to come up with something to say to bring her back down to his level; he was such an arrogant asshole, but possibly a good cop only time would tell. Her mind's a million miles away when she walks right into Daniel Forthsythe again, and she shakes her head as if to let him know no more questions. He stands at the ready with his mic in hand and his ever present smile on his face.

"So, Detective Steele, you've had a chance to get a look at the body," he's trying to shove the microphone into her face, "is there anything that you can give us?"

Maxine tries to step around him, but he's ready and moves with her blocking her way. She turns and sees Raymonds heading her way and wonders if he's going to make a scene, and her mind is in avert danger mode as she tries again to push her way around the edge of the reporter.

"Just one comment, Detective, that's all we need. Can you confirm the Fitzwilliams case?"

"Look, Mr. Forthsythe, I've already told you that there will be an official statement given downtown later. Please leave it at that."

Forthsythe looked over her shoulder and nodded as he saw Raymonds headed their way. He pushed back at his cameraman giving him the signal that the interview he was trying to have was now over. "Thank you for your time, Detective."

Maxine stood there watching as the two men hurried off and shook her head again. Raymonds lightly placed his hand on her shoulder and she turned to face the man who had been coming to her rescue.

"You ok?"

"Yea," she smiled, "just a pesky reporter trying to scoop the other stations. Nothing too big."

"Do you think he would be here… watching?" Raymonds stood there staring at the crowd of people all standing around watching everything going on.

"To be honest, I'd be surprised if he were standing out here watching. To him that would be too cliché. He would sit at home knowing we would be thinking he's standing out here watching, but he would be watching for us to see how we are accessing the scene."

"It's almost like you're getting into his head, Steele," he remarked with a raised eyebrow. "How do you do that?"

"Damn good question," she looked around taking in all of the faces at the edge of the crime scene. "Its just what I do I guess you can say.

"Come on, let's get out of here. We still have to meet with the Captain, and we need to see what's on that letter."

***

"So have either of you read it?" Salter asked staring at his two detectives.

"No, Raymonds and I figured it would be best to bring it in first since you still had to do that interview with the press."

Maxine reached over and picked up the evidence bag from the Captain's desk. She had pulled on a pair of gloves before grabbing the bag and now reached inside to pull out the letter and read it. Afterwards she passed it to Raymonds who read it and then he passed it on to Salter. Maxine was not shocked that once again it was addressed to her because she was almost sure that in some way or another she and this unsub was connected; the question was how? She picked it up and read it once more.

My dear Maxine,
It is so grand that they have bought you
back and put you right back into the fray of

*things running... blind. How so very easy of
them don't you think? If I know you I'm so
very sure you've already Accessed that
there are more than just these first two of
my lovelies... oh I'm sure you know, but you
just don't know how much you know. I have
so much more to share with you, Maxine, so
very much to show you. We have so far to
go and I will be in touch with you my dear
Maxine... very, very soon.*

Folding the letter she placed it back into the evidence bag recording it to memory as she'd done the first letter. This one was definitely more personal than the first right down to him repeating her name several times. In her mind she was trying to process the letter and travel back in time to see if anyone she knew could fit the bill of a serial killer, but for the moment she was drawing a blank.

As a kid growing up her mother pretty much kept her away from people to the point that she was home schooled right through her first year of college. Living in a single parent home and never being able to speak of the father she'd never known was often times tough. Her mother wasn't the most pleasant of women, loving her alcohol more than she loved her own child, and she endured plenty of beatings that often came for no reason.

"I need a moment," she said almost at a whisper and stood from the chair and hurried off to the women's restroom.

"Where are you, you little bitch," her mother's words were so clear in her head. "I know you're hiding and you know when I find you I'm going to beat the fucking skin from your little body."

She'd found a way to squeeze into the smallest area in the back of her closet and that's where she hid. She was careful not to breathe as her mother stumbled into her room screaming out at the top of her lungs looking for her. Tears were slowly dripping from her eyes before she closed them hoping to disappear into the dark of the space in the closet.

"I know... I fucking know you're in here," her mother ranted. "Come out now and I promise I won't beat you. I promise. I just need you to help me with dinner."

She almost most stirred, but something made her wait.

"Come out now goddammit. Come out now or I'll tear up this entire fucking room."

Maxine sat in the back of the closet fearful to the point of screaming. When her mother pulled open the closet door she sat there frozen pushed as far back into the corner of the closet as she could get her body. She sat there watching as the drunken woman got down on her knees and began pushing things out of the way and pulling them out and throwing them back into the room. She trembled just knowing she would find her this time and she would be beaten again.

"I'm going to beat you to within an inch of your fucking life," her mother hissed and then turned away from the closet to crawl and look under the bed. "Where are you? Where the fuck are you?"

Her mother stood and moved towards the door of the room. "I know you're here somewhere and when I find you… when I find you."

Maxine sat there and listened to her walk out of the room and then down the stairs still mumbling. She sat there still afraid to breathe… still afraid to move. When she was certain her mother was still downstairs she allowed herself to breathe out and cry, but she refused to allow herself to move from her hiding space. She trembled and prayed to be away from there, maybe with the father she didn't know, but anywhere would be better than staying with her mother. She had to go to the bathroom and she knew she would have to clean up the room before her mother saw it again.

She sat there for as long as she could before her legs and butt got numb from her being on the floor. Quietly she moved things out of her way and eased out of the closet. She could tell it was late, but she had no idea how late. She slowly moved downstairs hoping not to run into her mother. The television was on and turned up loud as she tiptoed into the living room. Again she was holding her breath as she moved towards the back of the sofa. Her heart was pounding in her ears as she slowly peeked over the back and stared down at her mother sleeping soundly. She ducked back down and sat on the floor behind the sofa saying another quiet prayer of thanks before running to the bathroom and locking the door.

Maxine stood in the mirror staring at herself. There were tears slowly running down from her eyes and she was breathing heavy. It had been years since she'd even thought about her life back home with her mother, and even now it had her trembling as if she were back there sitting in her room's closet. She coughed, but it wasn't enough. She wanted to scream, but looking around she knew she couldn't because she was standing in the bathroom at her job.

"Damn," she whispered as she pulled paper towels from the holder and wiped her eyes. "And you wonder to this day why I fucking left you, or why I'm as much an alcoholic as you? I am definitely a product of you, Mother."

She stomped from the bathroom slamming the door in her wake, and returned to her desk to get back to work.

Chapter 10

He slowly pulled up to the gate of Mount Pleasant Village and waved at the guard standing there in the booth. They were always so friendly and unassuming. As he stopped and gave the older man his identification badge he smiled and tipped his hat and waited for him to check for his name on the list. It was like this in all of these gated communities they knew him but not really because he was merely a name on a check list to be allowed within the realm upper echelon. He took his badge back and hung it from his rear view mirror and waved again as the man hit the button to open the gate to allow him in.

He slowly drove in and followed the road around the large pond with the costly fountain in the center and off onto the next road to his right. The houses were so immensely extravagant sitting semi-isolated on their plush expanse of lawn, and unbeknownst to them this made each and every one of them the best of targets. He slowed down and took in the different men all moving around with their mowers roaring or their edgers buzzing as they plied their trades of landscaping these expensive lawns. There were other trades also being adhered to; he saw a couple of guys working on windows, another set working on a home alarm system, and another working on a family's car right there in the drive way.

He turned down the next street being careful not to be noticed as someone out of place. He picked up a tablet beside him and appeared to be looking for a particular address, but the truth of it, he already knew exactly where he was going. He shook his head at the waste of land from house to house as he slowly pulled off the road and across the street just short of the house he was looking for. He sat there looking around watching as people slowly moved around taking care of their daily chores and he lit a cigarette.

The family he was concerned with he knew they were all gone for the day. It was a family of four, and they had just recently moved into this neighborhood. He'd been following the woman for well over a month as they prepared to move from their old home and into this one. It wasn't that hard to find out where they would be moving, and he'd already gotten inside of the new home and made himself familiar with everything except how it would be furnished. The new home had a great basement area where he could hold up and the windows on the lower levels were old enough that even if the family were to lock them he could jimmy the locks and slip inside. He was all prepared for them to move in.

He sat back in his seat pulling on the cigarette and wishing he could stop smoking the rancid things, but it was a habit he was no used to and there was no stopping. He reached down on the seat and pulled up the picture of her and stared at it again. She was as beautiful as all the rest with her long blonde hair was pulled back into a tight ponytail and he could recall the day that he took the picture that her hair bounced around on her head as she walked. He caught himself from moaning out as he closed his eyes and then opened them again to stare at the picture. In this one she was dressed for jogging which she did every morning on the trail that went off into the small park area just outside of the gates. The trail is off through the trees on a man-made walk made for the joggers and bikers of this community. He ran his finger along the picture as he took in her standing there in the tight fitting sports bra and the loose fitting jogging shorts on down her bare legs to her small feet in her running shoes.

"Look at you drooling over a picture of one of those dirty little bitches," his mother's voice was so loud in his head. "What? Did you think I didn't know about your little books under the mattress of your bed, you nasty little fuck?"

"I need for you to go away, Mother," he whispered.

"What did you say to me, Boy?" she was shrieking now and he could feel the heat of her smoky breath on his ear. "What the fuck did you just say to me?"

He ducked his head down expecting to be hit. The still burning butt of his cigarette dropped from his lips and he was able to pull himself free of his torment to beat out the cherry sparks as the butt rolled down the front of his shirt to the floor. He stomped on the cigarette snuffing it out as he checked to make certain he wasn't burning anywhere and then he sat back again trying to calm himself.

He checked his watch. "Good, it's almost 10… you should be heading home here soon."

He looked around to make certain no one was watching and he drove off to park his van in the copse of the trees just beyond the house so that it was out of sight. He stepped out and walked around the back and he opened the doors and pulled out the camouflage netting and moved about covering the van to blend it in with the richly green of the trees and shrubs. He stepped up into the back of the van and spread out the plastic and the cloth covering over the floor so that it would be set and ready for him once he returned. Stepping back out he closed the door after grabbing his toolbox and placing it on the ground.

This was the time of the day he loved. The morning was pleasant and cool but the sun was up and warming everything up quickly. He pulled on his gloves and then zipped up the light leather jacket he was wearing. He always felt as if he were dressed for battle and that he had to go through a checklist to make certain he was covered properly for his mission. He pulled the large, Bowie styled knife from the sheathe at his back and stared at it. He loved the weight of the heavy hilt in his hand as he looked along the curved, sharpened edge. He slashed it about for but a moment listening as it whistles in the morning breeze. He placed the blade back in it's sheathe and picked up his toolbox and made his way towards the side of the house that was shielded by the tree line.

The window he'd jimmied open was still unlocked and he was able to slowly slip inside of the house without worry of noise. Once inside he moved towards the stairs and slowly made his way up to the main floor and he looked around. Again he glanced at his watch and calculated how much time he had left and then ran up the next flight of stairs to the bedroom floor. He marveled at how large this home was as compared to the others he'd been in and wondered for a moment if this was what spurned him on. Shaking his head she moved down the hall towards the double doors leading into the Master's bedroom.

He stepped inside and moved towards the extremely large walk-in closet and closed the doors. Knocking along the walls he found the secret door he'd made that sealed itself in firmly to the wall. He pushed against the wall and the latch clicked and the door slowly moved aside. He looked inside and then stepped in pulling the door closed and making certain it locked in place. He was amazed at the amount of space he had between the two walls and quickly moved about to find the spot where he'd drilled his small peepholes to stare out into the bedroom and the bathroom. He stood there staring out into the room waiting for her to get home.

She didn't disappoint. She was always very prompt and always on schedule. Nothing short of what he would have expected from the CEO of her own large company. He smiled as he pressed his eye to the hole and watched as she walked into the room and sat down on the bed to remove her shoes. She was such a beauty to watch being a woman who was in her early fifties, but she did not look it. Hers was a natural beauty and not enhanced at all through any cosmetic surgeries or any chemical enhancements.

He held his breath as she stood and slowly removed her clothing and stood there in the bedroom naked and walking around putting away her dirty jogging clothes and he shoes in their proper places. He could hear her moving around in the closet and he turned to peep through that hole he had drilled for there. She moved about so casually, and this surprised him as he'd imagined her being very uptight and very stiff. He couldn't take his eyes off of her bouncing breasts and the way her butt cheeks seemed to dance with each step.

She gathered her clothes for the day and moved off towards the bathroom and soon he heard the shower running. At some point she had turned on a radio because he could also hear music playing, some old Kenny Rogers serenading her as she stepped into the water. Again he moved to where he'd drilled his hole and looked out into the bathroom and watched as she moved about behind the opaque glass doors. He was breathing heavily and he could feel his penis growing and hardening as she rubbed her sponge across her body and he could just imagine her covered in soap before rinsing off.

He stepped back from the hole and dropped to the floor his body shaking as he grabbed at his penis and squeezed hard. He bit down on the heel of his other hand to keep from making any sounds that she may hear if she had stepped from the shower. He closed his eyes and pressed his body hard against the wall trying not to kick out or move about in any way as he waited for everything in his body to settle down once again.

"Why you sick, sick little fucking boy," he looked up through teary eyes and saw his mother standing over him with her belt in hand. "This is why I fucking hate you. Why couldn't you just be a good boy?"

"Please, Mommy," he quietly begged as he looked down at the wet spot now visible on the front of his pants, "I'm so sorry."

He dropped his head as he waited for her to swing the belt down at him. His heart was racing as again pictures of the beautiful woman in the shower flashed through his overcharged mind. His body is on sensory overload and again he begins to shutter and shake as he holds his breath trying not to scream out.

The music was turned up and it slowly helped to settle him down as he realized she'd finished her bath was most likely preparing to dress for work. He forced himself to stand and he started at the bathroom hole looking for her and not seeing her in there mostly due to the steam from the shower. He quickly moved to the bedroom hole and pressed his eye to it and found her sitting at her vanity with a towel wrapped about her body and one around her head. He watched without any other incidents as she applied her makeup and then dressed for the day. She stepped back into the closet and grabbed her briefcase and he watched as she walked from the room knowing she was headed towards her multi-million dollar business.

He slumped once more against the wall breathing heavy and again tears filled his eyes. He could feel her staring at him and shaking her head. He could almost feel that belt she always had with her striking his flesh and he had to keep from screaming out as he did as a little boy. He shook as he sat there and he sat there until he finally fell off to sleep only to be plunged into the nightmares of his dreams.

***

He stood there silently watching. As always he was in the shadows as he watched the boy growing up. He was so shy and so withdrawn and that's just how his mother wanted him. From the time he was able to walk he'd been beaten and abused by her in all manner of ways, and she never felt she'd done anything that warranted any kind of an apology. Her belt was always her favorite because he never seemed able to run fast enough to get away from it and it just struck from all directions. He barely ever talked, and when he did it was primarily to apologize and beg for her to stop.

The boy was sitting at his desk most likely trying to finish up a homework project. He'd been home school his entire life because she didn't want him getting away from her and out into the real world. Her excuse was always that the real world would corrupt him and he was already such a bad boy. He was about sixteen at this time and had found ways to slip off when she was asleep and into town. Under his bed at this time were several magazines he knew she would kill him over if she were to ever find them. And he'd also seen her…

She was absolutely beautiful. When he'd seen her that first time she was running down the sidewalk with a group of her friends laughing and talking and the first thing he saw was her hair. It was so long and so blonde flowing behind her loose as she ran. He stood in front of the little dime store he frequented just watching her when the clerk came out with his broom to sweep. The older man stood there watching just as hard as he was and told him, after whistling, the girl's name.

Sybil Danning… and he fell in love that day.

He stood there staring at the boy as he sat there now daydreaming. He slowly pushed away from the desk and walked to the door and peeked out to see if he could hear where she was at in the house. He eased out of the room and made his way to the stairs and quietly tiptoed down to the main floor hoping not to run into her. The television was playing loudly as he made his way towards the living room and he peeked around the corner looking for her. A smile crept across the boy's face as she lay there on the sofa sleeping, and he turned and headed out the backdoor through the kitchen.

The boy raced down the few steps and then off towards the shed at the back of the house. He slipped inside and quickly locked the door and then he slowly walked up to the door in the ground that led down into the cellar. Lifting the door he could hear a murmuring that caused him to look around, but then he quickly descended into the belly of the hole closing and latching the door. He got down to the floor level and his hand slid against the wall there and he flipped the light switch.

He stood there in the shadows watching as the young boy turned towards the area where he had a bed set up. There was something squirming there and as the boy got closer he smiled as he looked down upon Sybil Danning. She was absolutely gorgeous with her hands tied behind her back and her legs tied at the ankles. There was a blindfold around her eyes and a piece of duct tape over her mouth so she couldn't scream out. He'd taken off all of her clothes except for her bra and panties, and just looking at her laying there like that excited him… excited them both.

She mumbled as she realized that someone was there, and he leaned down and whispered into her ear. "Don't you scream and I'll take the tape off. Do you understand?" She nodded her head and grunted as he ripped the tape from her lips.

"Please," she whined, "please don't hurt me." She flinched as she felt his hand roughly grab at her breast and squeeze.

"I wouldn't have ever hurt you," he whispered again in her ear. "I have loved you from the moment I saw you."

"Then why am I here? What are you going to do to me?"

He stood there watching his younger self toy with his very first. He'd almost forgotten this time, and it was a major milestone for him. He watched as the boy walked away from the girl and retrieved the large blade from his makeshift working table. The first of anything done can definitely be messy, but under the right circumstances it can also be exhilarating. The boy moved back to the bed where the girl was laying and he stood over her just staring down at her. He was sweating and he was nervous, but he was so excited that his little penis was throbbing painfully.

"Why are you doing this to me?" the girl cried out.

"Because," the boy raised his the knife, "you FUCKING laughed at me."

As he growled out, he brought the knife down swiftly and began stabbing and hacking at the girl. At first she screamed out and she cried as the blade bit into her over and over. His movements were timid to begin and he noticed that the blade was doing damage but not enough and the girl was still moving and crying out. He got angry, stabbing her in the belly the blade sunk half way into her body; she jerked violently drawing in a very deep breath as her eyes stretched wide. He slowly drew out the blade; marveling at the wet, sticky sound, and he was rewarded with the heady stench of her spouting blood.

"Die," he said as he stabbed her again and again. "Die, you bitch, die."

She stopped moving. She stopped breathing. He kept stabbing until his arm got sore from pulling the blade from her body as it would go deeper and deeper. His hand and arm were completely covered in her blood and all he could do was grin. He licked his lips as he now stood over her dead body, and that's when he heard her voice.

"Where are you? You need to get your ass in this house now. I know you hear me calling for you."

He picked up the dress she'd been wearing and wiped off his hand and arm. There was no time to really clean up so he left everything as it was and raced up the ladder. He made certain everything looked as natural as possible before leaving the shed and he raced towards his mom standing in the backdoor staring at him.

"You need to get your little bitch ass in here and get cleaned up," she grumbled as she pulled on the cigarette and released the smoke. "Don't you make me stand out here calling for you again or I'll skin you alive."

"Yes, Ma'am."

"What the fuck were you doing? Why do you have blood on you?"

"I was playing with a dead dog I'd found," he quickly lied.

"You are a nasty little bastard."

***

"No, Babe, you don't get it," he woke to the sounds of the couple in their bedroom talking. "I've told Evelyn on more than one occasion that she's to handle that account and yet every time I turn around Rob is doing something with it, and I'm done."

"Charlene, you can't just fire her for being lazy. I think the Board is going to want more than you telling them she's not doing her work. She get's the numbers that everyone is looking for."

"But that's just it, Henry, they aren't her numbers."

He slowly stood and looked through the hole out into the bedroom and watched as they continued to talk as she walked around in nothing but her bra and panties. He looked down at his body and he was naked and he couldn't remember taking off his clothes; he shook his head and looked back out the hole into the room. He took a deep breath knowing that he couldn't allow himself to get over excited again and risk being heard behind the walls, but his hand was slowly stroking his penis. She was breathtaking standing in the middle of the room with her hands on her hips as she was telling her husband more about this woman she did not like.

"I just want her gone and I don't want to be put into a position where we have to pay her anything including her severance. She not deserving."

"She has a family, Charlene."

"That is not a concern of mine, Henry," she exclaimed. "She's a fake and I want her gone. This is my company… why must I subject it to bullshit like her?"

Hearing her voice stopped his hand as he pealed his eye away and pressed back against the wall behind him. His mother's face popped into his head and he had to fight from screaming out. He slid to the floor and folded his body up into a fetal position and he quietly wept. She haunted him, every waking hour, and every sleeping hour his mother haunted him. He feared her.

He looked up and she was standing there over him and all he could do was cringe back away from her. She didn't move. She didn't speak. She just stood there staring down at him. Tears streamed from his eyes as he tried to shake away, but she wouldn't move. He tried to cover his nakedness up from her eyes hoping she wouldn't beat him again, but she did not move at all. Her eyes bore into him and he could see the disgust she felt for him. He tried to stiffen his back, but just seeing her standing there he felt as he always did as a little boy.

"You're the devil," he whispered deeply under his breath, "and I fucking hate you."

He turned away from her murmuring, "Go away, please… just go away and leave me alone."

***

He sat in his chair waiting for the news to come on with a big smile on his face. There was no way this one would not be on all of the channels. There would be no way to hide her disappearance from the public. He rubbed his hands together trying to be patient, but he was failing miserably. The last minutes of some obnoxious comedy show was ending and the credits were running with the studio audience still laughing. He sat back holding his breath as he waited for the head anchorman to show his face.

"Good evening," the man sat behind his desk with a very grim look upon his face, "this is White Chapel News 9 and I'm Neville Dern and in our top story tonight we take you directly to the home of former Senator Henry von Dermott with out correspondent reporter Daniel Forthsythe who has been following a series of similar stories.

"Good evening, Dan, can you tell us what's going on there?"

"Well I'll be honest, Neville, it's not a very good evening here at the home of Senator von Dermott. Police received a call this evening around 6pm after the Senator got home from a business engagement stating that his wife was missing. The Senator has told the investigating officers that he last saw her this morning before he left for his out of town meeting and that it was their plans to meet early this evening to go to a dinner with some friends. The Senator went on to say that when he got home that his bedroom was in shambles as if someone had been fighting in there and that he has been unable to get his wife on the phone. After all that's been going on, we feel that the police believe she may have been kidnapped."

"Dan, do they believe that this was committed by the same man who kidnapped and then staged Chief Councilwoman Grace Muldoony?"

"Right at this moment, Neville, the police are not saying anything about either of the cases, but we will definitely keep an eye on all of this and report more as it comes to us."

"Thank you very much, Dan, and in other news…"

He sat there staring at the television as if he'd just been slapped. Just a few words said about a woman so prominent. She was not only the wife of a former Senator who did absolutely nothing for the state or the country; he merely sat in his chair and took a very nonverbal, noncommittal stance on everything and was able to keep his chair for over a decade. During that time his wife has built a little company from the ground floor and built into a very lucrative empire of her own. As the

Senator, he's benefited from her company as she was one of his major contributors that kept him in office for as long as he'd been there.

He picked up the glass that was sitting on the table next to his chair and tossed it across the room to smash against the wall. He screamed out and pulled at his hair until he finally calmed himself breathing in deeply. He wiped away the tears that had fallen from his eyes and again stared at the television. Slowly he sat back in his chair and thought as he tried to consider how he would be able to get the news involved.

He grinned as he stood and walked off towards the kitchen. "Time to up the ante."

Chapter 11

The entire news room was in chaos as they prepared for the early morning news. Nothing was settled as to how anything would proceed and the anchor was still arguing with those in control as to what was to be said and what was not. The stage was set but no one was in place as the cameramen and the gaffers all moved around in the background checking the lighting and sound just to keep themselves busy. Someone was going around shouting for there to be quiet on the set, but this only created a need to be louder by everyone moving around. On one of the screens there seemed to be a reporter trying to get anyone's attention but he was failing miserably and getting irate for his efforts.

Daniel Forthsythe sat at his desk leaned back in his chair looking at a news report he'd been writing on his computer screen. He shook his head as he read through it not satisfied with what he had, knowing that it was incomplete. There was so much more going on with these disappearances and deaths than anyone was letting on to, and he was sure the police knew more than they were saying. If he could only get Detective Steele off alone so that she would talk to him he was sure she would give him more than what he had right now.

He rubbed his chin and grimaced at the stubble growing there. He hadn't been home in two days as he'd been trying to track down more information on this case as he could. He hadn't been on any of his street reports because this had now taken precedent over everything else that he was working on. He was sure that he had heard one word whispered that definitely piqued his interests and he wanted to be the one to break the story before any of the other news groups in the city.

"We're definitely looking for a serial here." He was sure those were the words she'd used as she knelt down examining the body of the latest murder in White Chapel. Of course it was a bit distorted because the equipment he was using was not capable of capturing sounds at the distance the police had them corded off, but there was enough there for him to almost be certain that's what Steele said.

He shuffled through some of the folders that he had on his desk until he found one that he had marked with her name and he quickly looked through it. He'd done his research on her as well because she was undoubtedly the primary detective on the case even though the big tough guy assumed the roll. He ran his fingers through his unruly hair as he perused her file and then smiled as he again came to the conclusion that he had to talk to her and soon.

"We're definitely looking for a serial here." Those words continued to roll through his head as he read through her file and then read over what he'd written. There was just too much missing and he didn't even know where to begin looking because the police had a media block out on all of the case information. All any of the newscasts had to report at this time was the death of Mrs. Muldoony, but he knew a little more than that thanks to the look on Steele's face when he asked about Mrs. Fitzwilliams. Something was being withheld and he was bound and determined to find out what.

"What are you working on, Dan?" the sound of Aaron's voice startled him as he looked up at the frazzled man walking around with a make-up cloth around his neck.

"Just trying to get my head around these murders," he began as he pointed at his computer screen. "There's more going on with this but I can't seem to put my finger on it."

"So what are you thinking?"

"I can't be sure just yet, but…" he glanced up at the head anchor once more, "what if there are more bodies and we just don't know about them all? What if the police is keeping quiet about what's really happening?"

"Are you saying," Aaron leaned down and whispered, "we may have a serial killer?"

"I don't know yet," Daniel looked around, "but if we do I want to be the first to break this out. We have to keep this quiet for now until I can talk to her." He pointed to the picture he had of Maxine Steele.

"You be careful with that one," Aaron stared at the picture.

"Do you know her?"

"Not personally, but I know some guys on the Force who says she a real powder keg. They say she's good at what she does, but she's quite unstable. I know for a fact that she's been off the Force for a while and on Administrative leave."

"Well they have her back on duty because she was at the Muldoony crime sight," Daniel closed the file and slid his chair back from his desk. "I need to talk to her; I think she can give me some insight as to what's going on with this case."

"Well once you find out more get with me and we'll take it to Harry and see if we can run with on the air, shit, we need something worthwhile to report."

"I'll get with you post haste, Aaron, but I'm going to need some time. She looks like a tough nut to crack."

I guess you'll have to let me know," Aaron waved off the girl who was calling him back to make-up, and he walked off leaving Daniel at his desk.

"We need to meet, and soon, Det. Steele," Daniel whispered as he again opened the folder and stared down at her face. The picture was in black and white but he could still see her grey eyes staring back at him. There was something a little intimidating about her, but he was bound and determined not to let that detour him from tracking her down.

Because she had the answers…

He stood from his desk and finally made it over to the coffee pot and poured him a fresh cup of the sludge that had been brewed. He stood there at the counter trying to doctor the bitter taste to make it somewhat palatable enough for him to drink, but he still wrinkled his nose at that first sip. He leaned against the counter and stared around the office area as he stirred his cup and wondered just how he would get this woman to talk to him. He frowned, damn; he had nothing to offer to her that would even begin a conversation.

That was where he had to begin; he had to find something that he could bring to the table and maybe then she would open up to him about what's going on. He could even promise to keep any and everything she gave him under wraps as long as he got the exclusive story directly from her. He took another swallow of the stuff he had in his cup and looked around for someone he could send to the Starbucks right down the block. Shaking his head he walked back to his desk his mind full of thoughts about his next move. At this point he was at a complete standstill unless by fortune something was just dropped into his lap.

Sitting down he once again stared at the computer screen in the hopes that something jumped out at him that made any kind of sense. If he could only get the police to release any information from the coroner that he could use in his research, but every call he'd made thus far had hit a stone wall. He'd even talked to Captain Salter but was given the standard police statement that left more in the air and giving out any answers. It was all so frustrating to him as a reporter because it didn't give him anything to fucking report.

"I need someone to go get me some goddamn Starbucks before this shit kills me," he said aloud to anyone walking by, but no one came to his rescue.

"Excuse me, Sir?"

Daniel looked up and then waved the young boy off. "If you're not here to run to the damn coffee store for me I don't want to talk to you."

"I have a couriered message for a Daniel Forthsythe, I was told that is you."

"A message from who?" Daniel looked again at the boy and ran his fingers through his hair.

"There was no name given," he explained. "It was dropped off this morning and I was told to deliver it directly to you." The boy passed an electronic clipboard to him and asked him to sign it and then passed him the envelope.

Daniel sat there watching as the young man walked away and then stared down at the parcel he'd just left him with. Years of caution had him wondering if he should open the letter and take a chance that there was nothing inside that would explode out and cover him in something that could possibly kill him. He shook the envelope and didn't hear anything moving or shuffling around inside. He glanced around to make certain no one else was near and then he pulled out his letter opener and slowly slid it into the top of the letter and pulled it across watching carefully for anything to spill out. Finally, taking a deep breath he reached in and slowly pulled out the folded piece of paper and opened it up laying it out on his desk.

Greetings Mr. Forthsythe,

I am Death and as such I'm offering
you a look into my world through my eyes.
Are you ready for such a challenge?
Because I am ever willing to give you what
the police are holding from you...
Information. Information about what's
going on in this wretched city you call home
and where Death has come to dip his scythe.
And just to give you a taste of the blood I'm
offering I'll let you know now that I am
responsible for the lives of Margaret

Daniel stared down at the letter with his mouth wide open. He looked around as if expecting someone to be standing over his shoulder reading what he had just read. He felt the slight moisture building on his forehead and the thoughts of coffee went out the window and he suddenly needed something stronger… a lot stronger. He picked up the letter and read it again slower making certain he hadn't missed anything and he felt himself shiver at the thought that this man had contacted him. He sat there with what he considered a confirmed letter from a serial killer.

There were more, but the question now was how many more and how could he find out? He continued to read and re-read the letter hoping for more to just bounce out at him, but there was no more just this little tease of more to come. He stuffed the letter into the folder he had on Steele and slammed down the top. For the first time since the first break in this story he had a little something to smile about.

"I think its time we had a sit down, Maxine Steele," he murmured to himself.

"Hey you," he shouted to one of the passing girls, "yes, you come here I need you to run down to Starbucks and get me a decent coffee."

***

Sheryl Evans sat at her desk looking at the multi-screen system that she was literally tied to on a daily basis, and she smiled. She was the best at what it was she did and she didn't have to brag about it because her work did all of the talking for her. She was a master behind the scenes of almost each and every case being handled by the workforce of the White Chapel Police Department, and they all knew it. Her phone was constantly ringing requesting information that only she and her dynamic computer could come up with at but a moment's notice. It was like being an all-seeing goddess with her fingers at the hub of the universe of information. She'd even been approached by the FBI's Behavioral Analyst Unit on a couple of occasions hoping to steal her and her skills away from such a small department of law enforcement, but she was happy where she was.

Her fingers whizzed over the keys of her keyboard faster than the eye could follow and she watched as the dual screens flipped and churned information as fast as light. Another hit of another button and things she needed were quickly whisked away to the printer to be compiled for which ever officer needed them at that moment. Even as she typed and researched her phone would ring and she would hit yet another button and the voice on the other end was transferred to the microphone piece in her ear and this call only prompted her to open yet one more page on either of her screens to gather that information needed. She was a beast, and didn't get the proper respect for what she did.

"This is the dungeon and I'm the mistress of the roost," she said into the microphone hanging by her mouth, "how may I torture you?"

"Cute, Sheryl," the familiar voice was Maxine Steele. "I was wondering if you found out anything for me?"

Sheryl had been waiting for this call and had things all set up and prepared including a folder that was full and thick sitting for a courier to run upstairs. She clicked her mouse over one of the tabs she had sitting there on one of her screens. As the tab pulled up on the screen it was like multiple folders opening up and information just spilled out as if she'd opened a faucet.

"I'm glad you called, Detective," she began, "I have quite a bit of information for you and I'll be sending a folder up for you to go through. But, just to give you the highlights… there is definitely a trail that goes back at least a decade. Using the primary M.O. of the stab wounds I'm counting at least fifteen victims, but what gets me is that the ages of all of the victims are pretty much the same. They are all between their mid-40's to early 50's and they are all blondes, but they range from prominent to having no real community status at all. Each victim was stabbed no less than 30 times in their pubic region and with each case it eventually goes cold. "

"Damn," Steele sat silent for just a moment, "I wasn't really expecting him to have been active so damn long. When can you get those files up to me?"

"I'll have them on your desk within the hour," Sheryl answered.

"Excellent, excellent. You did a great job… thank you very much, Sheryl."

A smile creased her face at someone actually acknowledging the work she'd done for them. She gathered all of the information Det. Steele had requested and closed the folder that she had placed everything in. She stared at the screen once more and flipped through a few of the folders she had saved to make certain she had not missed anything that she wanted to send, and with a nod she closed everything out and made the call to have someone come down and take the folder she now placed off to the side of her desk.

"This is definitely a sick one you're dealing with," she said as she patted the top of the folder. "I hope all of this helps."

***

Maxine sat at her desk looking at the phone before placing it back into the cradle of the base sitting on her desk. Her conversation with Sheryl Evans was more than she'd anticipated and now she was at a loss. His history was deeper than she had expected meaning that he was evolving slowly and meticulously. As she sat there, she wondered if maybe he'd done some time between the murders, but she wouldn't be able to remotely determine that until she got a look at those files. This only compounded the case as it was and now she was almost certain there was a new missing person to add to the workload.

"Did you hear from Sheryl?" Raymonds stood at her desk with his hands stuffed into the pockets of his superbly pressed slacks.

She looked up at him and wondered just what motivated him because he always seemed ready to move on to something more to her. He was so clean up with his fresh haircut and his clean shaven jaw line and upper lip; not even a sparse five'oclock shadow there.

"I just got off the phone with her," Maxine looked about her desk as if searching for something. "It appears there are similar cold cases going back a decade."

"Do you really believe it's our perp?"

"I really won't know until I get a look at the files, but…" she looked up her partner, "from just what Sheryl said it sounds like our man has been busy for quite a while. Just from the way our bodies have been laid out I can tell this is not his first time. I just need to know what does it all mean and why is he picking the women he's picking."

"Just don't get caught up on this "serial killer" bullshit until we can directly pin him to more than one case. The last thing we need is to panic the entire city that we have a maniac out there targeting certain women."

"I'm all about the evidence and where it leads me, but I'll be honest with you, Raymonds," she took a drink from her near empty cup of coffee, "everything points to a serial killer even if we don't want to admit it."

Raymonds pulled his hands from his pockets and placed them on his waist. He was trying to keep his composure but he could feel a tinge of anger building as he could feel Steele just not following his lead. He wanted to point out to her that he was in charge but that in itself would have made him look and feel really petty so he stood there staring as she shuffled through her files.

"We just have to keep our heads on about this one, Steele," he said rubbing his hand over his head. "The last thing we want is to do is create a bigger issue with this shit than needs to be. I'm sure that the Captain would agree with me on this."

"I'm not going to the top of the White Chapel Cathedral and screaming out that we have a fucking serial killer," Maxine stared up at the nervous acting idiot and then turned away from him before she really got rude. "I'm just letting you know that based on what I've seen so far he has the potential of being a serial killer, but I promise I won't say anything out of turn before I'm able to prove what we have on our hands."

She pulled out the last letter and looked it over again. Just from what he was saying she knew he was telling her that there were more bodies; not only in his past but more to come very soon. Her only thoughts were finding a way to get ahead of him and bring him out before he could ruin anymore families. She looked around hoping that someone would step up with the folder from Sheryl so she would have something more to read through than what she had on her desk.

"Go the fuck away, Raymonds," she thought to herself as she shuffled through her papers once more. *"Go away now or I swear I'm going to rip you a new one."*

"I'm glad we got that out," Raymonds said softly. "There were no problems with that reporter, were there?"

"Nah," she said with a smile, "he was harmless. I'm sure he was just looking for an inside scoop on a story he has no clue about."

"Ok, well I have a few things I need to confirm," he stuffed his hands back into his pockets and turned to leave. "If you need me… ummm, I'll be at my desk."

Maxine grabbed the two letters and nodded as he slowly walked off. *Things to confirm at his desk…* what a joke; he was waiting for her to

come up with something just like the Captain was. He had no fucking clue
what was going on and was in complete denial as to the unsub being a
goddamn serial. She shook her head and again wished she had something
stronger to go in her coffee cup to lift up the drab liquid already coating
the sides of the cup. She took a deep breath and looked at her watch, it had
been too long since she'd had her last cigarette and she was definitely in
need of one. She looked around once more hoping for a courier, but it was
just the normal hustle and bustle that met her glance.

"Excuse me, Detective Steele," a young, female officer had
stepped up to the front of her desk. "I have a message for you."

Maxine looked up from her desk and stared at the girl before
reaching out hand to take the note that she was holding. Dropping the
paper, the officer did a quick about face and walked off without waiting to
see if the note was opened or tossed aside. Maxine unfolded the paper and
glanced at the note within.

> *Detective Steele,*
>
> *I do believe that we got off on the
> wrong foot the other day and I'd like to
> make amends. Please forgive me for being
> rude and abrupt and downright pushy, but
> in my defense I was merely trying to get a
> jump on my comrades in arms. Every
> reporter is looking for that one story that
> will propel him beyond his peers and I do
> believe that this is "that" story for me. I
> would like to meet with you very soon, I
> believe I have something in my possession
> that you will find very appealing, and I'm
> sure that for some reason "He" wants us to
> meet.*
>
> *Maybe we can meet this evening for
> dinner... say around 7pm at the Grey Goose
> off of Kentucky and Lennox. I will be there
> waiting for you until 8:30... I do hope that
> you will grace me with your company.
> Again I do believe I can make this worth
> your while, and I give you my word that this
> is strictly between you and I.*

Maxine glanced around to see if anyone else had seen her getting that message and then she stuffed it into the pocket of her jacket. Her mind was atwitter as to what this man could have that he felt she would find interesting; especially interesting enough that he had to set up a paper note rather than just calling her and speaking to her directly. Such cloak and dagger antics caused her to grin, but she figured it was at least worth going to see what he had to say. She sat back in her chair and contemplated something he'd said about being sure "He" wanted them to meet. She could feel it in her bones that things were about to get worse long before they got any better.

She heard her name called out over the din of the office and she looked up to see a plain clothes office scanning the room for her. She raised her hand and whistled out to get his attention and waved him her way. He was carrying a file box that he dropped on the edge of her desk that was marked Important Documents for Detective Maxine Steele.

"This is case files and research folders from the Analyst downstairs. She asked for all of this to be brought up to you, and there are about three more boxes to come."

"Excellent, just have them all brought to here me and I'll sign for all of them once I get the last box."

"Very good," the man didn't stand there waiting for anymore directions. He walked off leaving her there staring at the box.

Maxine felt like a kid at Christmas as she pulled open the box and dove into the papers that were within. It was going to be a long day, but a very productive one as she looked around once more before tackling her new task. It was time to find out some definitive things about her new pen pal because it definitely seemed that he knew a few things about her.

***

The Grey Goose was a very upscale, well to do establishment on the upper West side of White Chapel in what was considered the Blue Light District. It was a small restaurant that was still family owned and ran by the oldest son of the original owner, and he was a very skilled chef. It catered to more of a prominent clientele that enjoyed what most would consider a very good four to five star restaurant. Their food was country Italian with its primary dish being a rustic style veal parmesan with a homemade tomato sauce. They were known in the city for their very large wine collection that would complement any meal prepared. The waiting list just to get a seat was said to be months out, unless you were someone or knew someone.

Daniel Forthsythe was someone.

He walked up to the door and was immediately recognized by the doorman who greeted him with a handshake and a pat on the back as he moved him past the line and into the restaurant foyer. The smells from all the varieties of foods attacked him as he moved to the hostess stand and waited for her to return. As he looked around, he waved to a couple of people as they were enjoying their meals.

"Good evening, Mr. Forthsythe," the hostess had returned with a beaming smile. "Are you dining alone tonight?"

"Actually, Alex, I have a guest that needs to be watched for. Her name is Maxine Steele."

"I'll make certain that we keep an eye out for her and I'll have her sent to your table immediately. Come and I'll take you to your table." She stepped from around the stand and led him through the restaurant to a private table near the back.

Daniel is almost like a local celebrity and well-known for being the reporter that he is. He doesn't mind what people say behind his back about his reporting style, he merely looks at himself as being aggressive and willing to take those "out of the box" chances to get his story. Thinking about it, that's why he was here tonight.

"Shall we start with your usual wine tonight, Mr. Forthsythe?" the Sommelier asked as he held the bottle of deep red wine to pour.

"Thank you, Gary, but I have a guest coming and I'm thinking something softer, maybe a light white wine."

"Give me a moment, Sir, and I'll find you something nice."

Daniel sat back with a smile and nodded the man off. His waiter finally made it to the table and placed a basket of bread sticks for him to snack on as he waited. He informed the young man that he would wait a bit longer for his guest to arrive before ordering dinner and watched as the Sommelier returned with a new bottle of wine in his hand.

"What I have for you, Sir, is a very fine bottle of Baron Philippe de Rothschild's Viognier. This is a candied and fresh fruit flavored wine which is enhanced by some subtle floral notes, and I must say it pares well with fish."

The man poured out a taste into Daniel's glass and watched as he swirled the glass around, sniffed it breathing in the fragrant floral essence of the wine and then he took a sip letting it sit in his mouth for a moment before swallowing. The man smiled as Daniel swallowed with a smile and then drunk the final bit in his glass before sitting the glass down and nodding for him to pour.

"Enjoy your meal, Mr. Forthsythe," he left the bottle in the ice bucket he'd brought with the first bottle of wine and made his way through the restaurant to his next customer.

As he was pouring his first glass, he looked up and Alex was ushering Maxine to his table. He quickly stood and waited for her to be seated before he sat back down and offered her a glass of wine. Not taking no for an answer he poured her a glass and then sat there taking her in. She was nothing like any other woman he'd ever entertained, but it was definitely refreshing. There was just something about the way she looked, right down to the fact that she was definitely uncomfortable here, but she would never let it seem like she was nervous at all. He took in the fact that she hadn't dressed up, she in fact looked as if she'd come straight from work to the restaurant, and this didn't fall lightly on others in the restaurant as they all seemed to stare at the woman in the slacks and leather jacket.

"Thank you for joining me, Detective Steele," he greeted her even as he stared at her.

"I'm not sure how to take this place," she leaned over and whispered to him before sitting back and taking a sip of her wine. "Please call me Maxine."

"Then you must call me Daniel, that way we're on equal grounds here. I really hope that you don't mind the restaurant because its one of my favorites."

"Its very beautiful in here," she smiled as her eyes went from the man across the table from her to her surroundings. "I've always wanted to come in here, but the waiting list is fucking ridiculous."

Again she surprised him because he was not ready for a woman who literally speaks her mind. She's definitely a street cop and that is for some reason very sexy to him. He shifts in his chair as he takes a big swallow of his wine. He could sit and watch her all night, but he was positive that she would voice against that rather quickly. He waved over the waiter for his table and put in an order for an appetizer of shrimp scampi for the both of them and told him they would be ready to order dinner by the time he returned.

"I hope you don't mind me taking the initiative and ordering a little something to get us started," he tipped his wine glass at her with a smile.

Picking up the menu and wrinkling her nose that it was all written in Italian she merely smiled placing it back down on the table. "Well it looks as if I'm going to have to trust you ordering the full meal."

"I think I can handle that for us both," again he flashed his smile at her in an attempt to be charming.

"So, do we enjoy our meal first, or do we just get right down to why you invited me here tonight?" she looked about the room taking in the scenery. For some reason she could see potential victims for her unsub and she tried to shake away the thoughts, but there were a number of those same kinds of women she could see fit his particular M.O.

"I was hoping that I could at least enjoy your company for a bit after the ass I made of myself the other day," he answered. "I hope that this makes up for it."

"You have nothing to make up for, Daniel. Trust me I know what it means to be headstrong about what you're working on."

"True, but there are ways of doing things without being, dare I say, an asshole."

Maxine couldn't help but to giggle at him as she tipped her glass to drink. It has been a good two months since she'd had a drink and even though it was not her usual poison it felt pretty good to have a little something alcoholic in her system. She tried to see him as she had the day they'd first crossed paths, but tonight there was something very different about him that she found amusingly comfortable.

The appetizers came and they both sat enjoying them over a bit more small talk and she marveled at how fluently he spoke Italian when he ordered their dinner. She was amazed at how prompt they were at getting their food out to them and she was completely pleased with the fish dish he'd ordered. Dinner was stellar and they even enjoyed dessert and a second bottle of wine was ordered before they finally decided that it was time to talk about why they were both there.

"So tell me," Maxine said putting her glass back down on the table, "what is it that you think you have that I'd want to know?"

"Would you believe," Daniel leaned over the table whispering conspiratorially, "that 'He' contacted me?"

"Why would 'He' contact you? How would 'He' even know about you?"

"Are you kidding? My face is always all over the television, that's the how, but I have no real idea as to the why. Maybe he wanted us to meet? Or, maybe he wanted me to put him all over my reports?"

"How exactly did he contact you?"

"He sent me a letter," Daniel said smugly.

Maxine leaned over the table staring at him to the point he felt uncomfortable; like she may jump across the table at him. Her steel grey eyes were so piercing at that moment that it scared him.

"Do you have the letter," she asked. "I'd really like to read it."

"Uh," he began feeling his forehead beginning to sweat, "no, I didn't bring it with me. I forgot it on my desk when I left the office this evening."

"Anyway," she sat back again, "what did 'He' tell you?"

"Well firstly, he stated that he was responsible for the deaths of Fitzwilliams and Muldoony, and he went on to say that there was more to come. The creepy part was that he told me that he would be in touch with me again.

"Oh yea and he gave me a name to call him. He called himself Death and said that I could call him Reaper."

Maxine sat there staring at him not allowing her anger for him not bringing the letter to show her appear on her face. Her unsub was reaching out because he wasn't getting the type of press he was wanting for his endeavors, and of course he targeted the most influential reporter in the city. He wanted people to be fearful of him and he was willing to personally invite the press into his madness. This was not good, but what she really needed was that letter.

"Do you think you could fax me a copy of your letter to my office tomorrow?"

"I can do that," he took a deep breath watching as she seemed to calm down, "but why do you think he contacted me? Really?"

"He's longing for his 15 minutes of fame I'd say. We've been trying to keep a lock on what's going out in to the press so's not to panic the entire city."

"That makes sense, but," he was about to put his cards on the table, "I need something from you."

"I'm not surprised," she mumbled under her breath. "And, what might that be."

"I want the exclusive to the story," he sat there staring at her.

Maxine said nothing as she considered how she would take this to the Captain and explain it to him. She wondered what he actually considered as giving him the "exclusive" to the story and just how much she would be allowed to give him just for sharing a letter with her.

"I guess you know what I'm going to say next," she took on last drink from her wine glass feeling an end to the night coming. "I'll have to take this up with my Captain, but I'm sure he'll have no real problem with it as long as you don't agree to report on what we ask throughout the investigation."

"I won't have any problem with that, as long as you keep me in the loop."

Maxine stood to leave and watched as he jumped up just as quick snapping his finger for the waiter. The young man ran up and passed him his receipt which he signed and then grabbed his coat and pulled it on. She was impressed that he was bound and determined to walk her out to her car. He moved them through the crowd and out the door into the cool of the night and she pointed him to her car. As she unlocked her door, and turned to say goodnight and he handed her one of his business cards.

"Call me with an answer tomorrow and I'll fax over a copy of that letter."

"Thank you," she smiled as she accepted the card and then sat down in the car letting down the window. "I'll call you first thing."

"You know," he had that smile on his face that made her nervous, "we don't have to end the night so soon."

"We don't, huh? So what are you suggesting?"

"Why don't you let me come over, or you come to my place and we can… talk some more."

"I really don't think all that you want to do is… talk, Mr. Forthsythe." She grinned up at him.

"Well we could begin by talking," they laughed.

"Sure, we could talk some more, but you'll have to follow me."

She watched as he jogged off and jumped into a very nice Lexus and quickly started it up. As she pulled off, she glanced into her rearview mirror and smiled as he pulled in behind her and they drove off. There was a part of her trying to tell her not to get involved with this man; that he would be just another conquest of her played out from a drunken stupor, but the other part quickly screamed out that she wasn't drunk. She turned up the radio and headed home not paying either of the voices anymore attention.

But, what she missed was the dark van sitting across the street from the restaurant and the fact that he pulled off following them.

Chapter 12

In anger he began beating at the steering wheel as he watched them standing there all giggles and talking. In more anger he began screaming and howling as he watched the man run off and jump into his fancy little car and they drove off together. He followed thinking that maybe he just wanted to make certain she had got home safely, but no, once they parked they both went into her complex and he watched until her light finally came on. In anger he sat there smoking cigarette after cigarette as he watched the light and the front door to see if the lights go out or he came out the door.

He could feel his heart pounding in his chest and he could feel the sweat building across his forehead as he sat there. He could almost see them sitting there on her sofa and that man's hands are all over her. He could almost see them ripping each other's clothes off as he tried to take her right there in the living room on the same sofa he'd pleased himself on a dozen times. He opened the door to his van and stepped out and paced around trying to decide what he would do, and the thoughts of murder screamed at him.

He stared up at the window and the light was still on and he began to wonder what the hell they were doing. He pulled off the skull cap he was wearing and scratched at the thinning dirty blonde hair on his head as he lit another cigarette.

"Aww poor little whiny boy," his mother stood there at the back of his van, "can't have your way so here you are stomping around like a little girl."

"What do you want, Mother," he mumbled. "Why are you still fucking with me?"

"I want you to be a fucking man," she hissed into his ear. "I want you to be more than some sniveling little pansy looking for me to whip his little ass, but that can never be you can it. You think that with all that you've done, with all of the women you've killed, that at some point you would become stronger. At some point you would become a … Man."

"I am fucking stronger, you bitch, I am a fucking man," he looked her standing there. "I don't need you anymore and that's what you hate the most."

"Oh, you think because your infatuations have turned to that little bitch you can do without me now?"

"I don't need you anymore, Mother," he growled as he looked at where she was standing. "I don't need you and that's why I…"

"Say it," she stepped closer to him and he backed away. "You weak little shit, with your nasty, sick thoughts. I should have put that belt to better use on your sniveling ass."

"Go the FUCK away," his voice seemed to carry into the dark of the night and as he looked around there was no one standing there but him. He looked up and down the night street and took a deep breath as even the little bar seemed scarce of people at the moment. He had to calm himself before he went to check on her, or else he would not be responsible for his reactions.

He looked up at her window just in time to see it shut off and he knew that the man was not coming back down. He cursed in his head but didn't allow himself to get out of control again as he locked up the van and made his way across the street. He let himself into the building with the key he'd copied from hers and made his way to the stairs, he slowly walked up allowing that time to completely calm his mind before he got to the door to her floor and peeked out. He slowly stepped out into the empty hallway and crept down to her door, looking around once more, he slipped the key into the door knob and twisted it quietly unlocking it and then the same with the deadbolt.

As he stepped into the apartment, his ears were assailed with the sounds coming from her room, but he remained calm as he closed the door and silently moved about in the dark. The door had not been closed and he stepped over the clothing that they had both thrown about the floor. There were no lights on in the room so he quickly settled into the shadows of the room that he knew hid him best and he stood there watching.

His eyebrows furrowed across his forehead as he watched the pale man with the fake, painted on tan hovering above her while she had her legs hoisted up with him in between them. He could see her eyes widen in delight as he finally pushed forward and slowly enter her and his body fell down atop hers. Their lips met as the man began to grind and pump his ass around between her thighs and she moaned like a little whore in the red-light district with one of her tricks. He stood there staring as their naked bodies seemed to become one and it was hard to tell her from him, and the sounds from both of them was sickening to hear.

He could feel that anger rising again and he held his breath to keep from making any sound. It was like watching a train wreck; no matter how much he wanted to turn away he just couldn't take his eyes off of her. Her face was twisted in ecstasy as her body continued to bump up to his. His lips were locked into hers and his hand had one of her breast and he was squeezing it hard as he pumped and pounded between her legs. He watched as the man pulled all the way out and flipped her over onto her belly and then pulled her up onto her knees and he reentered her fiercely. Just watching them made his stomach lurch even as his own manhood slowly became erect inside of his pants.

He stood glued to the wall watching, wiping the sweat from his forehead as they continued rutting around on the bed until at last he grunted and groaned out as he pushed up into releasing his seed. His body reacted before he could stop himself and he slapped his hand to his mouth as he too moaned out and leaked his seed out into his pants. He bit down on his hand as he slowly moved from the room and back out into the living room. Frustrated and embarrassed he sat down on the floor behind the sofa and allowed the tears to slowly drip down his face.

She was right…

As much as he wanted to beat it out of his head, she was right. He was weak. He could never be strong. He froze up as he heard the sound of someone running through the living room and into the kitchen. The refrigerator door opened and he could hear someone moving things about.

"All I have is a couple of cans of Sprite," she yelled out, "will that be ok?"

"That's perfect; just hurry your ass back to the bed."

The sound of her giggling was almost weird as he'd never heard her laugh ever. He pressed up against the back of the sofa and held his knees to his chest as he waited for her to go back into the room. Once he heard the door close he stood and made his way to the front door. Slipping out, he relocked everything and made his way back down the stairs and out of the complex to his van. He sat there staring up at the window and with shaky hands he pulled out a cigarette and lit it. He took a deep drag and began to feel his nerves slowly returning to normal.

"Poor little whiny bitch," her voice was like a church bell ringing in his head. "Now what are you going to do? I know, just sit here and watch her dark window while you imagine her getting fucked over and over by that stud she's found herself."

"No," he said as he blew smoke from his lungs. "It's time to make them pay for this shit… to make them understand that I'M in Control… it's time to pull their fucking heads from the clouds."

His van roared to life and he sped off into the dark without looking back. He was angry beyond words and someone would have to pay for that.

An hour passed quickly as he made his way into Dryper's Lane, the lower East side where the lower working class all seemed to huddle together in their small neighborhoods. Mediocre homes with their small yards all mostly built the same way like from a cookie cutter mold, and all so close together that you could follow the conversations going on in each home. He liked hunting in this area because of how close things were, but no one seemed to watch anything going on in their neighborhoods much like the people in the big cities.

He pulled up to the small fenced in park and turned off his motor as he sat there watching the house just across the street. The lights were on in the living room and also upstairs in the Master's bedroom, and he could see her shadow as she walked around her bedroom. He couldn't see her clearly thanks to the curtains in front of the window, but he knew it was her and he took a deep breath as he smiled. He'd noticed her a few weeks ago as she was coming from across the street from where she'd parked her car. She was just his type, and he watched her just as he'd done all of his other women and learned everything about her.

Her husband worked at one of the banks downtown, nothing fancy but he made a fair wage for his day's work. She was a waitress at her family owned café a few blocks from where her husband worked and they met for lunch every day. Her father owned the café but she'd been working there since she was a teen, and that was how the couple met. They have no children at home, but tend to keep her sisters kids for them when ever they need to get away.

He sat there patiently waiting for all of the lights to go off. The street itself was already dark as if the entire neighborhood had fallen asleep, and he sat there waiting. He smoked the last cigarette in the pack trying not to think back to Maxine's house, but he wasn't succeeding as images flashed into his head of their naked bodies twisting and turning all over her bed sheets. He could see the sweat on their bodies and smell their odors in the humid room. He wanted to scream, but bit down on his lip until he could taste his own blood dripping into his mouth.

The lights finally went out and he started up his van and backed up onto their driveway in front of the garage. He glanced up and down the sleepy street before moving into the back of the van and gathering up his toolbox. Slipping on his gloves he finally made his way out of the van into

the cool of the night and moved towards the front door. He fished the key
he'd made from his pocket and gently pushed it into the knob unlocking
the door quietly. He stepped into the home and quietly closed the door. He
stood there on the foyer taking in the sounds and smells of the house
before slowly moving up the stairs to the top floor.

He walked towards the bedroom door just missing the board in the
floor that he knew squeaked. He pushed on the slightly closed door and
looked into the dark room at the couple sleeping on the bed. He quietly
settled his tool bag down on the floor and opened it pulling out some duct
tape and rope. His anger was building again as he saw flashes of Maxine
with the reporter. He grabbed a pair of handcuffs and quickly reentered the
room; he moved around to the other side of the bed and grabbed the
woman's arm and handcuffed her to the bed's headboard, and watched as
her eyes flickered open. He pulled his knife from his back and pressed it to
her lips letting her know she was to be silent.

He climbed up onto the bed and straddled her husband and
watched as he slowly woke up. The man's eyes stretched as he stared up
his eyes seeming to cross as they bore into the edge of the knife just above
his face.

"I would like to apologize," he said to them as he looked from one
face to the other. "This was not how I had this planned, but they have
pushed the envelope and now I have to make them pay.

"Your sacrifice will not go unwarranted," he stared at the man
beneath him. "Your death shall all but cleanse you of your sins and
transgressions and I'll make certain they remember you."

The wife began crying as she thrashed about the bed with her
hands cuffed above her. She kicked at the man sitting on her husband but
it didn't faze him at all. He merely looked at her and shook his head as he
placed the blade to her husband's throat.

"And you, Mother," he stared down at the woman, "we have so
much catching up to do… again."

She watched as the man slowly moved the blade of the large knife
across her husband's throat and the blood quickly welled up and began to
drain from his neck. Her eyes bugged out as her husband reached up and
grabbed at his neck trying to keep the blood from spilling out and a silent
scream gurgled from his open mouth. She wanted to scream out herself
but couldn't force her throat to make a sound, and she watched as the
knife went up and came down forcefully into her husband's chest several
times causing blood to spray out and drench her. Her eyes rolled into the

back of her head as the smell of her husband losing his bowels and his blood swam in her nose making her sick. She fainted with her last thoughts being that all of this was a bad dream and she would wake up soon and shake it off.

He sat on the man plunging the knife deeper and deeper and over and over. He could feel his manhood growing and his excitement was building as he stabbed him again and again until at last… he stopped. There was blood everywhere; all over him and all over her. She was no longer watching but he could see she was still breathing so he was sure she'd just fainted. He stood from the bed and stared down at the body his chest completely caved in from his knife. He wanted to count the holes so he could make record of it later, but the man was not as important as the woman lying beside him. He wiped the sides of the knife off on the cleaner part of his legs and placed it back into the sheathe on his back.

He moved to his bag and came back with the duct tape and rope and then made his way back to the woman. With practiced ease he tied and muzzled her in preparations to move her to his van. He moved about the room and then found something on her dresser that captured his attention. He slowly picked up the necklace and stared at it and himself in the dark shadows of the mirror and he smiled as a tear slowly slid from the corner of his eye and down over his cheek. He then stared at the chain, more so at the charm and his smile faded. He then wiped his bloody hand against the mirror writing out the word… "Reaper".

***

Maxine sat up in her bed and looked around. It was late into the night and she was tempted to wake up Daniel and send on his way as she'd done most of her lovers, but he looked to cute stretched out on his back with one hand behind his head and the other lost beneath the covers. She looked about again catching the faint smell of an odor she didn't recognize, but seemed very familiar. She ran her fingers through her hair and moved to get up.

"And where do you think you're going?" she jumped at the sound of his voice and then turned to face him.

"Just to check the door," she smiled at him, "an old habit of mine."

"The house is locked up, Maxine," he whispered. "Just come lay with me."

She moved back into his arms and slowly dropped her head onto his chest. She could hear his heart slowly beating. She'd never allowed any man to get this close especially this fast, but something about this

Daniel Forthsythe made her comfortable. Slowly she slipped back off into a very pleasant sleep as he gently stroked his hand across the back of her head.

When the alarm clock buzzed they woke and stared at each other both with teenager-ish smiles on their faces. Maxine didn't feel her normal sick to the stomach need to get rid of him, and even allowed him to kiss her lips before they both slipped from the bed. They raced off to the bathroom and she made it there first playfully closing the door in his face. Taking turns they relieved themselves, and then together they showered. She even smiled as he sat on the bed in his boxers watching her as she went through her morning make-up routine. They dressed and then went into the kitchen area and she pulled out a box of cereal and they had breakfast together. He walked her to her car and watched as she got in and closed the door; she sat there a moment with a big kid like smile on her face before she finally let down the window.

"This is kind of awkward for me," she began before he put his finger to her lips.

"I don't want this to be too forward or too pushy, but I do want to see you again," he leaned into the car window. "How about you just call me sometime today and let me know how you're feeling and we go from there... no pressures... no anxieties."

"Thank you, Daniel," she leaned forward and pressed her lips to his sharing one more kiss. "You have a great day, and I'll text you the number to fax me the letter he sent you."

"Oh I hope you'll text me for a whole lot more than that," he laughed. "You be safe today."

"I will" she started the motor to her car and slowly pulled away watching him through her rear view mirror. The van caught her attention and for a split second she could have sworn she saw a man sitting there in the front seat staring at her, but the windows were tinted too dark to get a clear view. She glanced into her rear view again just in time to see Daniel's car heading off into the opposite direction, and she smiled.

She turned up the radio and pressed the gas speeding off towards the downtown cityscape laid out before her. The sun looked radiant this morning shining off of the buildings of glass and concrete rising up to kiss the clouds. The sky was the bluest she'd seen in years and the clouds were painted multi-hues of orange and pinks of the morning sunrise. It had been a long time since she'd actually felt this good as she merged with the breakfast traffic and sped along towards police headquarters.

It was if the entire morning was going her way. Her mind was not even on the day ahead, but on the night she'd had. From the restaurant to their parting this morning she felt as if she were on her prom night with the most perfect date. She could still feel his eyes on her staring from across the table as they talked and enjoyed the sweet of the wine. She could still feel his lips as they kissed her lips later and then every part of her body, and she was still tingling. If only the rest of the day could remain as her night had been.

But, that quickly came to an end. As her phone rang, she wanted to slam her hand against the dashboard.

"Steele," she finally answered.

"This is Raymonds," the voice came back over the phone. *"We have a new one. I need for you to meet me over on Dryper's Lane over on the Lower East. The address is 1631. I'm in route now."*

"Damn," she grimaced, "I'll be there in about twenty."

Maneuvering to the far right lane and then dropping off into the exit lane she drove off quickly weaving her way through the busy city streets to get her back down toward one of the most poverty stricken sides of White Chapel. Years ago this was a thriving side of the manufacturing boom that hit the city in the late 60s. There had been an influx of hearty Irish immigrants fresh from the Old World looking for their own place in the New World and the big factories were places of hard work and low wages. Then there was the scare of the Irish and Black gangs with their weapons and drugs wreaking havoc in the streets in the 70s. Finally, the factories began closing down and between the 80s and 90s the streets were filled with the unemployed crowding the soup kitchens as the people struggled.

She slowed down as she came around the park and stared at the line of cookie cutter homes spread across the street. The colors were different and there were some slight differences in each home but they were all too similar in shape and general design that you could tell the same construction company was involved in their building. It was still early in the morning and a couple of school buses were going through the neighborhood picking up the kids to haul them off for the day to the number of schools covering this district of town. She spotted Raymonds car parked on the side of the park and she pulled in behind him as more emergency vehicles were pulling up to block off the rest of the street.

She stepped out of her car just as she saw Daniel's news van pull up and she hurried off before he could get out and try to corner her for another interview. Right now she didn't need to be seen staring at him like he was some kind of movie star; she need for all of her faculties focused on what she was about to walk into. She moved across the street quickly and disappeared into the home everyone was crowded around. She kept her hands in her pockets as she quietly looked around taking notes of things she would write down later. She noticed that the door in the kitchen leading out into the garage was unlocked and noticed something that looked like mud on the kitchen floor. She poked at one of the crime scene techs and pointed out the mud substance and moved on through the house.

She found Raymonds in the Master's bedroom standing by the bed. She moved to his side and grimaced at the sight laying there. She didn't even try to count the number of holes in his chest, but what did get her attention was that his eyes were stretched open in horror.

"His name is Emmanuel Ferro," Raymonds say without looking up. "We don't know too much about him, yet, but the one thing we do know is he's missing his wife."

Maxine takes the picture that he hands to her, and immediately she notices the resemblance. She stares at the picture taking in everything as she always does and then lays it down on the nightstand beside the bed.

"Why are we even here, Raymonds?" She doesn't want to be a smartass just yet. "Shouldn't this be something for another homicide dick?"

"He left us an autograph," Raymonds pointed to the mirror, and she walked over and stared at the word written there in blood.

"He poked around on the dresser top here," she said as she used her pen to move away a few things to see the streaks of blood on the top of the dresser.

Raymonds moved to see what she was looking at and then pointed to one of the techs to come over and picture and take samples. He then stepped out of the room leaving her in there to look around. There was nothing more he wanted to see as he waited for her. He took several deep breaths trying to clear his lungs and nose of the scents of the room. He wanted to spit because he could almost taste the coppery tinge in the air and he just wanted it all out of him. He stood there with his hands stuffed into the pockets of his pants wishing that the Bureau would finally just accept his application and get him out of this fucking homicide hell.

"He's taken the wife," Maxine stated the obvious, "I have a feeling she's still alive, but what's bothering me more is the amount of anger he put into killing this man."

"What do you mean?" he turned to face her as she continued to stare at the man laying there on the bed. "This can be no worse than what he's done to the women we've found so far."

"First, up until now he's never touched the husbands," she pulled her notebook from pocket, "he's always laid in wait until they were gone, but this one not only did he kill him… it was extreme overkill."

"Every killing this maniac does is complete overkill."

"This is true, Raymonds, but just from the way those kill blows look he was sitting right on top of the man driving the blade right down into his chest. Something really pissed him off for him to do this.

"I'm sure we'll know more once the M.E. has had a time with him. The blood on the mirror is most like the victim's, and I can almost guarantee that he took something personal to the woman from the dresser. We may want to put her picture on the news just to see if we can get something from somebody who may have seen our guy coming or going from the neighborhood."

Raymonds glanced in at the body laying there once more and felt as if he was going to vomit right on the spot. His legs felt weak and his breathing was caught in his throat.

"Yea, yea I can believe he was angry," he stepped away from the door and headed down the stairs. He didn't stop until he was outside and taking in deep breaths of air and shaking his head.

"Did you hear what I said about the news?" Maxine was suddenly standing beside him with her hand on his shoulder. "Are you ok, Raymonds?"

"Yea," he whispered, "yea, I'm good. Just tired of seeing all of these fucking dead bodies."

He moved his shoulder away from her hand and reached into his coat pocket and pulled out a pack of Black & Mild cigars and quickly rolled it between his fingers to loosen it up and then he lit it taking in a deep breath. He's normally not a smoker, there was the occasional "bud" sometimes with his boys, and every now and then he'd slip away to the cigar shop because his wife allowed him that as long as it wasn't a habit. But, here lately he needed something almost daily and parts of him wanted to blame his new partner. He looked up at the morning sky and blew out the smoke from his lungs before taking another long drag and releasing it.

"I'll talk to the Captain when I get back to the station and let him know about the missing woman and getting her flashed on the news stations. I just have a bad feeling that he's watching and don't give a rat's ass about this woman we're now looking for."

"Raymonds," she had lit her own cigarette, "I doubt she's the only one. Just from the looks of things this was spur of the moment; like I said he was pissed off bad. I have a feeling he had already had his newest victim. Something changed. Something major changed for him."

Raymonds stepped away walking towards the garage. Looking down he slowly cased the area stopping just off the side of the concrete and he squats down. Staring at the vehicle tracks he points to Maxine and motions for her to get a tech to come over. He stands and watches as she and another younger girl strolls over.

"I need a cast of this vehicle print," he points down and then steps away not wanting to hear anymore of Maxine Steele's mouth. "I'll meet you back at the station."

Maxine stands there as her partner walks off his head clouded by the smoke of his cigar. She shakes her head as she turns and walks back into the house.

***

He sits there watching. There's a calm, serene feel about him as she slowly goes back into the house. He'd been sitting there since earlier this morning after he'd loaded the woman into the back of his van. He had been waiting, and now they were all there and for the first time in a few hours… he smiled.

"I told you, you Bitch," he hissed, "I'm stronger than both of them. I'm stronger than all of them." He stared at the necklace lying in the palm of his hand and again the charm held his attention. "I'm stronger than all of you."

Chapter 13

"Good evening and thank you again for joining us… here's a recap of tonight's top story." Aaron McMannis filled the screen with a very solemn look upon his face as the face of a female filled the side prompter. "The police are asking for any help of the citizens in the Dryper's Lane area. This morning the body of Emmanuel Ferro was found mutilated in his bed and his wife Liza is now considered missing. Please look carefully at her picture, this is the most recent picture of Liza Ferro given to the police by their family, and if you have any information that could lead to the apprehension of the kidnapper or if you have any information about any suspicious vehicles in that neighborhood please contact White Chapel police as soon as possible. We'll have more on this story as it comes to us through the remainder of our programming."

He sat there in his chair with his head laid back. The news was playing on the television, but tonight his head wasn't into it. There was something completely different about his mood since he walked through the door and after he deposited the woman downstairs with the other one. He wiped away the sweat on his forehead and closed his eyes. He suddenly felt… Empty.

The chain from the woman's house had slipped around his closed hand atop his brow and grazed his head. He sat up and brought his hand down to stare it once again and his eyes were dazzled with the crucifix charm at the end of it. He held it close up to his face watching as it dangled at the end of the chain. He was pretty much mesmerized by it as it spun about before his eyes. He drew it up into his hand until the charm finally stopped spinning around and he stared at in closely.

"She" had always worn one about her neck. Sometimes she would clutch it as she pulled her belt from her shoulder to beat him about the house. She would always clean it the night before church as if to clean away the shit she'd done throughout the week, and they would sit near the front so that she could make certain he paid the utmost attention. She would always make him pray at night before he went to bed and she would stand over him rubbing at it as she pressed his face down into the bed. She would literally pray over his bath water as if to make it holy water before he stepped into it to bathe.

He stood there watching from the back of the church as she lead the boy to once of the confessional booths and pushed him in. He could almost hear her standing there praying as they both waited for one of the priests to finally make it back to the other booth to take the young boy's confession. At his age, he was guilty of so much now, but no one but him and his diary knew of all the things he'd already done by the time he was almost 16 years old, and he smiled. He would keep and hold on to those journals and he would read through them often just as a refresher of what he'd done and what he still plan to do. The side door slid open and a kind faced man sat on the other side of the screened opening.

"I am here, my son."

"Forgive me, Father," the young boy cleared his throat, "for I have sinned. It has been a week since my last confession."

"Much can be done by way of sins in a week, my son," the man's voice was so soothing. "Tell me what are your sins for this week, Abel"

It always shook him to hear one of the priests say his name, but knew it was because his mom was standing just beyond the door that they knew it was he in the booth.

"This week, Father, I have not been able to concentrate much. It's like my mind has been preoccupied with a bunch of dark thoughts, and this has kept me from being a good son to my mother."

"Dark thoughts?" the priest asked. "Such as what?"

"Well there are these boys at my school who keep harassing me, and well," he sat there contemplating his stories as he always did, "I want things to happen to them just so they will bother me no longer."

"Do you wish for these boys to die, Abel?"

"No, Father, not die, but I want them to hurt as bad as they constantly hurt me. I sometimes wish I was bigger than them so that I could be the one to beat them up, or stuff them in a locker, or push their heads into a toilet. I know I shouldn't have such mean thoughts, Father, but it hurts the things they do to me."

"You must always remember, my son, that we all must suffer our trials and tribulations just as Christ suffered his. Remember the trials he suffered at the hands of the Romans right up to his death and never once did he ever wish or harbor any harm against him. He chose to pray for them that they find salvation in the heart of God for all that they did against him. You must practice to be as humble as Christ."

"I can only promise to try, Father," he dropped his head as if ashamed of what he'd said, but in truth it was just another story he'd made up to keep his mother appeased with his confessional. "They are pretty much terrorists and I'm their prime target. I just want some kind of peace."

"You'll find peace within, Abel," the priest says as he raises his hand does the sign of the cross, "I want you to say a Hail Mary with me and then tonight before bed I want you to say another as you ask for forgiveness for your thoughts."

"Hail Mary," they began together, "full of grace. The Lord is with thee. Blessed art thou among women, and blessed is the fruit of thy womb, Jesus. Holy Mary, Mother of God, pray for us sinners now, and at the hour of our death. Amen.

"In the name of the Father," they continued together, "and of the Son and of the Holy Spirit. Amen."

"Thank you, Father."

"Go in peace, my son."

He stood there watching as the young man exited the confessional booth with a very satisfied smile on his face. He hugged his mother as he always did after clearing his soul of his sins and he would always forgive her. She would kiss his cheek and tell him what a good son he was as the priest exited his booth and he would give her a curt bow. If anyone only knew that this was just the face she gave the public, but the one he knew, her true face was so much more evil than this beautiful, smiling woman.

At church was the only time he loved his mother. In the church she was so pure as she would sit on the bench with her eyes going between the priest and his sermon to the large wood carve statue of Christ as he was nailed to the cross. There were many times he would look up at her face and he would watch as she would sit there and cry, and he would wonder if she ever shed a tear for him and the things she'd done to him. Even if she didn't, he still loved her while they sat there in the church, and there were times he would even feel guilty about the things he'd dreamed of doing to her.

"I believe in God, the Father almighty, Creator of heaven and earth, and in Jesus Christ, His only Son, our Lord. He was conceived by the Holy Spirit, and born of the Virgin Mary. He suffered under Pontius Pilate, was crucified, died and was buried. He descended into hell. On the third day He rose again. He ascended into heaven, and is seated at the right hand of God the Father Almighty. He will come again to judge the living and the dead. I believe in the Holy Spirit, the Holy Catholic Church, the communion of saints, the forgiveness of sins, the resurrection of the body, and life everlasting. Amen."

He stood there watching them as he whispered to himself.

It had been years in truth since he'd last stepped into a church, and he wondered if the priests there would even remember him.

"Of course they would remember you, Abel," his mother whispered into his ear. "Who could ever forget you, always playing the innocent, always playing the shy little boy, but always holding such evil in his little heart."

He spared a glimpse over his shoulder to see her standing there dressed in her Sunday best as if prepared to sit for Mass. He glowered at her again remembering how he only loved her in church, and here she stood ready to take him to the confessional before services began.

"You never truly loved me," she moved in close and whispered softly in his ear, "your heart would never allow you to love me, oh but I did love you, my beautiful boy."

He turned away from her and watched as mother and son walked off towards the front of the church and took seats where she could see both the priest and the statue without much effort. He moved to stand beside her and again he was so amazed at how beautiful she was. Her make-up gingerly applied and hair combed and pulled back into a neat ponytail, and she wore a dress with a pair of small heeled shoes. Her hand was caressing the charm on the necklace as she sat there with her tears in her eyes even before the sermon began.

"Those tears are for you, Abel," she stood there beside him also with tears in her eyes. "So much evil in such a gorgeous boy and I could never get it out of you."

"Get it out of me?" he hissed. "You! You put it in me."

"I did nothing more than love you," she reached up to touch his face, "I only wanted you to love me in return, but I could never get through to you. You were such a distant little boy. I cannot count the number of times I'd come to your room and you would be hidden inside of your closet."

"That's because I was scared of you, Mother," he ran his fingers through his thinning hair. "I hid because of you. I pissed my bed because of you. I ran away because of you. I FUCKING killed… because of you."

"Watch your mouth, we're in the church."

"No… no we're inside of my head. We're where things are always clear and twisted and sick. We are where you completely ruined me."

He moved away from the woman sitting on the bench that represented the mother he loved, walking away from the fake woman he truly remembered her as. The doors of the church slowly opened before he got to them and he stepped out into the rain and he pulled his hood up over his head. This was his favorite time in the city, and why he would always return to it after taking a few of his ladies captive. He slowly strolled down the streets leading from the Holy Divinity Catholic Church of Saint Mary and headed off towards an area he knew best.

The prostitutes all looked the same no matter the race or the age; they were all used up and still trying to hustle a buck. Most of them were drugged out and looked it making it hard to want to do anything with them, but he loved coming down here. This is where he got a lot of practice. It never amazed him at how many looked a lot like her, and they were all expendable. He stood against the building watching them and then he saw the boy… slowly walking and smiling as all of the women would walk up to him and run their hands through his light mane of dirty blonde hair and tell him how cute he was. His smile was so unassuming as he walked those streets from a young age with his little notepad in hand and he was categorizing them as he posted up against the wall just watching them as they marketed themselves out to the passer bys.

"Such a dirty, nasty little bastard," she spat, "look at him standing there with his dirty little thoughts as he gawks at those tramps. Of all the things I've taught him and he takes nothing I say to mind, but he hangs on the words of these nasty bitches."

"If you only really know what he's thinking," he grumbled over his shoulder."

"Oh but I do," she lit a cigarette, "remember I'm in your sick, fucking head and I know exactly what you want them for. I know you want to lay them out and pull out your dirty little no-no and stroke it as you watch them bleed."

"You just don't know."

"Is that what happened when…" she stepped away and glared at him.

"When what?" he sneered as he turned back to watch his younger self studying the hookers. "So much happens when I kill and all of it excites me, Mother. Much like how you would go to your room and pull out your little toy after you'd beat the shit out of me. I guess you didn't think I heard, but I heard you every time and it sickened me that you could get so much joy from causing me so much pain."

"You're so full of shit, Abel," she pulled on her cigarette and blew the smoke out over his head. "You just have to play the victim don't you.

Poor little Abel, his mother beat him a few times and it turned him into a weak, sniveling pussy of a man. Someone please cry for him, oh wait, he does that quite well on his own.

"You're no fucking victim, you sick little fuck," her words were right in his ear. "No you're just a pitiful little man who uses violence as a means of getting off."

"No… goddamn you, no."

He pushed off the wall and walked across the street as the boy, a little older now, picked his first woman. He followed them as they made their way to an alley as she held his hand and then pushed him against the wall. She looked around quickly before dropping to her knees and unzipping his pants. She whistled low and gave him an approving smile before opening her mouth and slowly slurping him in. The boy felt his back smack against the wall and one of his hands dropped to her head and his fingers dug into her hair and her head bobbed up and down his length. She was making a lot of noise and didn't notice that his other hand had slipped behind his back.

Abel looked up and down the alley as he pulled the large blade from behind his back. Just the thought of what was about to happen excited him and he could feel his heart pounding against his chest and his blood was whizzing through his veins. There was a pounding in his head as he closed his eyes and began pumping his pelvis against her face and she seemed to happily take the beating. He could hear her gurgling and swallowing around his length as he pulled the knife free into the night and pulled her head back from his penis.

It was the look in the woman's eyes that created his true orgasm as she watched in horror as the blade swung up and then down and slashed across her throat. She took a deep breath in even as he ejaculated all over her face and her own blood sprayed out and over the both of them. She tried to scream out but the only thing that came from her mouth was a spray of blood as her mouth filled quickly from the backwash of her throat. She reached up and grabbed at her throat as he held her head in his hand by her hair. What seemed to last a lifetime for her was only moments as he reached into his pocket and tried to wipe her face clean of his semen before letting her drop to the ground. Slowly her life ebbed away as she kicked and continued to fight to breath but only choked on her blood as it spilled out upon the asphalt. Her eyes closed and she took her final breaths before fading away.

"See," he hissed at his mother, "I am in control. I am not a victim of you or anyone anymore."

"All I saw was you with your dirty little no-no in that whore's mouth," she answered with a tinge of disappointment in her voice. "Such a dirty little boy to be such a beautiful boy. No wonder you got your ass beat, you needed it for all of those thoughts running around inside of your head."

He closed his eyes and shook his head. When he opened them again he was standing over his sleeping mother, and she was passed out drunk upon the sofa which was something he was used to seeing. He leaned over her and could smell the nauseating scent of her cigarettes and the cheap beer she loved to drink all over her breath as she snored deeply. Her hair was a mess upon her head and there on the floor was her ever present belt. He felt a slight shiver run through him before standing up.

He made his way through the house and out the back door through the kitchen. He could almost hear Abel working down in his little private work shop, and he didn't want to miss a thing. Not waiting to see if "She" would follow he closed his eyes and waited until the sounds in the workshop were clearer and when he opened his eyes he could see the naked boy sitting at his desk sharpening his knife. There was always something liberating about doing his work down here naked. He was never ashamed as he would be in the house, and she never came out here. The sound of the grinder against the steel of the blade always made him smile, and to this day it's the one thing that always seems to calm him. Small sparks flew and the few that bit into his skin were always electrifying as he moved the blade slowly against the spinning drum.

The boy, well he wasn't a boy anymore he was a young man in his early twenties, stood from his desk and walked to the bed against the wall. There was a naked woman laying there with her hands tied down to the legs of the bed with some very hearty straps, and her legs were taped together with duct tape. Her mouth was taped closed and she stood over her waiting for her to wake up. Her blonde-ish hair was flared out around her head as if she'd been struggling, and he reached down and gently touched her forehead. He could feel his body heating up as he stood over her watching her breast rise and fall as she lay there breathing softly. The blood in his body was jetting around his veins and his breathing was shallow, he was no longer nervous at this time; no, for him it was all about patience now. He longed to see her eyes as he took everything from her.

"I took nothing from you, you whiny little bastard," she was there pressed against him as she looked over his shoulder. "I gave you everything when that bitch that bore you did nothing but toss you away. I gave you everything but fucking life."

"No, Mother, you took my life from me," his voice was quiet as they stood there watching. Abel was so calm right now, and it made him smile watching his younger self. "I could have been a good kid, I was smart, hell I was smarter than those bastards I went to school with. But, all you saw was your own little whipping post because he left you with me alone. I was your fucking excuse to be the bitch you were."

"My whiny little boy," she turned him and stared deeply into his steel grey eyes, "you need someone to blame for your transgressions."

"Now I know you're in my head," he smiled. "She would never use a word like transgressions, and yet it just flowed from your pretty mouth. You're definitely not my mother."

"Is that why your nasty little no-no is growing, you dirty boy," she pressed her lips to his and kissed him. "You want me on that bed don't you? Both of us naked and you holding your little knife in one hand and your dick in the other."

"Stop it," he pushed her away but she pulled herself back into his arms and kissed him again pressing her body to his. "Stop it now goddammit."

"Look at me," she was suddenly naked and writhing around in his arms, "look at me, Abel, and tell me that you don't want me. I can feel you growing."

The woman on the bed woke and tried to scream through the duct tape covering her mouth. She tried to move her body about to get away realizing that she was completely trapped. Her eyes were bugged open and the tears were flowing as she stared up at the naked man standing over her.

"He's so fucking excited," whispering into Abel's ear as she began to grind against him. "You want to watch, don't you? I bet it would excite you for me to take you into my mouth as he killed her. Think of the whore and how much it excited him."

"You wouldn't understand," he said as tears filled his eyes. "You fucking killed me, and I can never get that back. You fucking killed me… I just wanted a regular life. You fucking…"

"And you fucking killed me," his mother stepped away staring at him as he stared upon her naked body. "Or did you forget that, Abel? Did you forget how you came into my bedroom, tied me down… how you raped me repeatedly for days on end. How you pissed on me and forced me to piss in my own bed over and over. Did you forget you fucking ungrateful little bastard, how you drove that fucking knife of yours into my pussy over and over and OVER and you just stood there watching as I bled out?"

His body shook in his chair as he sat there with his head back enjoying the orgasm that ripped through his body. His mind was filled with the images of his mother lying there in her bed covered in blood and he stood there watching with his dick in his hand stroking it and ejaculating all over her twitching body. Her eyes were stretched wide open as she stared lifelessly at him, mocking him even in death, but at this moment it didn't matter because he had finally taken from her everything she'd taken from him. He stepped back on shaky legs and tried to catch his breath as he just continued to stare at her.

"I am powerful now," he said aloud and scaring him as he looked around.

"I am powerful now," he screamed out as he threw the chain across the room and then stood and kicked the television knocking it from its stand to crack upon the floor.

"I am powerful now," he said again as he dropped to his knees trying to catch his breathing. "You can no longer hold me, Mother. I am powerful now."

He rolled up into a ball and began to cry. He never noticed that she was standing there naked staring down at him with her belt over her shoulder and a cigarette hanging from her lips. She smiled before turning and disappearing off towards his kitchen… more time to haunt his mind later.

Chapter 14

Janice slowly opened her eyes and looked about her room. It was quiet tonight. Even her medication pump seemed to be silent, but as she looked into her arm and stared at the tubes she knew she was in no dream. I was just quiet tonight. She stared across the room and at the shaded window that would be looking out into the hall and she could see shadows moving around, so, she knew the nurses were there… no need to push the button this time. She looked up at the only light source on in her room at this time and stared at the television and cocked her head because even it was quiet. She took a deep breath and she could hear the intake of air and when she exhaled, but as she looked around…

It was just so quiet.

She sat up in her bed and ran her bony fingers through her unruly hair and took another deep breath. Her mind was so clear tonight that it felt as if she hadn't taken any of her medications in a very long time. She pinched her arm and flinched as the pain streaked along her nerves and triggered her brain letting her know… she was not asleep. She pulled on her gown and straightened it some because it felt like it was keeping her pinned to the bed and then she turned to hold her legs over the side of her bed. It was so tempting to just get out of bed, but she had a sudden fear of them big men suddenly appearing and strapping her down again. She smiled as she just sat there letting her legs swing.

It felt as if she had her own mind about her. Nothing was cloudy. Nothing seemed to be keeping her from thinking for herself. There were no panic attacks. She just felt so calm. Looking around the room she pinched herself once more and winced again as the pain of her taking her own flesh between her fingers and kind of torturing it hit her brain. She smiled as she pushed forward and placed her feet down upon the cold of the floor beneath her… it felt so good. She stepped off the bed but held on as she tested the strength of her legs… she felt so weak, but her legs held her up. Reaching out she grabbed the post holding her medications and she slowly walked towards the door… it felt so good to be moving without the help of anyone.

She made it to the sink and she pinched herself one more time. "Ouch," she giggled.

Slowly she walked around her room getting a feel for having her feet under her and moving her about. She kept looking at the window as if waiting for them to come rushing to her room at any moment, but for now they never came. Her legs became tired and her lungs were beginning to hurt from excursion so she slowly made her way back to the bed and sat down. She ran her fingers through her hair once more and looked about with a big smile on her face.

"Did you enjoy yourself?" the sudden sound of his voice almost made her scream as she turned on the bed and stared towards the window that held back the outside world. She could barely make out the shape of him, but he was there sitting in the chair with his legs crossed.

Slowly she pushed back up onto her bed and pressed her back to the pillows. Her breathing quickened as she stared at him sitting there.

"Amazing what the body can do when it's not all drugged up… isn't it?" his voice was deep and scary and yet he didn't seem to be so dangerous. He just sat there and even though she couldn't see his eyes she could feel them staring at her.

"I know you," she whispered. "I've seen you before and not just in my dreams. But, I'm not who you think I am."

"How do you know you're not who I think you are?"

"Because I know who you're looking for, and I am not her," she moved her hair from her face. "I am not who you are looking for and I'm so sorry."

He stood and slowly moved to the end of the bed, but he remained cloaked away in the darkness. She could barely make out his face, but his steel grey eyes burned into her mind. He pressed down upon the back of the bed and leaned forward just a bit so that she could definitely stare into his eyes. He watched as she pushed herself back deeper into the pillows behind her as if trying to scurry away from him, and then she saw him smile.

"You don't know me…"

"Not by name, but I know you," her voice was timid and she could feel her body shaking in fear. "And I know you've seen her, my daughter, and she is not who you are looking for either."

He slammed his hand down on the bed frame, "You don't know," he stepped back and took a deep breath before turning around and facing her once more. "You don't know what you're talking about. You can't have a clue as to what I'm here for."

"My son died…"

He stumbled backwards glaring at her. "What do you mean, your son died?"

"I remember that night so very well," she began as she wiped her eyes. "It was so cold and the snow was just beginning to fall. My husband was on shore leave from the Navy and he was so excited as I screamed out that we needed to go to the hospital. He held me to his body as he helped me to the car and I screamed out again as my water broke… he kept telling me to breathe. To breathe and then he would do the lamas class breathing from the last class we had taken together. I remember trying to smile through the pain because it was so cute what he was doing, but it felt like something was wrong. It felt like my insides were trying to tear itself out and I stumbled over in pain just as he was helping me into the car.

"Karl, 'I cried out as the pain twisted my stomach and buckled my knees,' we have to hurry. Oh dear God hurry, please.

"He dropped me in the car and hopped over the hood and he had us on the road and the car racing towards the hospital. The roads were so bad and he almost spun out a few times, and there were no police out anywhere so he drove like a madman getting me to the hospital in no time. He drove right up to the emergency room doors and ran in screaming for them to come out and help me.

It was so maddening. They got me into a room with another girl and I could hear her over myself as she tried to keep count of her contractions. I could hear her telling someone that they were a little less than two minutes apart and then another female's voice telling her to breathe. I looked up and I was surrounded by nurses and a doctor all screaming for things that they needed as yet another pain ripped through my abdomen. And then, then I started bleeding. I looked over at Karl as he stood near the door with tears in his eyes.

"It's going to be ok, 'he mouthed to me,' and then a nurse rushed him from the room."

"Stop it," he growled from the shadows of the room. "Stop it now, you're lying. I've done all of the research. I followed all of the clues. These are all lies."

"Not lies," she whispered as her words caught in her throat and she sat there crying. "I celebrate his birthday every year even when I am totally screwed up on their drugs. November 30, 1978, it was the year of the worst winter we'd ever had, and my son was born to me dead at 11:02pm. They tried to revive him even covered in my blood, but his little lungs had collapsed and his heart had only beat for two minutes. They cleaned him up and they let me hold him for just a moment before taking him.

"The girl beside me had her baby just moments later and the woman with her took the baby just after he was born and she never brought her back. I could only assume that the girl was most likely a teenager with no means of supporting herself and a baby.

"But my baby died. My husband blamed me. He left to go back to the Service and he never returned."

He stumbled back to the chair he was in moments ago and dropped down into it. He fell forward catching his face in his hands as his elbows dug into his knees and he broke down sobbing. His head swam with everything he'd been through because of "her" and because she wasn't his real mother. He thought of all of the beatings. He thought of all of the words of hate. He thought of all of the times he sat with her in church and she treated like he was the best son on Earth, and then afterwards she would get her first beer and get her first cigarette and grab her belt and she would beat him just because he was sitting there. He thought of every bathing with the scouring pad. He thought of all the times he'd wet his bed and was afraid she would find out.

He looked up and stared at the crying woman across from him and noted how she looked so much like "her" that it was scary. They all had looked like "her" every last one of them including the first girl. He sat there huffing and wheezing like he couldn't catch his breath. He rocked on his seat as his mind felt as if it were about to collapse.

"No," he said as he stood, "you're lying. They lied to you and now you're lying to me. He did not die because is standing before you. You are her, you are my mother, and I hate you. I hate you for not keeping me. I hate you for letting "her" have me."

"No, I am not your mother. I don't know her but she was there in the room with me. I sat there listening to her cry after they took her baby, and then I sat there crying myself as my husband stood at the door staring at me as if I were diseased."

He stepped around the bed and put his face down into hers until their noses touched. His hands twitched as his mind boiled into overload. He could feel the sweat popping out on his forehead and around his neck as he stood over her breathing hard and through his teeth. "Her" face flashed before his eyes and he could see the cigarette, he could smell it, and he could see the belt. He growled deep in his chest as his hands went around her neck… squeezing.

"You are a fucking liar. You are her I know you are and you're going to pay for my life…" he released her neck watching as she sat there coughing and choking. "With your fucking life, and then I'm going to laugh as she stands over your corpse."

Before Janice could move he swung down and hit her across her temple. The room began to twist and turn and swirl as she fluttered her eyes. Her stomach suddenly soured and she felt as if she were about to vomit. There was a ringing in her ears as the room began to darken and she looked up at him as her eyes closed and she swam in a world of nothing.

***

Maxine ran through the doors of the White Chapel Adult Living Facility with Raymonds close on her heels. The look in her eyes was not something anyone wanted to see and they dropped their head as she ran by. The girl at the front desk didn't say a word when the two people ran by her and through the doors leading into the patient area. The entire ward was unnervingly quiet as the orderlies and nurses parted like the Red Sea to give her room to run on by. Everyone knew where she was headed, and everyone knew why. The rumor had spread around the facility like wild fire, and they all knew that the Detective was going to raise hell once she got to…

Her mother's room was empty. The bed was turned over and the bags that held her fluid medications were spilled all over the floor. There was one pillow with no cover over it laying near the bed, and the sheets were missing. There was a smell in the air that caught her attention, but she couldn't place where she knew it from as she slowly walked into the room and stood in the doorway. She flipped on the light and just stood there quietly.

"Detective Steele," Dr. Thine's deep voice echoed in her head as he stepped up behind her and placed his hand on her shoulder. "I don't know where to begin. We have been going over everything to figure out how this happened."

"I'll need to see all of the video from this area."

"That will be," Thine dropped his eyes, "umm, a bit of a problem."

"A problem… why?"

"We cannot seem to find them," Thine answered. "It's as if everything was taken offline in this area and all of the video recordings were taken."

"This is bullshit," she said more to herself than to the doctor as she walked into the room to look around closer.

"Had she been getting any visitors that you noticed, Doctor?" Raymonds asked as he watched Steele.

"None that I know of, Detective…"

"Raymonds, I'm Det. Steele's partner," he explained as he scribbled on his note pad. "How could anyone have taken the video recordings? Are they in a secured area?"

"We've never had this kind of problem before, Det. Raymonds, and yes we do keep all of our security recordings in a secured room. We have one of our trained staff go into that room to download the night's recordings and stored away."

"So for anyone to get into this room they would need to know the code, correct?"

"Yes, and we even change the code every six weeks."

"Interesting," Raymonds scratched his chin as he looked in on Steele.

"I want a Crime Scene crew in here A.S.A.P.," Steele said from the middle of the room, "I want everyone who has ever been in her room finger printed so that we can see if there's been someone we don't know of in here. I want you to check all of the employee time sheets find out if there's someone missing. And, I want every recording checked from about two months out, I need to know if someone has entered my mother's room."

"I'll have someone get on that right away," Thine answered.

"Not you, Doctor," she glared at the man, "I do not trust you or your fucking people. Our people will handle everything from this point on. This is officially a Police investigation."

"I understand, Detective," he sounded wounded. "I'll make certain all of my people comply."

"That goes without question, Doctor," she glanced over at Raymonds. "I have some blood right here make certain this isn't missed, and I want these chairs checked for any hairs just incase he sat before he attacked."

"I'll make certain they get on it the moment they get here," he said staring at her as she moved around the room.

***

He stomped and stormed around in the living room as his anger rose to levels he'd never experienced. There was no way he was wrong; no, she was wrong… she was lying to him. She was trying to save herself and she lied about everything. She was the "Mother" he'd been searching for, and he knew it.

"And what if she wasn't lying," her voice carved through his head like a knife causing him to scream out in pain. "What if, after all you've done to me and all of those women calling yourself searching for her… what if, she was telling you the truth and she isn't your precious real mother?"

"Shut up, you Bitch," he screamed out. "She's lying. You know she is. I know she is. So you just shut up. Shut up and go away."

"I cannot go away, baby," she mocked him, "I love you. I would never leave you to this world alone."

"Leave me alone," he dropped to his knees groveling in pain. Looking up he watched ass she materialized in front of him in her classic night gown and an unusual smile on her face. "You are not here. You can no longer be here."

"What? You think that your killing me would keep me away for your sorry, miserable ass?" she kneeled down beside him and he could feel her hand sliding through his hair. "I am the one that makes it so easy for you to love all of those other women the way you so uniquely love them. I give your desires merit, you sick little shit."

He rolled out on the floor and closed his eyes tightly. He could see her just lying there on the sofa in another of her drunken stupors and he was so tired of it. At sixteen he needed more and she could no longer provide that at all. He stared at the belt she had dropped to the floor, and there was a lit cigarette slowly burning down to the filter perched between her lips. He took the cigarette and placed it to his lips and sucked in the last draw of the acrid smoke and held it in lungs before spitting out the butt to the floor. He slowly blew it out and stared down at her prone body.

"I don't need you anymore," he whispered into her ear and smiled as she slowly turned away and pressed her face into the sofa's back cushions.

He pulled his knife from behind his back and stared at the edge. He had spent about and hour on it just for this moment. He felt a surge in his heart and then another in the crotch of his pants. He licked his lips as a smile slowly creased his lips. He raised the knife above his head and stood there as she woke and rolled over to face him.

"It's about time," she hissed through and ugly smile. "I've been wondering when you'd finally come for me. I love you, Abel, I always have my beautiful boy."

He had an orgasm the moment the blade sliced into her neck. She never screamed and that only made his excitement that much stronger as he hacked at her body. Her body spurted blood all over him as she slumped down into the now drenched sofa onto her back. He positioned himself at her waist and began to stab the point down into her privates over again and again until his arm finally got tired.

"Look at the fucking mess you made, you little bastard," her voice made him jump and he turned to look over his shoulder.

"No," he murmured, "no you're dead. See? Right there you're fucking dead."

He ran upstairs and took a shower. When he returned back downstairs he checked on her and she was still on the sofa. He looked around and shook his head feeling relaxed that he was alone. No voices to be heard. No ghost like visions to be seen. He felt comfortable as he went out to his little work shed and grabbed a gas can he had ready. He doused everything around him and lit a match dropping it as he walked out. He then hurried to the house and did the same with the gas and lit another match as he walked out the backdoor.

He began walking down the street and he turned to look back once more. A smile split his lips as he thought of what he'd done. That had been his home for his entire life and now he was walking away from it with nothing more then the clothes on his back and his favorite toy. When the cops and fire department finally make it there they would find two bodies in the house and a body down in his shop. Everything would work itself out and they would be able to close up a couple of unsolved cases by blaming it on the now dead boy.

He slowly rolled over and looked around the room. She was gone… again. He took a deep breath and eased his way up off of the floor. He walked into the kitchen and pulled the refrigerator open and grabbed a bottle of water. He popped the cap open and stood there drinking it down until the cool contents were completely gone. He wiped the cool surface across his forehead before throwing the bottle away. He grumbled to himself as he turned and faced the door leading downstairs and he stared at it unsure of what to do next.

"FUCK…" he shouted out before turning away from the door and storming off back towards the living room. Too much was going through his head; he would have to deal with the three of them another time. He grabbed his keys and rushed out to his van. He needed to see her again.

Chapter 15

Maxine sat at her desk staring at everything scattered across it. The pictures and the notes and all of the boxes that had been brought up from archives, everything was just there and none of it was coming together. She wanted to pull her hair, but she didn't move as she read and re-read again and again the notes he'd left for her and the one she'd got from Daniel. Her head hurt. Her eyes hurt. The coffee was stale and undrinkable, and her perp remained several steps ahead of her.

She pushed her chair back and slammed her fists down on desk. "FUCK!"

Everything got quiet as she beat on the desk over and over. She didn't see any of them all she could see was the clutter all over her desk, and she stood beating her desk even more. She screamed out and pounded the desk until she felt as if finally all of her frustrations had been sated. Then she dropped back into the seat and took a few deep breaths finally realizing that the office had gotten deathly silent.

"Steele," her Captain shouted across the room. "My office… Now."

She stood grabbing the first note and walked off to the room shaking her head as she read it once more. The word "Mother" again stuck out like a sore thumb causing her to wonder. She took a deep breath as Raymonds met her at the door and they both walked in to sit before the Captain's desk.

"What the fuck is your problem, Steele?" he stood over his desk glaring at her. "Do I need to make an appointment for you?"

She dropped her eyebrow and glared back at him. "It's been two fucking months, Captain. My mother has been gone for two months as well as the last woman he kidnapped and we've heard… nothing."

"What makes you think it's the same person?"

She pressed the first note down on his desk and waited for the Captain to pick it up. He read it and didn't seem to get it before dropping it back to his desk.

"He was warning me then that he was watching her and I missed it. There's something I'm not seeing and it has everything to do with this first note, I'm sure of it."

Salter and Raymonds both stared at her and then at the note just laying there on top of the desk. Raymonds remained silent because for once he felt he almost understood why she was so angry. He'd done a little research on Steele's past and knew that she and her mother didn't have the greatest of relationships. He knew that her mother was an alcoholic who had been in and out of a few rehabs over the years and that she was diagnosed as a borderline psychotic. He had learned that Steele dropped out of high school to care for her mother, but had managed to get her diploma through an alternative school and then got herself into the police academy the next year. He knew that she loved her mother, and was definitely in over her head with the bills for the older woman living at the Adult Facility.

"He mentioned 'mother' in the first note," she began to explain, "it was like he was letting me know that our pasts are connected. Now I need to figure how."

"Where do you even begin?" Raymonds finally spoke up.

"I guess I need to dig deeper into my mother's past," she said quietly. "I need to find out why she would drink like she did, and why it seemed as if she hated me. There has to be something that I don't know about that she's kept from me all of these years."

Raymonds pulled out his cell phone and punched in a quick number and held it to his ear waiting. "Hey, Sheryl, I have something big I need for you to do for me that takes a bit of an upper precedence to what you may have on your desk at this moment. I need you for you to do an extensive background on Janice Rollins, and once you get the information I need you to forward it post haste to Det. Steele." He paused for a moment letting the tech analyst get the process started.

"Thanks, Sheryl, we need this information as soon as you can get it to us."

"Thank you, Raymonds," she pushed back into the chair thinking. "I know that she was married once. I cannot remember his name because I never met the man, but I know he was in the Navy for a while. I think I need to find him as well and see if maybe he can give me some information."

"Now that you have your head straight, I need for you to get busy with this shit. We have a killer out there that needs to be caught and I need you two to kick this shit in the ass and bring this psycho in. I have everyone crawling up my ass straight up to the goddamn Mayor. The Chief says he's looking into bringing in the fucking Feds and we don't need that kind of attention here.

"I need something to give them and I need it soon. Do you two understand me?"

They both nodded and stood to leave the room. "Steele," Salter called out, "sit I need to talk to you."

Maxine turned back around and sat again. She reached out and picked up the note she'd forgot and then looked up at her Captain. "Is there a problem?"

"You tell me," he intertwined his fingers and then leaned forward on his desk resting his chin on his fingers. "Are you sure you're ok? I know I brought you back and just dropped you right off into the think of things. So I need to know that you're… ok?"

She stared at him and then down at the note again. Her head was hurting from the lack of sleep she'd been suffering since her mother had been kidnapped, and she was dying to just go to the bar and breakdown and drink herself stupid. She took a deep breath and then looked back up at her Captain.

"I'm fine, Captain. I just need to stop and figure out where this guy is going with all of this so I can get myself back on track. The last two months I've just been spinning my wheels and its got the better of me."

"I need you on your A game, Steele," he stared at her intensely. "I need for you to get into this asshole's head and not the other way around. You're the best at what you do I in this department, and I need you to remember this.

"So the question remains, Maxine, are you up to this?"

"I have to be, Captain, my Mother is depending on me."

She stood and walked from the office and out to her desk. She stood there looking again at all of the stuff cluttering the top and shook her head. She needed a new perspective to look at of this from. She needed a new direction, and that definitely wouldn't come from sitting around here. She reached into her desk and retrieved her weapon and her credentials and she started to leave. Raymonds caught up with her just before she made it to her car.

"Where are you headed to?"

"I need to look at this from a different direction. I have a storage room with all of my mother's stuff in it so I'm going to go there and see if I can find the name of her first husband. I think he can help even if it's just a little bit."

"Do you need me to come with you?"

"No, but if you can I need all of the CSI information from her room at the adult facility. Check again to see if anyone hasn't been in since she's been kidnapped, and if so find out where they live so we can go check them out tomorrow."

"Gotcha, and Maxine," Raymonds put his hand on her shoulder as she turned, "if you need me call me… ok?"

"Thanks, David," she slowly stepped away. "I'll be fine."

***

Maxine sat on the floor in the middle of a host of boxes with just the light from the hall illuminating the small room. She had placed all of this stuff in this storage room just after moving her mother into the White Chapel Adult Living Facility with the sorrowful hope that one day she would be able to take her out of that place and put her back into her own apartment. But, her mother's psychosis only worsened over time and she'd been in that facility on a multitude of medications now for over five years with no positive outlook in the near future.

She ripped open a box that had been labeled from her mother's bedroom and slowly went through the items within. The pictures brought back memories of a childhood she longed to forget. Memories of a mother who was never emotionally there for her. Memories of a mother who just never seemed to care. Memories of a mother who always picked her drink over her daughter. She picked up a picture of her and her mother sitting in front of their old house and her mother was holding her as she laughed; if she remembered it right her mother was tickling her. It was one of those few days her mother wasn't staring at the bottom of an empty bottle of gin or vodka which were her primary drinks of choice.

A tear slowly dripped from her eye as she tossed the picture aside and continued her search. She grabbed a handful of letters tied together and placed them off to the side for a moment before picking up a small crystal tiger that had been wrapped in newspaper. It looked very familiar but it wasn't something that she'd ever given her mother. She remembered her mother crying when she got it and then running into her room locking the door for most of the night.

"What's wrong, Mommy," she remembered asking her when she finally came from the room. "Why were you crying?"

"Just leave it alone, Maxie," her mother answered, "and never let me see you touching that. Ever, do you understand?"

"Yea," she told her mom as she went back to playing with her dolls, but in her mind she wanted to get a closer look at what made her cry. She kept her head down as her mother slowly moved off to the kitchen and she waited until she heard her making dinner before she quietly made her way to the bedroom. Looking back to make certain her mother was still busy she moved into the room; finding the small crystal tiger she held it up to watch the lights reflect through the colored glass and she smiled. Why would this make her mom so…

"What the fuck are you doing in here?" her mother's voice scared her and she almost dropped the little tiger. "I thought I told you not to bother that."

"I… I just wanted to see it."

The feeling of the leather striking her bare leg at the edge of the dress she was wearing caused her to shriek. It was a good thing she had sat down on her mother's bed or she would have dropped the glass figurine on the floor. She cried out and the tears burned her eyes as the belt reached out and touched her again and again as she rolled over the bed trying to get away from it, but her mother was fast.

Her mother held a glass in one hand and struck her with the belt in the other hand quickly. She squealed and cried and begged her to stop, but the belt continued to drop down harshly against her body. She was hit on her legs, her back and her butt as her mother didn't let up. Through her tear drenched eyes she looked at her mother and just didn't recognize her face; it was as if she had been possessed and she was taking her fury out on her small body. Finally, it all stopped and her mother stood there breathing hard.

"If I tell you not to touch something, I mean don't touch it. Now get your little ass out of my room."

Maxine sat there on the floor in the middle of all her mother's stuff staring blankly at the small glass figurine. This was the first time that she'd seen it since that day she had been beaten and right at this moment all she wanted to do was throw it across the room and watch it shatter against the wall. She slowly wrapped it back up in the newspaper and gently placed it back into the box and wiped away a tear. Too many bad memories.

She picked up the letters again and untied the string holding them together. She slowly thumbed through glancing at the names on the front of them. The names on the first ones she looked at were from her own father, a man she hadn't seen since she was about six years old. She could barely remember his face, but she could remember how it felt to rub her small face against his furry face and she would always giggle from the feel of his beard rubbing against her face. She wanted to read them, but she didn't want to face his truth.

Her fingers continued to slowly move through the letter until she came across a name that she didn't recognize. She pulled it free of the stack and stared at it. The envelope was so very old as she gazed at the upper left hand corner wrinkling her nose at the nearly illegible but it was definitely her mother's handwriting. She stared at the name in the center of the dingy paper… Karl Mezzeric with an address directed towards some ship in the US Navy.

"Karl Mezzeric," she whispered as she opened the letter. She sat there reading it and she could suddenly see her mother sitting at the dining room table trying to write this one letter. There were tear stains all over it and some of the words had been almost washed out because of them. She held it tightly as the words poured out and she couldn't help but cry again before slowly folding it up and placing it back into the envelope. She'd never sent him that letter … *I wonder why,* she thought to herself.

She didn't worry with packing away anything she'd pulled out. She stood holding on to that one letter and she walked from the storage room and locked it up. After sitting down in her car she stared at the envelope once more and then she called Sheryl Evans.

"Hey, Sheryl, sorry to be a bother but can you look up a name for me real quick?"

"Sure, Suga," the younger lady answered with a smile in her voice. "What's the name you have for me?"

"Karl Mezzeric, I just need to know if he's still living here and if so the address."

"Give me just a sec," Maxine could hear her fingers tapping at her keyboard through the phone and she sat there waiting. "I do have a Karl Mezzeric, he's a retired Naval Sergeant… worked for Maritime Shipping for about twenty years and has recently retired from there… he's a widower with two sons… and,"

"And… what?"

"Well that name that Raymonds gave me earlier today, Janice Rollins? Well he was married to her while he was still in the Navy."

"Do you have a current address for him?" Maxine asked without acknowledging what had just been said.

"Yes, 3312 West Immorsen Street. I'll send it to your phone so you'll have it."

"Thanks, Sheryl, I appreciate it." She hung up the phone and drove away from the storage house.

***

She looked down at her phone and then again at the numbers against the wall of the house, 3312, she was at the right place. She held the letter in her hands as she stared at the door wondering if she should knock or just walk away. There was so much she wanted to know about her mother's past because it could answer so much about why she treated her as she did. She slowly raised her hand and gently knocked on the door. She could hear footsteps making their way to the door and she held her breath as the knob suddenly turned.

"May I help you?" his voice was so deep and she could only imagine him as he was when he was in the Navy. He stood there in the door taking up almost all of the space there as he looked down at her.

"Mr. Mezzeric?"

"Who's asking?" he had a very commanding presence and that almost made her smile. She could imagine him being her father and the difference he would have made in who she would eventually become.

She pulled out her police credentials and flipped them open so he could see her picture and badge. "Maxine Steele, Sir," she answered before placing it back into her coat pocket. She watched his face as she stared at her.

"Yes, I'm Karl Mezzeric. How can I help you, Officer?"

"I… damn," she murmured. "I think you know my mother, Janice Rollins."

"Goddamn, Janice Rollins," he smiled as he said her name, "now that's a name I haven't heard in a lifetime. Please, please come in."

Maxine followed him through the foyer and into the living room. It was a modest home he had with just a plain little sofa and loveseat combo and he was sitting in a lazy boy easy chair. The small screen television was set on some talk show that she didn't recognize and he had a still steaming cup of coffee sitting on this side table. She could tell that a woman's hand had decorated this house but it had been a long time ago and he had just never changed a thing. She smiled as he offered a seat on the sofa.

"How's Janice doing these days?" he took a sip of his coffee.

"Mr. Mezzeric," Maxine rushed through her mind trying to pick her words, "I don't want to come off as harsh or brash but I need your help with something."

"Something's happened. What's going on with your mom?"

"She's been kidnapped and I have no clues to go on. I came to you because I just came across your name in some letters I had of hers in storage, and I was hoping you could tell me a little about my mother's past."

"Why her past? I'm not sure how much help I can be."

"I believe that something she went through caused not only her depression and alcoholism, but it also triggered her kidnapper. I just need to know if anything happened while you and she were married."

Karl sat there and his face softened. He closed his eyes and took a deep breath before looking at Maxine.

"I was so mean to her," he began. "I mean so very mean to her, and I blamed her for everything when none of it was her fault."

"I don't know what you mean," Maxine sat at the edge of the sofa.

"When I was in my second year in the Navy, your mom and I were expecting our first child. We were both so excited and when we found out it was a little boy I was on top of the world. My first born was going to be a son and I immediately began to think of everything he and I would do…"

"I have a brother?"

"No… no he died the night he was born," a tear slowly slid down the side of his face and he gently wiped it away. "I was home on shore leave for my two week furlough and she went into labor. The weather was so bad that night and as I was trying to help her to the car she told me something was wrong.

"I rushed to get her to the hospital and when we made it there I ran in and got them to come out and help me get her. They said that the baby was breached and that they couldn't find a heartbeat. There were so many people in the room and your mom just kept screaming and trying to hold on to something and they wouldn't let me into the room. And she kept screaming.

"I remember standing there trying to look into the window to see what was going on but they had her bed surrounded. I think I walked a rut into the floor as I paced the hallway just waiting to hear her stop screaming and the baby crying. And then… I heard it and I wiped the sweat from my head and ran to the door, but it wasn't her. There was another girl in there with her on the other side of the curtain. I opened the door and stood there watching as the doctor was doing compression on such a little chest as a woman was carrying the other baby out of the room.

"Our little boy died, and," he sat there choked up. "I didn't even go into the room to comfort her. She reached out for me and I turned away in anger and walked off. I blamed her for letting my son die, and for years I wouldn't forgive her. I never went back to the hospital; I even moved out of our house while she was still in there by herself. I wasn't even man enough to tell her I wanted a divorce, I just had the papers mailed to her while I was back out at sea."

Maxine just sat there staring at him as he talked and now she could understand why her mother was so mad all of the time. She could also understand why her father was sent away and she rarely ever saw him. She pushed back into the sofa and tried to catch her breathing as her thoughts ran to her mother being locked up somewhere with no one just hoping that she would save her. She could hear her calling out to her and she almost broke down, but she swallowed hard and sat back up.

"Two more things, Mr. Mezzeric," her voice was shaky. "When was your son born, and what can you tell me about a little glass tiger she got?"

"He was born on November 30, 1978 at 11:02pm. I'll never forget that date. I keep it marked on my calendar. It was the most shameful I've ever felt in my life. He was such a small thing… so very small."

"And the glass tiger?" Maxine asked again.

"That I do not know. I never saw a glass tiger and I never sent her one. I do know your mother loved tigers, she would always call them the most majestic of the big cats."

Maxine stood and thanked him for his time, and again apologized if she'd been rude at any point. He didn't stand he just sat there staring at the floor lightly sobbing and she could only assume that it was because of how he left things between him and her mother. She looked about again and took in that he must have had a pretty decent life with his second wife, and she again wondered what it would have been like to have had him as her father… to have had any kind of father.

"Maxine," he voice was low as he finally stood and walked towards her, "when you find your mother can you please let me know. I want to be there for her and for you if either of you will allow me to be. Tell her I said I'm so sorry for everything."

Before she could step away the big man had grabbed her and took her into his arms and hugged her. Unable to hold it in anymore she began to cry against his chest as everything from the past few months flooded her head. He held her as if she were one of his own and didn't say a word, he just allowed her to cry as she held on to him. The feel of his hand rubbing gently at her back was like everything she used to dream it would be and she cried harder.

"Its ok," he cooed softly, "everything is going to be ok, and if you ever need me you can always call me."

"Thank you, Mr. Mezz…"

"Call me Karl."

"Thank you… Karl."

When she finally left her mind felt so much clearer than it had in weeks. She had left the letter her mom had written with him so that he could read it. He sat back down with it as she slowly walked away his hands trembling as he slowly opened the envelope and pulled the pieces of papers out. She watched for a moment and then left hoping that the words on those pages would ease his heart some because her mother had forgiven him a long time ago.

Chapter 16

"Hello," she answered her cell as she sat down in her car. "Hey, Daniel, it's been a few days I'm sorry I've been so out of it."

"Hey, Beautiful," she could hear the smile in his voice. "I've been wanting to check up on you after all of that with your mom, but I figured you would be busy trying to get that figured out. Any news yet?"

"Nothing yet, and its driving me crazy. What are you up to."

"I need to see you about something," now he sounded secretive. "Something you really need to see."

"When?"

"As soon as you can," he answered. "Can you drop by my office?"

"I'm on my way. I can be there in about thirty."

"Excellent, I'll see you then."

Maxine sped off back towards the downtown area with her mind full of everything her mother's first husband told her. So many new things were now running through her head and she would need more time than a quick drive through the city to put it all together, but one thing that was definitely put itself in the forefront… she almost had an older brother. She grabbed her phone and called Sheryl again.

"Come on, come on…" she murmured as she waited for the woman to answer.

"You've reached the offices of Debts and Merits, I'm your host how may I help you?"

"I honestly believe you have way too much time on your hands," Maxine giggled. "But, I do have something new I need for you to look up for me."

"Anything for you, Sweetness," Sheryl answered as her fingers flew over her keyboard. "What can I do you for?"

"I need for you to go through the hospital records and look up a child births on November 30, 1978, I'm looking for two children around 11pm and most likely two boys."

She could hear the woman typing away and could only imagine what she was looking all across her screens. It was amazing the information that could now be obtained with just a few strokes of a keyboard, especially if you knew what you were looking through. As she pulled up to the television station, she sat there pulling out her pen and pad waiting for her answers.

"This is making no sense," Sheryl suddenly said. "I'm getting some conflicting information. On the one hand its showing that there were two recorded boy births that night, but then its saying that there was only one and that baby was a still born to Janice Rollins. I'm going to have to dig a little more because if I'm reading everything correctly… there was another girl giving birth at the same time and in the same room, but there's no information of who she was."

"Damn," Maxine pressed the phone to her ear with her shoulder. "Its like every time I get close something drops a wall. I think this other girl is very important, Sheryl, please find out more about her for me."

"I surely will," Sheryl was still typing. "The moment I find something I'll text it to your phone."

"Thanks you're a sweetheart." She hung up the phone and slid from her car and headed into the news station's building.

He sat there watching with a sneering look upon his face. He'd been following her since she'd left her apartment and it still amazed him that she never noticed the tail. He lit a cigarette and sucked in the smoke and held it in his lungs then slowly exhaled. It was actually a beautiful day as he sat there contemplating walking inside the building. He wondered just how close he could get without being noticed as being someone who didn't work in the building. Without further thought he stepped from his van, stomped out his cigarette and made his way into the building.

***

Daniel was sitting at his desk when Maxine walked up and touched his shoulder. He was fully engrossed into the piece of paper he was holding that he had blocked out everything around him just so he could concentrate beyond the noise. He jumped and spun when she touched him and stared up at her a little bewildered before recognizing who she was. A smile slowly crept across his lips.

"Hey you," he grinned fully, "how are you doing?"

"It's been a long couple of weeks, and how are you?" she reached out to him but pulled her hand back because of where they were.

He smiled up at her and winked his eye. "I hope you don't mind me stepping back I know you needed the time to work on finding your mother, but please know I've wanted to be right there with you."

"Thank you, Daniel," she kind of shuffled her feet. Its been a very long time since she's actually tried to make any relationship with a man work, and he just seemed to real to be true. She stood there feeling like a little school girl staring at her high school crush.

"It's been really crazy and for the longest we had no leads, but," she felt this sudden urge to look around, "I've come across a few new things that I'm working on."

"We'll have to sit down soon so you can fill me in," he smiled up at her, "and not for any story. I want to know what's going on with you, Maxine. I don't want you to feel like you're doing this alone."

"That's sweet of you, Daniel," she could almost feel herself blushing, but she quickly drew it back. "So you said I needed to see something?"

"Yes," he lowered his voice and picked up the note he'd been looking at earlier. "I just go this today and well… read it."

> *Mr. Forthsythe,*
> *I want to start this by saying you overstepped your boundaries and for that I just may have to add you to my list. As you may well know I am not opposed to the disposal of men, and therefore your life as it is, is now expendable. You should have never touched her. You never had rights to her body, and for that alone your life is... Forfeit. Until that time just know that I now have two plus the mother... and this play shall soon come to an end... so say I*
> *Reaper*

"He's watching you, Maxine," Daniel whispered, "and from the looks of this note he's watching you closely. I wouldn't doubt he's been in your home."

Maxine stood there shaking. Everything in her head was swirling too quickly as she tried to catch her breath. The world was picking up speed as her thoughts went off everywhere at once. Her eyes flickered and she could feel her knees buckling as the letter slipped from her fingers and floated to the floor. She could feel Daniel's hands on her as he helped her to his seat and she just literally slumped down in it. Everything in her wanted to scream but she could only hold her breath before she felt the lip of a cup being pressed to her lips.

"Drink, Max, drink."

Her mind raced back through everything and it was always there.

"The smell," she said quietly. "I could never place it until just now."

"What smell, Maxine?"

She looked up at him but didn't really see him. Her eyes were focused on the homes of the victims and everything that she'd take note of, and the one very common thing was a smell that she could never quite recognize. The basement of the Fitzwilliams home first and then the Master's bedroom, and then the Master's bedroom in the Muldoony home. It was so subtle that each time she had almost missed it, but it was there. She remembered putting it in her notes as well. Then there was the Ferro home; her mind rushed through everything and she knew the smell was there throughout the house.

"Maxine," Daniel shook her shoulders, "what smell?"

"I don't really know how to explain it, but at each home I picked up this smell that just seemed out of place to everything else in the home."

She sat up and took another swallow of the water as her mind continued to play through everything. She was so used to being very detailed oriented and mentally bashed herself for just not paying attention to those particular details. In her mind she now walked about her own home and there in the bedroom she could pick up that smell.

"Fuck me," she growled as it all flooded through; not only the bedroom but also in the living room especially her sofa. "He's been in my apartment. He's been all through my entire home. How the fuck could I have missed it?"

She reached down and picked up the letter and read through it again. She got to the end and nodded her head. She knew something was off when he grabbed Liza Ferro; her kidnapping was so out of sequence and so arbitrary that she was almost sure he'd done it out of anger.

Out of anger…

"Goddammit," she slammed the note down onto the desk. "He was there when…"

She looked around and noticed that no one had stopped moving but something made the hair on the back of her neck stand on end. He was there… right now he was there watching her. No he was watching them and using this moment as another means of fueling his fire.

"He was there when?" Daniel urged as he too looked around to see what it was she was looking for.

"That night after the restaurant," she answered. "The night you came home with me, he was in my apartment."

"He was? How the fuck?"

"I don't know but I'm almost sure of it. I caught that smell that night, and something about the house wasn't right. He was there."

She stood up and continued looking around, but she didn't know what to look for. There was the obvious that he was most likely a white male in his mid-30s to mid-40s, but what else. He was undoubtedly very smart, and unworried about being in public so that means he was nondescript and could just fit in where ever he was. As she looked about, there were so many men just there on the set that could fit her description and this completely worried her. That definitely meant that Daniel was in danger, and she had no way of protecting him because she didn't know what to tell him to be looking for without him becoming paranoid.

"What are you thinking, Maxine," Daniel was a little panicked as he continued to look around. He stepped up and stood close to her wanting to reach out and hold her, but keeping his hands at his sides. "Is he here right now?"

"I'd definitely say that yes he is here, but I honestly don't know where he is, or who he is. I don't have a name for him… but I think I'm close. I think that the fact that I've made him mad is a clue and I'm closing in now that I have a new avenue to travel."

She looked at him and smiled. She then leaned forward and she kissed his lips in a long, hard and passionate lock that made the man swallow his breath when she finally pulled away. She winked at him and watched as he sucked in a deep breath and then slowly released. Daniel was already in the crosshairs of the killer so her kissing him should only spike his anger and make him step up what ever it was he had planned. She needed him to make his next move while she did her research. She knew he was out there, but the question was where was he and what was he thinking.

"I'm tired of him being in my head," she whispered into Daniel's ear as she pulled him into her arms, "its time to make this bastard a little madder. I need to get into his head from this point on."

"You know you're putting yourself in danger?"

"I'm more worried about you," she answered. "He already has his eyes on you."

"Don't worry about me, Baby," he grinned, "I'm a big boy and I can take care of myself."

"I have a feeling that this guy may be bigger than you, Daniel," she smiled back, "but I have a feeling you can take care of yourself. Just be careful because this asshole is definitely watching you."

She pulled away from him with a big grin on her face and pulled out her phone. She quickly dialed up Raymonds and waited for him to answer as she once again slowly looked around. After he finally picked up she asked him to meet her at her place with a CSI team explaining to him that she had a feeling that their Unsub may have been in her apartment. She almost had to laugh as her partner once again displayed a bit of his over protective nature, but she hung up after telling him that she would be there in less than an hour.

"I have a feeling we're going to know who his actually kidnap victim was in the next couple of days and then right after that he's going to put out the Ferro woman just to give us a little extra work to do. I need for you to keep a very close eye out around you because I don't know who this guy is or what he looks like, but he knows who you are and he's keeping really close tabs on me. You need to be very careful when you're out and about."

"I'll be fine," he responded, "I'm not at the top of his list, but you are. I have a feeling that if you are not able to figure this out and find your mom he's going to make you regret everything he's holding against you."

"Yea I know," she glanced in his eyes, "but I'm no longer afraid of him. I think that's what has been holding me back; my fear of him and my fear of what I can do. I'm ready to end this bullshit and I need to find my mother, and if he's hurt her I'm going to kill him."

***

If anyone could see him they would have dropped their head and walked on in fear. His eyes were a dark grey storm of anger and hatred, and his face was a grim mask as frightening as a gargoyles. He'd pushed himself deep into the shadows and was merely a ghost of a vision as he stared out across the room. He folded his arms about himself to keep from running out there right now with his knife out and screaming at the top of his lungs.

He'd sent him the note and warned him, and yet there they were kissing out in public with no shame. His heart was pounding in his chest as he watched them. His blood was seething and rushing through his veins and beating like a drum in his ears. He blinked several times hoping against hope that he was not seeing what he was seeing, but each time he opened them they were still pressed together and his hands were seemingly all over her body. He would make them both pay for this, but right now he had to get out of there before he exploded.

"Did you truly think she would wait for you, you silly little boy?"

"Not now," he growled under his breath, "I don't need your bullshit right now. I don't need your bullshit anymore."

"And yet, my dear disillusioned son, I am here to be the harpy of your fucked up soul."

He slipped away leaving the menagerie of his mother standing there watching him walk away. He didn't risk a look back to see if she was still there, nor did he look back out to see if Maxine was still in his arms. Hot tears slowly washed down his face as he rushed from the building and out to his van. He pulled open the door and clambered in looking for his cigarettes. He needed a smoke and as he lit the end and took that first deep drag he could finally feel his nerves settling down and his blood slowing down. After the cigarette was smoked to the filter he tossed it from the window and finally pulled away.

Tonight would be a very busy night for him…

***

Maxine sat on the edge of her bed as the Crime Scene Investigators moved through her apartment. They were taking prints and looking for anything that would constitute as suspect material and they were putting it all into plastic baggies to be preserved. She was doing her best just to stay out of the way as a team of about six of them worked her small home. For the first time since joining the Force she felt completely violated and just wanted everyone to leave.

She could hear Raymonds out in the living room area instructing them as to what he wanted to make certain they tested and gathered. He sounded aggravated as he stomped around trying not to trip over anyone as they were all vying for space to gather what they each needed. She reached over to her nightstand and pulled a cigarette from the pack and lit it drawing in the smoke as one of the CSI stood at her door staring at her.

"What do you want?"

"I need to start working in here, Ma'am," he answered. "Do you know of any place in particular I should begin?"

Maxine sat there smoking as she looked about the room. A shiver slowly slid up and down her spine as she stared at the spot right there just off the door. Closing her eyes she could see that area at night and for the first time realized just how dark it was there when the curtains were closed and the room light was off.

"Start right there," she began, "he's been in here and that's where he would stand just in the shadows so I wouldn't be able to see him. Check for dried semen I have the nastiest feeling he's left some of him here in my room. Also, tell someone to check behind the sofa and to test all of the sofa cushions."

The tech stepped out and relayed her message to someone in the living room and then came back and knelt down at the rug. She sat there watching as he ran through a series of steps and then looked up at her and nodded his head. He'd found semen stains there on her floor. Again she shivered as she wondered just how many times he'd stood there watching her as he relieved himself all over her goddamn floor.

"Why am I not too fucking surprised?" she grimaced drawing the smoke from the cigarette into her lungs. "I need to move."

Raymonds stepped into the room looking around. "He's definitely been all over your home, Steele. We may want to start with getting a locksmith up here to do all of your locks, that should at least slow him down and then I'd definitely say get an alarm system in here. But, we have bodily fluids all over your sofa, and we have prints that they are almost sure may be his all over tables and in the kitchen and even in the bathroom. He made himself at home here."

"This is making me feel sick all over," Maxine said as she stubbed out the last of the cigarette. "I can't believe I never seen this coming. I let all of this shit get too far gone and now I need to reel it in. I've allowed him to play with us for far too long."

"You have a look in your eyes that's making me very uncomfortable, Steele," Raymonds remarked as he stared down at her. There was something in her eyes that just made it seem as if a light had went off in her head and she was planning to do something very stupid.

"No need to worry," she gave him a very fake smile, "I got everything completely under control."

"I hope so."

The CSI tech stood from the floor and looked about the room. He had packed up his kit and seemed to be waiting for something before he finally cleared his throat to get the attention of the two detectives. Looking down he almost wondered how this would effect her security deposit, but then figured she would be back to make amends for it because she was a part of the police force and her apartment was now a crime scene.

"I think I'm done here, Detective Steele," he felt as if he were interrupting, "unless you know of any other areas in your room he may have been?"

"No," she glanced down at the part of her carpet that had been cut and half smiled, "I think we're good here."

The man nodded his head and walked from the room. Moments later she could hear the whole team of them leave her apartment making more noise than necessary. She sat there on her bed trying not to let Raymonds know that she indeed planned to do something very stupid and it would be very soon. She would discuss it later with Daniel once he came over just so he would be ready for what she had in mind. *Damn,* she thought to herself, *when in the hell have I cared so much what a man thought I did? This is getting crazy and I really need to figure this shit out as well.*

There was entirely too much going through her head, but the one thing she was almost certain of… he was about to leave out another body to be found. He was angry with her and to show that he was going to punish her. She tried not to think about her mother being the one he put out, but that thought kept rumbling through her mind. She was almost certain that he already had someone before he kidnapped the Ferro woman, but there hadn't been any kidnappings reported that she was aware of.

"He's escalating," she whispered more to herself than Raymonds.

"What do you mean?"

"I honestly believe that he had a woman before the Ferro woman, but something pushed him… angered him and then he took the Ferro woman, and to make things worse…" she took a deep breath. "Something else pushed him again and that's why he went after my mother. I think he feels that there's some connection between him and my family."

"That would make sense especially since he's talking directly to you in the notes we have, but the question is why?"

"I talked to my mom's ex-husband and I found out that there was a child before me…" she looked up at Raymonds and then stared away towards the window, "a boy."

"Do you think he believes he's her son?"

"The problem is, my mother's son died when he was born."

"Holy fuck, what if she tried to tell him that the night he took her? What would his mindset be at that point?"

"Exactly," she said bluntly, "that's why I have to find him now."

I'll get in touch with Sheryl," Raymonds began as he pulled out his cell phone.

"I've talked to her and I have her researching my mother's past. She said she would contact me as soon as she's found something for me."

"Ok, good… then we need to get out of here and get some work done."

"Yea, because I'm really tired of this son-of-a-bitch."

Chapter 17

Abel stood over the laid out body of Charlene von Dermott as she pulled against her bindings and cried pitifully staring up at him. Just like all of them, her eyes begged him where her mouth couldn't because he had it stuffed and gagged so she couldn't say a word. Her naked body was writhing and straining against the ropes he'd tied at her wrists and ankles. She was so superbly beautiful and he couldn't take his eyes off of her body, and he longed to just reach out and touch her but restrained from doing just that because he didn't want to overexcite himself.

He stood there just watching as her body trembled, and her breast rose and feel upon her chest. He took note of just how soft and silky her skin looked; there were no blemishes, no spots, and no varicose veins to be seen. He slowly followed the curves of her body from the top of her head down to each of her toes and he licked his lips.

"She would never want your sick, sick ass, my son."

"It's not about what she wants," he didn't look up but continued to stare at the woman before him, "it's not about what any of them wanted. This is about me."

"Yes it is my baby, it's all about you."

Slowly he turned and he walked away from the woman and made his way upstairs to his desk. There was so much to do and so very little time to get it all done. He sat there as he went through the possible places of showcasing his newest love, and a smile creased his thin lips as he quickly made his decision. So quickly that it was almost shocking, but it would be more shocking to everyone involved. Next he had to prepare his note; he had to let Maxine know that he was pissed at her and that she would have to pay for her transgressions.

There was just so much to do. He pulled his paper out and sat there staring at it as he worked on his words in his head. Slowly he began to scratch words to paper smiling as they flowed out so smoothly. This should put a bit of a fear back into her that will keep her motivated. She had to understand that her mind needed to be on the task at hand and not some swinging dick that just happened along because he intersected their paths, and next he would have to decide on just how he was going to handle said "swinging dick" to teach him a lesson.

Folding the note up he sat back in his chair. There was just so much going on around him that his head was pounding in a migraine that he couldn't shake. He picked up the bottle of aspirin and poured a handful out and swallowed them down with a chaser of whiskey. He lit a cigarette and took a deep drag into his lungs and held it there until he felt as if her were going to choke, and then he slowly released the smoke into the air around his head. He slowly looked around expecting to see her, but she was not around… anywhere. He allowed himself to smile and almost relax.

He stood and walked through the kitchen and downstairs to his waiting lady. He had a sick smile on his face and he flipped on the light and then moved to the closet. As he removed his clothing he looked over at her still squirming and writhing against her bindings atop the table she was on. He slipped off his boots and then his pants, he pulled off his shirt and the undershirt underneath and he wondered why he enjoyed doing all of this while naked. He slipped off his socks and then pulled down his underwear and he stood there naked looking around for "her" and again smiled because she wasn't anywhere around.

He stepped from the closet and moved to his worktable staring down at all of his toys. He had a thing for torture because there was something about the screams of his women that always seemed to make his insides sing. He took a deep breath and looked over at the cages where the other two women were stored, and grinned at how both seemed to be curled up into a corner fearful that they would be… next.

"Your turns are coming ladies," his voice was a low menacing growl. "I wouldn't want either of you to feel left out."

He stared at Maxine's mother and again everything she said the night at the adult home came rushing back at him. The headache felt as if it were a hurricane beating against the coastline sending cresting waves pounding inland causing him to grimace. He held his head and slumped for a moment against his worktable and held on waiting for that moment to subside. He words echoed in his head over and over telling him that her son had died. The gritted his teeth, grinding them, as she kept telling him that she was not his mother and that there was another girl in the room with her; another girl he could find nothing on.

"LIES…" he suddenly screamed out and he could hear all the two women in the cages scream and the woman on the bed try to scream out around her muffle. His knees buckled and he slammed his fist down upon the table as he tried to force his brain to calm itself. The pains of the headaches were becoming excruciating and more frequent. He could feel his stomach churning and the bile was boiling in preparation of forcing its way up his throat at any time. Dark spots appeared before his eyes and streaks of lights flashed as bright as lightning as he finally allowed his body to drop to the floor and he landed on all fours.

"It was all lies," he babbled. "It was all lies. I know the truth. She can't lie to me anymore. No one will lie to me… anymore."

Beating his fists on the floor until the pains in his hands surpassed the pain still throbbing in his head. He looked over at Janice once more and flashed her a sick smile before finally standing again. He could see the fear in her eyes. He could smell the fears of all three of them in the air and it excited him. He took a deep breath and forced away any pains he could feel and stared back down at his table. It was time to begin.

He grabbed his bottle of antibacterial gel and cleansed his hands, and then he followed that up with a handful of alcohol rubbing his hands together until that evaporated. From the corner of his eye he could see she had stopped squirming around and was staring at him; the all seemed to do that as if to see exactly what was coming. He didn't move for a moment as he stared down at what he had before him. His favorite knife he'd sharpened earlier sat there glowing under the table light, he had a few scalpels, some syringes with different liquids in the vials(for some reason she was going to be different and not just a stabbing), there were a pair of pruning shears, and even a hammer and some nails.

He grabbed a syringe he had a sedative in and stepped up to her and quickly searched her arm for a vein. She watched in terror as he stuck the needle in and quickly squirted the clear fluid into her body. Her eyes were stretched as the fluid hit her system and quickly a warmth spread through her entire body. Her eyes fluttered a bit and she tried to shake her head to clear away the drowsiness that seemed to hit her almost immediately. She took in a few large, gasping breaths hoping to bring in enough air into her system to keep her awake, but nothing seemed to halt the inevitable. Her body relaxed and her eyes drooped; her mind was fully awake and fearful as she tried to look up at the man she was sure was going to kill her. Silently, she prayed.

"I know you can hear me," he was whispering into her ear. "I know that you're scared, and believe it or not… so am I. You're not my first, but each and every time it feels like my first time. It's not your fault; nothing you did has brought this upon you other than the fact that you resemble her. I'm so sorry for all of this, so very sorry you've become a part of this story, but there are almost always some tragedy in every story.

"What I've given you a little concoction of mine. You will remain awake as I begin. Your body will feel the pain but you won't be able to move. I'm going to remove the gag because I'll want to hear the screams, and you will scream. You will scream a lot until the pain overcomes you and your body will finally shut down. The moment you're close to dying I will finally end it. This is truly a first for me, but I have been dreaming about doing this for quite a long time. Thank you very much, Charlene."

He removed the gag from her mouth and then placed a finger at her eye and gently wiped away a tear. He ran his fingers through her hair and then walked away back to his worktable. Grabbing the shears he stepped back over to the table and grabbed the woman's hand. They were so soft and beautiful, so unblemished with age spots, and her nails had been recently manicured and painted. He watched as her droopy eyes tried to widen as he slipped her pinky finger between the cutting edge.

Her droopy eyes stretched as far as they could as she only lay there and watch was he was doing. She could feel the cold steep brushing against her flesh and then she felt him tighten down until the metal had her finger pinched between the two edges. Her mouth opened first in a very silent scream that quickly turned into a shrieking wail as the shears bit down cutting into her finger. Tears flooded from her eyes as she watched in horror as he cut off the tip of her pinky and the small piece of flesh popped off and landed somewhere on the floor. She wanted her body to move, to thrash about making it harder for him to continue, but her muscles wouldn't move as she watched him take and do the same thing to her thumb.

Abel reached down and picked up the two finger parts and rolled them around in his hand almost admiring how cleanly they were cut off. He stared at the ends and marveled that even the bone had cut clean through with no jagged edges. The weight of the shears in his hand felt as comfortable as when he had his knife, and he's loved that knife for many years. He walked over to his table and dropped the two finger pieces into a small jar and filled that with his formaldehyde solution and capped it up.

He walked back over to her holding his growing penis and stroking it slowly. Leaning over to whisper into her ear and stroke her hair with his free hand. "Ever wonder why I've never raped you?" she shook her head vigorously her eyes stretched again. "No, not really? It's because the joy for me is your… pain."

Charlene watched as he stood there close to her face and he began to pleasure himself. His eyes were all over her body and yet he did not touch her at all, but she could see how excited he was as it was written all over his face. She didn't see him do it but he'd placed a leather strap next to her on the bed; she screamed out as the strap came down harshly across her breast. From the corner of her eye she could see his hand stroking faster, and then again the strap struck her quickly across her breast and her belly. Her tears drenched her eyes and her screams filled the room and he smiled and stroked faster.

She watched in horror as he began to grunt and her face was suddenly the landing spot for his seed as he ejaculated fiercely. Her head echoed with the sound of his howling out his joy at the top of his lungs.

"You see," he stared down at her grinning that her face was soaked in her tears and his semen, "I don't need your sex… just your screams and your terror."

He wrapped his hand around her throat and began to squeeze watching as she tried to catch her breath. He could feel her throat contracting beneath his hand as she forced the little air she was getting into and out of her lungs as he hand pressed down harder. Just from the twitching in her body he could see she was trying to move, she wanted to fight him, but there was absolutely nothing her body could do. He laughed at her as he released her neck and she coughed trying to fill her lungs with air.

"I think you're ready to continue."

Grabbing the hammer and nails from the table he proceeded to nail first her hands and then her ankles to the table. That began a new scream that was so much different from the first screams. He watched as her eyes rolled into the back of her head and her body began to shake violently. He could feel his heart pounding in his chest and his blood was rushing through him so quickly that he could hear it surging through his veins. He grabbed a few more nails and hammered them into various parts of her body shaking excitedly as the shock finally caused her to black out and her breathing became shallow.

Over the next hour Abel spent his time slowly torturing her entire body. Through the years he'd just enjoyed killing them and then stabbing their privates, but this was different. This was fun. He'd thought of just torturing and abusing his other women, but something always clicked and he felt rushed, but tonight he felt so calm and so excited. He watched as blood slowly trickled from different parts of her body. He smiled at the number of small black and blue bruises sprouted out all over her body. He watched her breast as they barely moved and he could hear her wheezing as she kept trying to breathe, and all at once he had an erection.

"Your body is broken," his voice was again like thunder in her brain, "so is your spirit. You're barely breathing and I know that by now you're feeling so very weak."

Trying not to cry anymore she looked up at him standing over her hoping that her eyes was telling him to just kill her. She couldn't move, but everything about her body told her that she could take no more. She couldn't count the number of times she'd passed out because the pain was too unbearable for her. Her throat was raw and she could taste blood as she swallowed. She tried to think of her husband and she wished she could see him just one more time, but her memories of him and their life were all great and this caused her to slowly smile. With one last look into this demon's eyes she saw an angry that shook her to her bones, but her smile held on.

"What the fuck are you smiling about?" he began to pace about the room not understanding what was going on. He screamed out again and again knowing she couldn't answer him, but wanting to know all the same why she was smiling.

"No," he screamed out, "no, you stop that right now. You stop that."

"You couldn't break her," his mother stood there as naked as he was and smiling as her cigarette hung from her lips. "With all that you've done to her, you could not break her and she's going to die with something happy filling her up."

"You shut the fuck up. Just… shut the fuck up!"

"My poor, little, stupid son. Such a wonderful little fuck up you are," she pulled the cigarette from her lips and blew the smoke into his face. "So big you are now, but you're still so goddamn weak."

Abel pulled the knife from the table and began swinging it around wildly. Slashing at thin air and cursing profusely as he moved about looking for someone. His screams bounced and echoed from the walls as his bare feet smacked against the concrete floor. There was a near feral look in his eyes like that of an animal being cornered and finally rearing back to fight its way free. He looked madly insane as he slung the large blade around cutting and cutting at nothing.

He turned and looked at the woman on the bed and growled that she was still smiling. He stared into her eyes and could see nothing there as she blankly stared at the ceiling above her, and he snapped. Nothing else made any sense as he stabbed the large blade down into her body; first her chest watching as the blade sunk down and finally through bone until it hit her lung, and her body jerked as she now tried to draw breath into her body. Then he sliced her throat watching as the blood spurted from the open wound and all over her body, and finally repeatedly in her pubic area he slammed the knife until his arm was too sore to even pull the blade free.

He slumped to the floor crying.

***

Abel stood there over her as she lay so peacefully in the bathtub of scented and bubbled water. He slowly looked about, it had been months since he was last here, and yet the husband hadn't changed a thing. So sure was he that she would be returned to him unharmed that everything was still as it was the day she'd gone missing. Abel smiled as he picked up her bottle of shampoo and popped the top to smell it, and then he placed it on the floor beside the tub.

There was so much that had to be done, but the good thing about it was that he had the entire day to do it all. He smiled as he thought of the number of police patrolling the Mount Pleasant Village area as if they had any chance of catching him coming or going. They would look right at him as he rolled through and some had even waved as he passed by, but none would ever stop him. He knew that the former Senator had left to go out of town and wouldn't be back until tomorrow morning, and this would give him time to prepare his dear Charlene so that she would be waiting for her husband.

He slowly knelt down and picked up her loofa sponge and the scented bath oil she had specially order from some Italian bath shop. Slowly he bathed her careful not to tear away at the skin around the wounds of the scalpel or his knife. He could almost feel her body jumping and jerking as he came close to the open wounds, and he didn't want her to be in any kind of pain. He held her tightly with his free hand to keep her from slumping to deeply into the water as he gently moved the sponge around. Gently he began to sing a song his mother would always sing as she was scrubbing and scraping at his body in hopes of keeping her calm.

"Shhhh, shhh," he softly cooed into her ear. "Everything's going to be just fine. We'll get you all cleaned up and I'll help you dress so that you can be ready for your husband when he comes home. He'll be so surprised to see you, and I know that you're ready to be with him again."

"She's dead, Son," the sound of her voice was grating and he tried to ignore her. "You killed her."

"He'll be happy to see her," Abel answered without looking up. "They are always happy to see them when I give them back."

"You poor, sick and twisted bastard," there was a hiss in her voice that caused him to shiver just a bit, but he remained to his task of cleaning his Charlene up to ready her for her reunion with her husband.

"You can leave now, Mother," he said calmly as he gently laid the body back into the water to wet her hair. Then propping her against the wall he squeezed the shampoo into his hand and slowly began to message the lather into her hair.

The smells of the shampoo and the bath oils filled the air of the bathroom around him. He felt like he was in heaven. He was always at his most calm when he had to bathe and clean them. He never brought the bodies back to their homes as they were on his slab at his home; they were always rinsed down to clean them up some, but they were never truly cleaned until he gave them a bath in their own body gels. He slowly ran his fingers through her hair making certain that it was clear of any tangles or snarls, and then he leaned her back and rinsed it making certain he didn't get any water in her face. He had a serious fear of water in his face and he went to all lengths to keep his ladies from suffering from that same fear.

Finally, he reached into the water and pulled her out; balancing her against him he wrapped a towel around her and carried her into the room and gently laid her out on the bed. Slowly he dried her again being very careful of her wounds.

"You lay here and cool off while I get everything else ready. You have to look perfect for him when he returns because we want him to always remember you."

He spent the remainder of the morning taking care of her. He oiled her body and even applied her make up. He sat her up and brushed her hair until it just seemed to glow to him. He then went into the closet and found the white nightie set she'd bought just for her husband and he helped to ease into it. When he was finally finished she looked like an angel, and when he laid her down on the bed she looked to be sleeping soundly.

"He's not going to be ready for just how beautiful you look," he whispered into her ear. "I think you are the most beautiful of them all."

He lightly kissed her lips and felt a charge of excitement flow through his entire body. He then pulled the note from his pocket and read it once more before folding it. Staring down at Charlene he felt a bit of sympathy for what he had to do next, but it was all apart of the game.

Maxine was now a part of his ritual and to keep her as such the note had to be there; she had to know without a doubt that it was him.

He stood over her moving her hair about to make certain it looked perfect about her head. Leaning over her he opened her mouth and placed the note inside and then slowly pushed it back into her throat. He had to swallow hard to keep from choking as it felt like his finger was pushing into his throat as well. Sweat beaded his forehead and he made a gagging sound as he tried to keep his breakfast down in his stomach. He'd come to hate this part, but it was a necessary evil, and he forced the folded paper down until it would move no further. Breathing through his nose, he took a deep breath in before pulling his finger out, and then he closed her mouth making certain that her lipstick didn't need to be reapplied.

"Perfect," he whispered to himself before stepping back to look at her laying there. He then pulled out his camera and took several pictures of her so he would be able to look at her later.

He moved about the room making certain to clean up everything wanting to leave nothing of his being there for anyone to find. The most that would be very obvious was the smell of her bath wash and her perfume lingering in the air, but he could live with that; he actually enjoyed knowing that even with the cops so out in force that he could still get in and out as he pleased. He pulled a rag from his back pocket and went about the room wiping down everything that he could remember touching before slipping his gloves back on.

"I don't want to leave you," he was standing at the room door just staring at her laying there peacefully on the bed, "but I have so much more that I have to get taken care of before you're found. The Senator will be home in the morning, and I'm sure that by midday your home will be filled with the police. Be sure to put on a good show for them.

"I love you..." he turned to leave as he finally whispered, "Mother."

***

Senator Henry Von Dermott slowly stepped into his home with the limousine driver following close behind carrying the couple of bags of luggage he'd taken with him on his trip. It had been a long and arduous meeting with a couple of gentlemen who didn't know the first thing about conducting a business meeting, and quite frankly he didn't care to see either of them again. He pointed for the man to put his luggage down as he casually looked around. He felt as if something was wrong or out of place but couldn't quite figure out what it was. He sniffed the air catching the scent of a fragrance that was familiar to him.

"Stay right here and wait for me," he looked at the man before making his way up the stairs.

The kids weren't at home so he moved on past their room doors and down the hall towards the door to his room. He hadn't be able to make himself change anything about the house just incase his wife was brought back to him, but the smell of her perfume in the air just didn't seem right. It has been over two months and he hadn't smelled that since the day she was last in their home. He could feel his heart pounding in his chest as he hoped that maybe she was in the room getting dressed. He slowly pushed the door open and closed his eyes as he walked inside.

"Charlene?" he called out smiling as the scent of her perfume became stronger. "Charlene, are you home? Please, please answer me."

He opened his eyes and almost shouted as he saw her laying there in their bed. She looked like an angel sleeping… he stepped closer.

"Call the police," he shouted to the man downstairs. "Call them now, my wife is dead."

Senator Von Dermott dropped to the floor at the door of his bedroom crying as he stared at the body of his wife laying there in the bed they'd shared for over thirty years. He'd longed for her to be returned to him, but this was not what he wanted. His mind raced as he heard the man shouting into his phone for the police to get there immediately, but nothing else mattered. He'd lost the one person in his life that mattered beyond his children. He wanted to go and hold her, he wanted to tell her that he'd missed her, but all he could do was sit there staring at her through tear filled eyes.

Chapter 18

Maxine parked across from the house and weaved her way through the growing throng of reporters and gawkers building in the street. She pushed her way through flashing her badge so people would move aside even though most continued grumbling about it being crowded. As she finally made it to the front, she nodded to Daniel as he and his crew prepared for the barrage of questions they had ready.

In her head she already knew what she would find; she already knew how the body was left and the lack of evidence that would be available. She was mentally ready for it all. She was almost glad that it had finally happened because she was beginning to wonder what had happened to him. She shoved her hands into the pockets of her jacket after showing the beat cop at the door her badge and credentials and he letting her into the house. Everything just seemed like some copied version of a bad dream as she looked around one more very affluent family's house. She pulled her hands from her pockets and slipped them inside of her latex gloves and turned to head up the stairs where everyone seemed to be crowded.

"You were right," Raymonds said as he made his way to her before she got to the top of the stairs. "I'm not sure how we missed this one on the missing persons reports, but she's been gone as long as the Ferro woman has been."

"Most likely he got this one first," Maxine stared at him as he looked through his notes.

"How do you come to that conclusion?"

"I'm thinking that he already this one, maybe even a week or so before, and then what ever set him off sent him looking for his back up victim and that's why he took out a lot of his anger on the husband."

"Well he's true to his M.O.," Raymonds glanced up towards the room. "We've found nothing out of place and yet everything has been wiped down. From the looks of things, he brought her here bathed and dressed her. Hell, he even put on her make up."

"And the note?"

Raymonds stared at her before allowing her to move on upstairs and then followed her as she went into the bedroom. The medical examiner was there already leaning over the body and making her own mental notes as Maxine walked up.

"Hey Dr. DeLong," Maxine stood on the opposite side of the bed staring down at the woman lying there. "So tell me what you have, please."

"Everything's pretty much the same, except, he went into full torture mode on this one. As you can see, she has lacerations all over her torso and there are even a few under the bottom of her feet and some along her back. He also took off two of her fingers and two of her toes. What pretty much signs this as your killer's work is the way he stabbed at her vaginal area repeatedly with a very large blade."

Maxine stood there watching as the doctor moved the night gown around to show her the slash wounds and the missing digits and then finally the woman's pubic area. It should have shocked her, but these things have never been able to shock her because she was well aware of what people could do. Staring at the way he cut into her pubic area she noticed that there was no pattern to it.

"He was very angry," she said pointed to the way the knife wounds just seemed all over the place.

"I would have to say he was very angry indeed, and it would appear that the angrier he got the deeper the knife would go until he finally hit deep enough for the knife to stick."

"I think he's losing it fast," Raymonds added in. "There has to be some way for us to get ahead of this maniac."

"Something will come along soon," Maxine picked up and stared at the woman's hand. "I don't get cutting off the tips of her fingers and her toes, or all of the slashing for that matter. Can you determine what he was cutting her with?"

"With the lines being that small and close I'd almost venture a guess and say a surgical scalpel, but I'm still not so sure about what he used to cut off her digits with."

"What about a note?"

DeLong glanced over at one of the CSI techs in the room and Maxine stepped up to the man. He handed her the note sealed inside of one their clear evidence bags. She stood there as if stuck in the rug reading it, and then she looked up at Raymonds.

"Have you read this?" he nodded and she looked at it once more reading it over.

Maxine,

Maxine said nothing. She stares at the note again and again but couldn't come up with anything say. Slowly she turned and walked from the room. Her body felt as is she were moving in slow motion as she made her way downstairs and into the main living room. Her body didn't stop until she was standing in front of a small bar area and she was reaching out for one of the decanters.

"What are you doing, Steele?"

The sound of Raymonds voice pulled her away from the sickly feeling she had in her stomach. She stared down at the decanter and wanted to pull the top and just turn the crystalline bottle up and empty its contents into her body. She hadn't had a serious drink in months now, but the need and the urge to lose herself into the bottom of this bottle was blatantly strong.

"Nothing," she murmured to the bottle as she pushed the top back down and stepped away from the bar.

"I don't pretend to know what demons you're still fighting, Steele," Raymonds had got close enough to talk low and not be overheard by the CSI techs still walking around, "but I need to know that you're still with me. Are you still with me… Steele?"

"I'm good, David," she answered as she looked again at the liquor and then walked away.

Her steps were hurried as she folded up the plastic with the note in it and pushed it into her jacket pocket. She pushed her way through the crowd of people crowding the front door with Raymonds on her heels as she made it outside. Taking a deep breath she made her way towards the street and was abruptly stopped by the throng of media hounds standing there.

"Detective, Detective," she heard Daniel's voice before she saw him. "Do you have a statement?"

"Sorry," she fought to maintain a semblance of calm, "I don't have anything to say at this time." She stuffed her hands into the pockets of her jacket and began to walk off. The crowd of reporters opened a path but kept the cameras rolling on her as if in hopes she'd change her mind.

Maxine stared up at the house and then thought of the letter in her pocket. Her mind was a race of thoughts as she turned and faced the cameras once more.

"Wait, I do have something to say," she walked back up into the middle of the cameras but quickly faced Daniel's cameraman and looked directly into his camera lens.

"I know you, you Bastard. You think you're scaring this city. You think that you're scaring me… but you don't scare me. I'm going to find you very soon, and when I do I'm going to treat you just like the rabid dog that you are. Nothing's going to stop me. You think you're ready for me? Well if you want me you son-of-a-bitch… come and get me."

She stormed off not caring that both Raymonds and Daniel were completely shocked at what she'd just said. The gauntlet was now dropped and she was preparing herself mentally for the aftermath on all fronts. At this point she knew what needed to be done and everyone was going to disagree and definitely question her rationale because she was inviting a known killer to come after her, but she had an ace up her sleeve and all she was waiting on was a phone call.

Her phone rang, but it was not the call she was hoping for.

"Yes, Captain?"

"Get your ass here pronto…" he was too calm and she knew the shit was about to hit the fan.

"I'm on my way."

***

"I'm not sure what the fuck you're up to, Steele, so you better make me believe that you know exactly what you're doing."

Maxine sat there in the chair before Captain Salter watching as he paced behind his desk. There was a coffee cup on the top of his desk but she could smell the thick, rich aroma of whiskey in the air and knew that he had been in his side desk draw before she got there. She reached into her pocket and pulled out the letter and unfolded it and placed it on his desk and watched as he snatched it up and read it. His eyes widen and he slowly sat down.

"He's fucking crazy."

"That's not the half of it, Captain," she said just as Raymonds joined them in the office closing the door behind him. "He wants me and he still has my mom so its time I called him out. He's been ahead of us for way too long. I have Sheryl looking into some things for me, and I have a feeling that with that info I'll be able to finally bait him instead of him baiting me and all of us."

"I don't like this plan," Raymonds piped in. "What's to say you don't get the information you're looking for. Now you have this maniac on a collision course with you."

"Its possible, but," Maxine closed her eyes as she thought back to what Karl Mezzeric told her about her mother's past, "I have a feeling I know why he targets the women he does. I just have to verify some things with Sheryl first to validate my reasoning."

She looked at Salter as he sat there behind his desk still staring at the note. She could almost tell what he was thinking and she knew he was fighting allowing her to do what she was planning. He was still questioning if she was ready to be back on the Force and she was quite tired of that. She was beyond ready, and she was determined to prove everyone wrong about her.

"Its time to end this bullshit, Captain.

"Do what you need to do," Salter placed the note down on the desk. He turned away and stared out of the window towards the city's downtown skyline. As much as he hated to admit it, Maxine was right. This guy had been five or more steps ahead of them since the beginning and he hadn't hesitated calling her out. The question had always been…

why? What was it about Steele that drew her to him, how were they connected, and how did this all revolve around her mother? He wanted all of this shit over, the Chief wanted it over, and between the Mayor crawling up his Chief's ass and the Chief crawling all up his… he needed for her to end this shit now.

"Get out of here," he grumbled. "I don't think I want to see your ass again until you have this asshole either dead or in shackles. Do you understand?"

"Yes, Sir," she reached across the desk and grabbed the newest note.

As she stood to leave her phone began to ring. She pulled it out and stared at the screen for a moment before putting it back in her pocket. At this moment she had more to worry about than Daniel and his angers and concerns over what she'd done. He knew that she had something planned, but she had refused to go into any details because she knew that he, just like Raymonds and Salter, would disagree and try to talk her out of it. What she'd done had to be done, this guy needed to be stopped and she was the only one who could do that.

"And, Steele," Salter called from his desk, "no more goddamn press remarks, do you understand?"

Without saying a word she walked off to her desk and slumped down in her chair. The more she thought about what she'd said, the more she realized that she had all but invited this maniac into her house. *What the fuck were you thinking?* She questioned herself. *Are you really that crazy?* She placed the note with everything else on the desk and then stared at her phone. She needed it to ring. She needed to talk to Sheryl so that she could finally put all of these puzzle pieces together.

"Excuse me, Detective," a young lady dressed in her well pressed officer blues stood at her desk, "I have a message for you from Sheryl. She wants you to come to her she has some things she needs to show you."

Maxine jumped up and followed the young office down into the belly of the precinct. She had heard Sheryl call this the "Dungeon" but had thought it was merely a coin of phrase until just this moment. The walls seemed to close in on her as she took each step deeper and deeper into the bowels of the building. She pulled her jacket tighter about her body as she picked up her steps to keep up with the young officer. At the foot of the stairwell they took a turn to the left and finally came to a stop before a door.

"She's right inside, Ma'am," the officer turned and left.

Maxine knocked and opened the door after hearing a muffled response from the other side. The room she stepped into was something out of a bad dream as it was dark of lights other than the multiple screens at the far end sitting a top a very cluttered desk that made her own desk appear neat. The room was freezing cold and the air seemed to be coming from the floor more than from the ceiling; Maxine figured it was because the number of computer terminals to help keep them from overheating and thus shutting down the entire police department. She stepped in and looked around but there was no one in there.

"Hello?" she called out.

"Give me just a second, Detective," a voice answered from a closeted room off to her right.

Stuffing her hands down into the pockets of her slacks she stepped closer to the monitors that were on the desk staring at a lot of nothing she understood. Her mind ached as she tried to decipher all of the information only to realize that this woman had four monitors running at one time and all filled with a mess of information. She refused to be beaten by a damn computer and so she stood there continuing to stare at everything, and slowly bits and pieces became familiar.

"That's a lot to absorb all at one time," a voice said behind her.

"I don't understand how you take all of this in at one time," Maxine answered as she stood to meet the woman she'd only know as a voice.

Sheryl was nothing like what she was expecting. She was a big girl but he weight fit her perfectly. She had full, big blue eyes that just seemed to shine behind her cat rimmed glasses. A pretty face with thick lips and her long black hair pulled back into two ponytails high on her head. She was dressed all in black like one of those little goth kids she'd seen in a lot of the high end clubs, but she wasn't moody like them. In fact, she felt completely comfortable with this other woman.

"Its good to finally meet you, Detective Steele," Sheryl said with a smile. "I hope you don't mind me saying this, but I know everything about you."

"I kind of figured you would," Maxine couldn't help but smile. "I hope you can help me piece together something on my killer."

"Boy do we have a lot to go through," Sheryl took her seat and then pointed to another one. "I have a seat right there for you. Pull it up so I can show what I've found out."

"Am I going to need a notebook, or do you have this all set up in color coordinated binders for me?" she sat down in the chair and rolled up next to her new "best friend".

"Well not in colored binders, but I do have a lot to give you, and I do mean a lot.

"The first thing I need for you to know is that I almost couldn't find out who this guy is… or was. The first time I lost him was right after his birth," she flipped around some information on one screen and then pointed out the information she wanted Maxine to read. "As you can see, I show where your mom was checked in, and if you look here there was another young girl there by the name of Ilyanna Russanovich, she was 15 and she came in with no parent and they had her in the same room as your mom. Now this is where things get hinky.

"Ilyanna's baby was born just moments after your mom's baby was born around 11:05, but if you look here," and she flipped the screen to another page, "there's absolutely no record of the baby being born here, but I'm showing two little boys being born on the same night and in the same room. This record here shows the time the doctor called the death on your mom's son."

"So what happened to the other little boy?"

"That's what I had a hellava time trying to figure out, but I finally did. He was put up for adoption through some private agency and ended up in the home of Frank and Madeline Hensworth. From what I've found Frank died when the boy was about 2 or 3 years old and his life was probably hell. I've found several emergency room visitations I'm gathering from a very abusive home life. There are several reports from the elementary school and Junior high school of unexplainable bruises and cuts, saying that the boy would tell them that he fell a lot. I also have a report here from the high school psychologist that the boy was pretty much a loner, very smart and creative, but with a very dark mood."

"Not a very good combination. So what happened to the mother, and do we have an address?"

"Madeline Hensworth died in fire about 25 years ago, and here's another twist for you; police reports say that your boy, his name is Abel, also died in that fire."

"I can feel a really big but coming," Maxine's eyes were glued to the computer screens as Sheryl quickly moved from one screen to the next loading pages of information on them.

"Well that but is this right here," Sheryl pointed to the screen to her right closest to Maxine. "We were fortunate that fingerprints of the unreported baby boy were taken as well as your mother's son, and well we had a hit from a print in your apartment on the unreported boy."

Maxine sat back staring at the screen. "So Abel Hensworth is alive? Two boys born the same night in the same room but one's records are lost. That's why he thinks she's his mother."

"So get this," Sheryl's hands were still moving across her keyboard, "I've done some digging. No, I've done a lot of digging and I've come across at least 35 killings that all have a similar M.O. to those you're investigating right now. My thought is this, what if after years of being abused by his mother, he killed her and faked his own death and over the years he's been looking for his real mother and killing this entire time."

"Definitely sounds like something to look into," Maxine was completely engrossed in all of the information dancing across the screens. Her head was swimming and beginning to hurt but this definitely put the ball in her court now because she has a name.

"Is there anyway to see if Abel is using his full name or any version of it and get an address on him?"

"I've been working on that, but I can do you one solid," Sheryl gave her a sly wink.

"I can give you a picture of how he should look based on a picture I pulled of him from his high school year book and a nice little aging program I have."

Maxine sat back watching as the man's face slowly came up on the screen and she sat there studying it. It was a face that would just disappear in a crowd, but one she was sure she'd seen somewhere. His eyes caught her attention because they were as grey as hers and almost immediately she understood his obsession.

"He thinks I'm his sister," she whispered. "This sick fuck thinks we're family."

She quickly stood and gave Sheryl a kiss on the cheek, "You're absolutely amazing. I need a copy of this picture and I need everything you've managed to get for me sent upstairs to my desk. Also, I need you to keep looking for an address, it will be something that most likely has a basement or an outside shed because he needs some place to work.

"Thank you so much, Sheryl, you did a tremendous job here."

Sheryl giggled as she stacked up a lot of the papers she'd already printed off and had ready for the detective, and then she pressed the print button for the pictured that she'd rendered of the potential killer.

"Here you can have all of this and I'll have the rest sent up to your desk today."

"Thanks."

***

Abel sat in his chair staring at the replay of the broadcast and he watched as Maxine finally stepped up. He could hear her words playing over and over in his head as she threatened him and then dared him. He leaned up in his chair and stared into her eyes and he could see the fire he'd been looking for and it excited him; he could almost taste it in the air.

"Oh I'm coming for you, little sister," he said to the television, "and when I get there you're going to welcome me home with open arms."

"And what if the little bitch's mother is right?" his mother's voice was in his head, "What if her name is not the one on your adoption papers?"

"That's just it," he screamed out, "there was NO fucking name on the papers. There are almost no records of you even adopting me, and if I hadn't found the few papers I had I would have sworn you fucking kidnapped me."

"Why would I be stupid enough to steal a little worthless piece of shit like you?" he looked up and she was standing there over him. "You're nothing to me, Abel, nothing but a houseful of trouble that kept any man from wanting to be with me. You were my death even before you killed me and the only reason I even went through the adoption is because my husband wanted you… I didn't want you. Do you hear me? I didn't fucking want you."

"And undoubtedly," he dropped his head, "neither did she."

Chapter 19

"Just what the fuck did you call that?" Maxine almost grinned at how protective Daniel sounded as he walked into her apartment; he didn't even notice that she was in nothing but one of his dress shirts and a pair of panties. She closed the door and watched as he stomped and paced around her living room ranting and raving about what she'd said to all of the news reporters that had shown up at the Senator's home. She turned her head and giggled a bit as he ran his fingers through his hair in an attempt to finally cool off.

"Just tell me that there's a plan, Maxine," he stared at her, his eyes softened, and his breathing calmed. "Please tell me that you and the police have a plan?"

"I'll be honest," she stepped around him and sat down on the sofa with one leg folded under her, "there was no real plan when I did that. I was just so fucking angry, Daniel, and I know that the shit he does is just to goad me. And, well, I had to make him feel that I am no longer his toy and I'm in a position to finally do the taunting."

Daniel walked into the kitchen and pulled two beers from the refrigerator and popped the top from both. He walked back into the living room and dropped down on the sofa next to her handing her the second bottle. Turning up his he swallowed until near half the bottle was gone before taking it from his lips. He was angry because she'd placed herself directly in the path of this psychopath, and he had no way of interceding.

"What are you going to do now?" he couldn't look at her at this moment.

"I know why he's so drawn to me, and I can use this against him."

"You know… what?" Daniel's look was quizzical as he placed the bottle down on the table and turned to face her. "What could you possibly know that would make you calling this asshole out seem; shit, I don't know… Reasonable?"

"I wouldn't say reasonable, Daniel," she laid her head back against the sofa and exasperated. "It gives me a bit of an edge. He's known my name, he's known all of these things about me, but I've know nothing. Now I have him. I have his name, I know who he thinks he is and I know the truth."

"And what is the truth?"

"That my mother is NOT his mother; because that is what he thinks. That is why he feels so close to me. He's gone through a lot to find me and to keep an 'eye' on me. This is why he's done nothing to truly hurt me. I honestly believe that he still has my mother with him and she's alive. I believe that he got angry at me for being with you that night he killed that woman's husband and took her.

"I have to show him I'm not afraid, Daniel. Fear is what he knows, it's what he grew up in so its all he knows. He thinks that the world around him needs to fear him including me, and I cannot allow him to be that comfortable anymore."

"He knows where you live, Maxine," Daniel dropped his head into hand.

"Yea," she smiled and took a swallow of her beer, "I'm counting on that."

Daniel stared at her seeing something in her eyes that made him uncomfortable. He sat there unable to move but wanting to pull her to him just to show he was willing to support her, but that didn't stop him from being afraid she was in over her head. There was so much going on and he felt as if he were completely on the outside looking in. That look in her eyes had let him know that she was planning something and she was not going to tell anyone… including him.

"I wish there was a way I could say be careful and trust that you would," he finally said as he stared out across the room. "He's going to come here, Max, and I don't think he's going to be nice about it."

"I can handle myself, Daniel," she responded. "Everything is going to be just fine and when it's all over he'll either be dead or cuffed up and ready to be transported."

He sat her bottle on the table. She stood from the sofa and moved in front of him gently pushing him back into the sofa. Straddling his lap she ran her fingers through his hair before leaning forward kissing him softly on the lips.

"I've never had anyone this concerned about me," she grinned down at him before kissing him once more. "I think I kind of like this."

"I more than care about you, Maxine Steele," he slid his hands up and down her back, "and now I have to add terribly worried to the mix."

"You let me do the worrying," her grin was very mischievous as she leaned into him, "and right now all I want you to do is make love to me."

"I think I can handle that right now."

Daniel slowly unbuttoned the shirt she was wearing and finally recognized it as one of his; he could still smell his cologne as he pushed away the shirt and it fell to the floor. He leaned into her and kissed her neck and then bit it lightly and grinned as she jumped just a bit on his lap. He licked his way down her chest and then between the valley of her breasts and felt her body relaxed and she cooed. His tongue moved on to lick up the slope of her right breast and he sucked into his mouth her hardened nipple. He gently bit down and stroked it with his tongue as she wiggled down on him.

Maxine took a deep breath as he toyed with her body. He had her nipple in his mouth and was just teasing it with his tongue. His hand moved down her body and was pressed between her spread thighs and now he could feel just how hot she was as he found her spot and rubbed at it gently but firmly. She was writhing on his lap as her body became hotter and hotter from ministrations. She closed her eyes and her head fell back as she moaned out loudly as his fingers dug in deeper between her thighs. She couldn't tell what her body was going through as she tried to push more of her breast into his mouth and feed more to his venturing fingers.

Daniel released her breast and then he ripped off her panties with a growl. Without standing he released his own beast from his pants and with practiced ease he slid slowly into her heated body. Their eyes were pinned on the others as she allowed him to pull her completely down upon him. She was barely breathing and he was breathing between his teeth. Holding her he spun her around to lie upon the sofa and he pushed deeper. Their voices mingled as they groaned and moaned out together.

Their bodies moved together as he kicked his way out of his pants. Her legs wrapped around his back and she pulled him down upon her body as her nails raked at his back. All thoughts of what she'd done that day and what may come tomorrow were the furthest things from her mind as they just seemed to melt together. Feelings that she'd never experienced washed over her as he began to gyrate and grind into her, and she called out to him as he took her to a plateau that she was ready to jump off of. Her body was now his and he worked it like a fine tuned violin.

They soaked her sofa, and most likely scared her neighbors as their passions finally came to and end with a crescendo of screams and moans. Maxine held on to Daniel for dear life afraid that if she let go he would simply disappear like all of those other men had. She held on and she cried as he held her and tried to calm her down. She didn't know how to tell him what she was thinking or what she was feeling, but she begged him to just hold her. He held her while they laid there on the sofa, and then he held her some more when he finally got her to go lay in the bed with him. He

held her through the night barely getting any sleep, but instead opting to
watch over her.

***

Her mind was the clearest its been since before she checked herself
into that nursing home. Back then she was so strung out on drugs and on
alcohol that she knew she couldn't take care of herself any longer and she
refused to pawn herself off on her daughter. Maxine had always been
tougher than she was and even as a little girl she'd let be known that she
would never grow up to be like her mother. Janice was hurting, not
physically, but emotionally as she thought of all that she'd done and put
her daughter through. She was not surprised that Maxine was so distant
and sitting here in this cage she hoped that there would be some way she
could make it all up to her. But, for now, she had to get through to him.

"I wish I could get you to listen to me," Janice sat in her cage
staring up at her captive. Over the course of the time she'd been there
she'd learned his name was Abel and the other woman there with her was
named Liza. She learned that Liza watched as Abel brutally murdered her
husband; she had described it in details after waking screaming from a
nightmare one night when they were both sure he was gone from the
house.

Abel had his back to her just staring at his desk. His hands were
firmly planted in place on top of the table and he seemed to be just staring
off into space. She had been trying to talk to him, trying to get him to talk
to her as she did every time he came down into the basement where they
were. In her mind she was hoping she could prolong her life and the life of
the Liza.

"You keep saying the same things over and over," he mumbled,
"and I'm so tired of hearing it. I don't wish to hear your lies or her lies.

"I know the truth," he turned and walked up to the cage holding his
favorite knife. "I know that you didn't want me anymore than she wanted
me. I know that you gave me away on the very night I was born. I know
the truth and all you do is lie."

"No, Abel," Janice kept her voice calm and sincere, "you have to
believe me that there was another girl there that night and…"

"AND what," he growled out. "You fucking lie. There were no
records of any others that night. There are no records of two boys being
born that night. You lie… you lie… You Lie."

"What do I have to gain by lying to you?" Janice was amazed at
how clear her head felt. For the last how ever long she'd been gone from

the nursing home her head has never felt this clear. No medications and no fears of talking to herself. Everything about her felt rational at this point; even though she was under circumstances where she felt like she should have been loosing her mind.

"I…" he hesitated, "I don't know, but you cannot be telling me the truth. The hospital would know. Why would they lie? Why would they say that there was only one birth that night?"

"That I don't know, Abel, but what I do know is that night was the worse night in my entire life… I lost my baby and I lost my husband."

Abel walked over to her cage and slowly dropped to his knees. His steel grey eyes reminded Janice of her daughter's other than the fact that there was a lot of rage in his eyes. She could see the hatred that he had for her and most likely all women and she just wanted to do something about that. She wanted to hold him like he was her son and just try to take away the anger and the pain he was in, but she knew it was too late. She reached her hand between the bars as he leaned forward and stroked his face softly.

"I can just see that she hurt you a lot, Abel, and I swear to you that if you had been mine I wouldn't have ever given you up. Karl and I wanted kids, we wanted a house full of kids, but that night…" she wanted to wipe away her own tears. "That night God took away my little angel. I had lost so much blood by the time we got to the hospital that the doctors say I drowned my son. He was dead before my first serious contractions.

"I'll never forget that night," her tears welled over and she began crying outright.

"Why do you all have to lie to me?" his voice was low and deep. He looked up and stared into her eyes and watched as she slowly backed away. He stood and began beating his fists down on the top of the cage watching as she screamed out and cried even harder.

"Stop the fucking lies," he ranted. "Just fucking stop. I don't give a damn why you didn't keep me. I don't give a damn why she did what she did.

He pressed his face to the cage top and glared at her, "All that fucking matters anymore is that all of you will pay… all of you. And, Mother, it starts with my little sister."

Janice stared at him in horror as he pushed away from the cage and moved to his desk. He grabbed the large knife he enjoyed using and he made his way up the stairs. Kneeling in the cage she began pulling and yanking at the door screaming for him to come back. Her words just seemed to bounce off of his back and into her face as he moved up the stairs and slammed the door. She fell back from the door and let out a shriek that scared Liza in her cage as she sat there terrified watching everything that had happened.

Abel stood there staring at the closed door. For the last two months she'd ranted and raved the same shit about there being another girl in the same room. For two months he'd gone over and over all of the information he'd got from the hospital and there were no mentions of another girl or another baby. He was sure of it and he was going to make her tell him the truth. He was going to force it from her and he was sure it would be at Maxine's expense.

"She won't tell you what you want," his mother stood there with her cigarette hanging from her lip, "she won't lie to you."

"She is lying," he said as he walked through her and into the kitchen. "She is lying."

***

"Hello, Detective?" Sheryl felt like she was whispering but it was so late at night that she didn't want to seem rude for waking anyone.

"I'm up, Sheryl, are you still at work?" Maxine was sitting on the sofa with one of Daniel's shirts on and a pair of panties. He's left hours ago because he still had a report to finish preparing and she needed the time to figure out she and Abel's next move.

"Yes, I am," Sheryl answered as she stared at her screens. "I think I've found him. He's almost a ghost, but I think I got him. The name he's using is Abel Stein and I have his address and vehicle registration. He doesn't use any kind of plastic and its harder to find a paper trail on cast, but everyone makes some kind of mistake and I caught him going into the bank on one of their cameras two days ago."

"That's excellent, I mean really excellent. What kind of vehicle does he drive? Is it like a van of some kind?"

"That's exactly what it is. It's a 1970s van and from what I'm seeing its not modded in any way just a plain black paint job."

Maxine stood up and walked over to the window and looked down. There it was just sitting there. She'd seen it so often that it didn't even stick out anymore. She watched as a plume of smoke slowly slipped through the top of the window and she knew he was sitting there… watching.

"He's here," she whispered into her phone. "He's here right now. Call Raymonds and give him the address to the house. Tell him I said that there's a basement somewhere in there and that's where my mother and the other woman will be. Tell him to call me as soon as he has them, but he needs to hurry."

"Right away," Sheryl answered and then hit the disconnect button. She quickly hit another button listened as Raymonds phone rang.

"Hey, Sheryl, what can I do you for?"

"I have his address and Detective Steele wants you to go there and search for her mom."

"What about him?"

"She says that he's there." Sheryl sounded terrified. "She said that there's a basement in the house and that's where her mom and the Ferro woman will be and she wants you to call him once you have them out safely."

"I'm on my way. I want you to send a couple of units there to meet me."

"Will do."

***

Maxine was dressed in a pair of jogging pants and a long t-shirt and standing in front of the window. She was determined to play this out since she now knew he was there and she had an idea of what he looked like. She had her small "toss away" strapped to her leg and smiled as she lit a cigarette and stood there smoking it as she watched the van. She needed Raymonds to hurry, but she was also itching to rattle a cage of his own.

"Hello, Sheryl," she had called into her favorite tech, "I need to know if he has a cell phone and if so… what's the number?"

"What are you planning, Detective?" Sheryl questioned even as her fingers flew over her keyboard.

"Just planning to be a pain in the ass," Maxine laughed lightly.

"The most recent that I'm showing is 925-555-3602, but I cannot tell if he still has that number."

"Thank you, I'll find out here soon enough."

Taking a deep breath she dialed the number and stood there watching the van. She felt butterflies in her stomach as she saw a light dimly shine through the tinted window and then she waited for him to answer.

"Who is this and how did you get this number?" he growled.

Maxine stood there waiting and listening to him breathe. She swallowed hard and then spoke slowly making certain he didn't miss anything. She wanted to anger him because he'd already made his mistake.

"I told you that I knew who you were," she said lightly. "What you didn't believe me, Abel?"

He sat there staring at his phone and then up towards her window. He could still see her shadow standing there and wondered if she knew he was sitting outside of her home. His heart was beating in his chest just hearing her voice and he could feel sweat beading on his forehead.

"It would seem that I did under estimate you, Maxine," he took a deep breath as he looked up again and watched as she moved her curtain around. "And what do I owe this call?"

"You have something of mine and I plan to get her back."

"You'll be with her all in due time, Maxine, all in due time. But," he smiled, "now that I have you on the phone I think we should take this time and get to know one another."

"I don't need to know anymore about you," she began, "I think I have most of it down. I know when you were born, I know who you were raised by, and even know you were abused by her probably almost every day of your miserable life. I think the most interesting thing that I've learned about you though revolves around your birth."

"And what is that supposed to mean?" Abel was fighting now to maintain his anger. She stood up there talking down at him like he was some common dog.

"What I know is that you aren't who you think you are."

"You're talking in riddles, that's so unlike you, Maxine."

"You want to believe that my mother is your mother, but the truth of it you sick fuck, you were born to some little bitch who got knocked up by her own father and was forced to give her baby up."

"Noooo," he screamed out. "That's a lie. There was no other baby born that night."

"Oh but there was, and that little bastard was you. And the doctors did everything that they could to hide your birth away. The made certain that there were no records of your birth or the fact that you was giving to a private adoption agency and that you were pretty much sold off.

"No one wanted you, Abel," she taunted. "They all but threw your mangy ass away and you ended up with someone as psychotic as you are. I'm thinking you killed her shortly after you turned 16. You killed her and planted someone there to be you and you ran."

"You need to shut up," he threatened as he slammed his fist on the dashboard of his van. "You need to shut the fuck up with all of those lies."

"But they are not lies, killer, it's all true and I have the documents to prove it. You grew up under some sick ass bitch and slowly turned yourself into a killer just so you could find your real mother, but you haven't. All you've done is made yourself sicker than your mother and terrorized my city.

"Now I'm going to put you down." Maxine hung up the phone and moved away from the window. She walked off towards her room and placed a pair of handcuffs and her service pistol under her pillow. She then walked back into the living making certain to walk by the window to make certain that he saw her moving about the living room.

She could almost feel his eyes on him. He was getting antsy and she didn't want him to jump the gun before she was sure everyone else was safe. She had thought of anything the last few hours other than making certain her mother was out of harms way, but as she stood here she was now thinking that a man as sick as this could have booby trapped the house. She stared at her phone trying to mentally force Raymonds to call her, but her phone remained quiet.

"Fuck…"

***

Raymonds had given orders for everyone to come in silent and without lights flashing. He sat outside of the track house he'd been given the address to and he waited patiently for his back up. He'd already walked around and knew that there was no one home and he'd knocked on the doors of the houses on both sides and asked the inhabitants to leave for a while because they were about to raid the house in the middle. He'd taken the time to ask a little about the man occupying the house between the two but they couldn't give him too much information because the man always kept to himself.

Two cruisers finally pulled up just as he was beginning to worry about the perp returning home. He had no clue about Steele talking to that maniac on the phone while he sat there waiting, but they were there now and he moved towards the door with four men in tow. The house was dark and when he got to the door he tentatively turned the knob. He watched as one of the officers glanced through one of the windows and another took up position to kick the door in. Raymonds pulled his pistol and then banged on the door.

"Abel Stein, this is the police… open up."

With no answer he nodded to the officer and watched as the man kicked at the door and it burst inward. Everyone filled in and quickly began to go through each room yelling out that they were clear as they went.

"Detective, you're going to want to see this," one of the officers yelled from the kitchen area.

Raymonds ran off towards the man and stopped as he came to a door leading downstairs. He turned on the light and slowly made his way down again with his weapon at the ready and just as he made it to the bottom he turned and shouted up.

"I need some bolt cutters down here… Now."

Chapter 20

"Raymonds, is that you?" Maxine had snatched up her phone and answered it on the first ring. "Was it his place? Did you find…"

She sat there and listened for a moment and then dropped her head down in relief as he explained that they had found her mother. She stood and walked over to the window and looked down at the van and now realized that it was time to finally end this. She thanked Raymonds and hung up the phone. Her mind was going a million miles a second as she dialed the number one more time.

"Hello, Abel," she whispered into the phone once he answered. "Are you comfy out there? I see you watching me and I told you that I no longer fear you. You think you're so bad. I dare you to come see me."

"You keep tempting me, Maxine," he responded with a sneer in his voice, "and I'll show up at your door."

"Would you like for me to leave it unlocked, or would you like to use the key you've made for my door?"

"You're pushing buttons you're not ready to see the results of, Maxine," his voice was hard and harsh and she could see him moving around in his van. He was agitated and that's exactly what she wanted. There was going to be a fight and she needed him off of his game before he came rushing up here for her.

"Did I tell you that your real mother was a junkie, and that after she had to give away you she got pregnant again from her father and was back in the same hospital? I found her, Abel, and damn does she look bad, but from the picture I've seen of you, you look just like her."

She pulled the curtains away from the window and stood in front of it so that there was no doubt that she was looking down at him. She knew he couldn't see her face but the contempt in her voice was as venomous as a rattler.

"Let me guess, Abel," she taunted him, "your adoptive mother was a junkie of some kind wasn't she. What? I'm thinking alcohol, she probably reeked of it on a daily basis. She probably walked around with a bottle in her hand at all times as she whipped your little scrawny ass all over the house.'

"You need to shut up about her."

"You want to know something, Abel?" she continued to goad him. "I visited the old house, and I've found that you are… predictable. I mean I found the little basement room out in the shed, and I went down into it.

You're like a gopher or something; you like to do your shit with the world over your head. And your mother, I bet you killed her while she was dead asleep in one of her drunken stupors. You didn't have the balls to face her, did you?

"I can see her calling you weak all the time. You little pussy boy…"

"Shut the fuck up, you bitch."

"Aww," Maxine was grinning as she stared out the window. He was so close to the edge she could almost see him in the front seat twitching. "Did mommy hurt your little feelings? She beat you ever day didn't she, called you names, made you feel so small?"

"I'm going to kill you," he snarled, "I am going to gut you and watch as you bleed out and then I'm going to throw you all around your fucking apartment. I'm going to enjoy every time I stab your dead body leaving so many holes in you that everything inside of you is going to slowly leak out."

"You know where I'm at you son-of-a-bitch, I'm waiting for you."

Maxine walked over towards the door and unlocked it letting him hear the latch. She then turned off the light and walked back over to the window standing in front of it so that he could see her shadow. She allowed her body to melt away into the shadows of her home knowing that he was watching, but she stayed close enough to keep an eye on the van below.

"Just come and get me."

"I'm on my way, Maxine," she watched as he stepped out of his van and looked up and down the street. "I'm on my way and I'm coming to kill you."

Maxine sat on her sofa in the dark waiting for the door to open. She could feel her heart pounding in her ears and her eyes were tearing up as she tried to remain as calm as possible. She knew his weapon of choice and she could just shoot him as he walked in, but would they hold that against her saying that she coerced him in. She laid her hand against the large butcher's knife she'd gotten from her kitchen, and she tried to smile. He was bigger than her, she was sure, most likely even faster but was he stronger.

The door slowly pushed in and she held her breath. She could see his head slipping around the edge of the door; he was hooded and couldn't see nothing of his features. He stepped in and she could tell that he was at least six feet tall; slender in build and in his right hand he held a very large blade that almost sparkled from the light in the hallway. Maxine slowly sunk to the floor from the sofa and crawled around the coffee table so that she could remain in the shadows of the room almost behind him as he stepped in and closed the door.

Quietly she stood up and pressed herself into the corner watching as the man she'd been taunting slowly walked into her home and moved about. She watched as he headed back towards her bedroom and felt sick to her stomach at how freely he just seemed to walk about. Her breathing was shallow and quick and she fought with herself trying to calm down as she waited for him to return to the living room. The knife she held on to tightly as she slowly began to relax and worked out in her head just how she was going to handle this.

"I hope you're on your way here, Raymonds," she whispered to herself as she crouched down and watched the hall.

His shadow filled the hall and she watched as he stood there trying to find her in the dark of the room. Again she could feel her heart pounding but this time it wasn't the fear but the anxiety. He was so near she could almost smell is anger from across the room. He was standing in a typical defensive stance as if he were waiting for her to step out and take a swing at him. This was a big mistake.

He wasn't huge but he was big enough to make these tight fighting confines a benefit to him. She would have to be fast, but if she wasn't able to hit something vital he would catch her. She watched as he moved slowly through the living room, he pushed the coffee table against the sofa, and slowly walked closer towards the kitchen. He would be upon her in seconds.

"I know you're in here, Maxine," he finally said. "I am going to find you… there's not too many places to hide."

She watched as he slowly turned his back to her and glanced back down the room towards her bedroom. The front door was still open and he made one step towards it and then stop… she moved, and quickly. She slashed the blade at the back of his leg and rolled coming to a stop just in front of the table. She stood tall as he suddenly crumpled from the cut right at knee. The sound of his screaming echoed in the room.

"It looks like we both know where the other is now, Abel," she resumed her taunting. "I'm going to take you a part a piece at a time, you good for nothing shit."

Abel stood and glared at her. She could finally see that he had a ski mask on covering his face so she could still see nothing of him but his eyes. The little light that shone through the door seemed to glint off of eyes near the same color as hers and that sent a small shiver down her spine. He resumed his defensive posture and with a limp he slowly began to circle her with his knife held ready.

Maxine began to think back to all of the martial arts training she'd received not only at the academy but also from a friend of hers as she was trying to prepare for duty. She watched in her head as she was attacked and she responded like a movie in her head as she began to slowly circle away from the man across the room. She wished she could see his face, especially see his eyes better, that way she could possibly know just what he planned to do. The laugh she heard from the beneath the ski mask gave her goose bumps and she dug her feet in for his first attack.

The knife flashed out and she struck back watching in slow motion as their blades struck together. They circled again and she took note that he was limping worse on that leg and wondered just how badly she'd cut him. Her next thought was how to get to the inside of his knife and attack that leg. His knife flickered out again and she bounced back out of its range and as he pulled his arm back she struck again slashing. She watched as he tried to avoid the move but her blade found flesh once more.

"It's a different story when she's fighting back, isn't it, Abel," she moved in and slashed her knife near his face. "You're not in control now, you're just a weak little pussy with a big ass knife in your hands. What happened to all of that bullshit about gutting me?"

He roared out and charged, but just as his knife flashed before her eyes Maxine moved; jumping out of his path she stabbed down and her knife stuck him in the back just below his shoulder blade. He howled out as he hit the floor and she felt her arm pulled as she tried to pull the knife free. She could see blood coloring the back of his top as he struggled to get back up.

"I'm in control," he murmured weakly as he pulled himself up to his knees and turned. "I'm in control."

Before he could he could get his feet under him she struck again. Her fist hit his jaw and he spit blood across the room as his head snapped back. A foot to his stomach and he double over trying to laugh as she continued her attack, and then another kick to the side of his head sent him sprawling across the floor.

"Is that all you got, you bitch?" he was slowly crawling across the floor towards his knife that had dropped from his hand.

Maxine stepped over him and kicked the knife away before kicking him across the face once more. She then knelt at his head and pulled his face up so that she could look into his eyes. She flipped back the hood and pulled away the ski mask and stared down at him.

"You took my mother," she hissed into his face, "you should have know I wouldn't stop until I'd found her."

"That's what I was banking on, little sister," laughing as the blood bubbled through his split lip, "and that's why I still have you by the short hairs. She's still mine and now it's my time to have her all to myself while you live without her."

"No, Abel, you're wrong about two things. I have my mother and you're not my fucking brother. My mother wouldn't have given birth to such a weak and useless sack of shit like you… ever."

She had to contain herself from the shock on his face. She reached into her back pocket and pulled out the handcuffs and she quickly pulled his arms behind his back. The sound of the metal as the ends pushed through to lock in place was like music to her ears. She pushed back away from him watching as he laid there on the floor crying now like a baby. She quickly checked to see if any part of her had been cut and almost laughed out as she found herself without a wound.

The door suddenly crashed in and Raymonds stormed in shouting as the light was suddenly turned on bringing spots to her eyes. She could hear more than see the room being filled with her fellow Police as she slowly leaned and laid back against the only piece of the sofa that the table didn't cover. She took a deep breath and closed her eyes finally feeling free. There were so many questions being shot at her at one time and all she could do was wave them all off as she finally forced herself to stand.

"Do you really think this over," Abel yelled out as he was pulled to his feet and forced towards the door. "This will never be over, Maxine… I promise you that I will be back and when I do you will die. I swear this, Maxine. I will kill you…"

She dropped the knife she'd been holding and watched as it was quickly snatched up by the CSI tech. She could hear Raymonds telling her that she needed to sit still so that they could process the area, but his voice seemed so distant. All at once she felt as if she were about to vomit and her head was swimming. The adrenaline was suddenly gone and all she wanted to do was drop to her knees and scream out, but her entire apartment was full of people that she just needed air.

"Where is my mother?" she asked Raymonds as she held on to the lapels of his coat. "I need to see my mother."

"She's downstairs in my car," he answered knowing that she would ask about her.

Maxine shuffled around people as she made her way towards the door. She could once again feel her heart pounding in her chest as she raced from her home and down the stairs. She made it to the lobby of the building she could almost feel the air from outside, but she felt as if all of the people around the front of the building were choking the life from her. She pushed at the door and a rush of more noises and voices and the flashing of lights angered her as she made her way towards Raymonds' car.

"Mother… Mother," she called out over the crowd as she pushed her way through the throng of people. She'd hope to see Daniel's face but the crowd was so thick that she couldn't really make out any faces.

She called out for her mother again as she finally broke free and opened the door. Her mother popped out and threw her arms around her neck and they hugged each other hard.

"I kept trying to tell him, Maxine," she whispered into her daughter's ear, "I kept trying to tell him that I was not his mother. I kept trying, but he wouldn't listen, and then we had to sit there and watch as he killed that woman."

Her mother was crying and all she could do was hold her. There was so much damage done and she had no means of fixing it, but for the first time in a long time she held her mother like a daughter should hold her mother. She was so happy that she was alive and had been found, and in her mind she was making promises that nothing like this would ever happen again. She whispered over and over that she loved her and smiled as her mother repeated it back. She slowly sat her down in the car and closed the door to protect her from the news force out. She pressed against the door and allowed her body to take in as much air as she could as the world quickly swirled around her.

A police cruiser slowly rolled by her and as she looked she could see the bloody face of Abel staring at her with a big toothy smile. Her mother wailed from behind the closed door as she moved to shield her from his face. His lips puckered up into a kiss and then the car drove off.

***

"How's your mother doing?" Capt. Salter asked.

"Better," Maxine answered as she stared down at her badge, "She's doing a lot better than I figured she would be. I've even had her moved into her own cottage and she's no longer in the infirmary being drugged up. Which is all good."

"And how the hell are you doing, Steele?"

"I'm making it as best I can to be honest with you. I'm more worried about what IA is going to do to me for beating the shit out of him."

"Well I think that you'll be just fine considering he had come into your house carrying something close to a sword. Just tell them what you put into your report and just let them go through the motions. Everything will be just fine."

"I hope that you're right, Captain. Is he out of the hospital yet?"

"They will be picking him up today to transport him to a Federal lock up."

Maxine stood and walked out of her captain's office and to her desk. She'd been pretty much on lockdown since the night that Abel had been arrested, but this allowed her to get all of her paperwork taken care of. She needed the down time because the last few months had been pretty much nerve wracking. She walked over and got herself a cup of that strong ass coffee and smiled as it burned all the way down on her first sip. Raymonds gave her the thumbs up as she walked back to her desk and all she could do was smile and nod. Her nightmare, as this case had become, was over and Abel would spend the rest of his life locked up being studied.

She smiled as she remembered his threats. "Let's see you come back, Abel," she whispered to herself. "They need to give your sick ass the needle and not just let you live reliving your bullshit for them to write papers about."

Her time with IA would come soon, and she would tell them how they worked the job and how he fixated on her. She would tell them everything that they needed to know leaving out how she continued to taunt and goad him after the remarks on the news. She would leave out how she waited for him to come into her house, but not how she defended herself. Then she would wait for her next case.

It was a done deal.

Fin

The air felt good on his face as the two officers led him out to their cruiser. His lip had been stitched up as well as the knife wounds in his back and knee, but neither of those mattered. He looked around and marveled at his city at rest and he smiled. His arms hurt a bit and being pulled behind his back to be cuffed had the pain throbbing. He was still walking with a bit of a limp from the cut she'd first delivered, and he had to mentally clap for that one. He'd had enough time to think about everything, and she was right, he hadn't been ready for someone who would fight back.

Never again.

"So you think, my son," his mother slid into the back seat and waited there for him to join. "She's going to always be better than you. You don't have what it takes to beat a woman like her."

"I can beat her," he mumbled not looking at the phantom sitting beside him. "I've already beat her."

"You say something back there, Inmate?" the transport guard said as he slide in behind the steering wheel.

"No," he looked up so that the man could see his eyes in the rear view mirror. "I didn't say a word."

"She's better than you, you sick bastard," his mother was leaning in whispering in his hear. "She's so much better than you and you'll never… ever… beat her."

He'd got to a point where he refused to answer her, but she continued to talk. He made himself as comfortable as he could while waiting on the two cops to get into the car. As they pulled off, he sat there as stiff as a sphinx as the one in the passenger seat kept looking back at him. He watched as the two of them made small talk and his mother continued her ranting. Everyone's attention was occupied as he sat there calming his mind for the pain that was soon to come.

Grabbing his thumb he gritted his teeth and pulled back listening for the snap of it dislocating. With a slight grunt at that first snap he took a deep breath and sat still for a moment allowing his hand to accept the injury. Slowly he wiggled his hand as he pulled it through the loop of the cuff and freeing it. And now it was all about timing, and he calmly waited.

"Soon, Maxine," he mumbled, "very soon you're going to hear from me again."

"What did you say?" the guard in the passenger seat asked.

"I said nothing," Abel smiled at him. "But do me a favor and let Detective Steele know that our paths will cross again really soon."

"Buddy, I don't know how you see that happening, but good fucking luck."

"Everything happens all in good time," Abel gripped the dangling end of the cuff in his hand and sat back quietly. In his mind he had everything timed out perfectly. In his mind he would definitely see Maxine again. In his head he could see her dying by his hand.

In his mind it was all working out… perfectly.

***

"Captain Salter," a young officer was running through the squad room yelling his name waving an evidence bag in his hand. "Sir, we have a problem."

"What's going on, Son?" Salter asked waving the officer to him

"This was found in Hensworth's cell after they'd picked him up for transport this morning. It's another note, Captain, and it's addressed to Detective Steele. I was told to get this too you pronto."

As he listened, his eyes were drawn towards the one television he allowed in the squad room just as the local news interrupted the current report with a breaking news story. The officer placed the bag in his hand and he looked down his eyes going wide as he recognized the handwriting on the paper. Cursing, he looked up again just as they showed an aerial shot of an overturned car on the road going towards the White Chapel prison.

"Someone get me Steele on the phone," he said as he pulled the bag open. "Now, goddammit, right now."

He looked at the television one last time and the caption beneath the scene read, "Reaper murderer, Abel Hensworth has escaped". He pulled the note from the bag and read it through before storming off into his office.

> *Hello, Sister*
>> *I want you to know that I*
>> *loved this little game of ours,*
>> *and now I understand the*
>> *fascination with having*

Salter stared at the overturned car still on the television screen and slammed his hands down on the top of his desk. They'd never been ahead of this asshole, and he'd been playing them from the start just to get to Maxine. He slumped down in his chair and pulled the bottle of whiskey he'd kept hidden there and poured his coffee mug full and swallowed deeply. This nightmare was just beginning and she was right in the middle of it.

"Maxine," he said dryly into the receiver the moment he'd been told she was on the phone, "we have a situation..."

"I know," she answered. "That bastard escaped."

"Yea, and you have a new note," Salter finished.

"I'm on my way, Captain," Maxine hung up the phone before he could say anything else. She stared at the television not listening to the female reporter's voice, she was just staring at the overturned car as she grabbed her jacket and pulled it on.

"I'm not too surprised," she said with a weird smile stretching her lips. "You wouldn't be you if you stayed locked up... now would you. I guess we'll be seeing each other again really soon won't we."